APEX PREDATOR

By S.M. Douglas

WINSTON PUBLISHING
APEX PREDATOR

For information address Winston Publishing,
P.O. Box 2326, Brighton, MI 48116.

ISBN 978-0-9976955-0-2

For my loving family, who spoil me with their tolerance of my varied interests

PROLOGUE

There is a wild part of Europe that straddles the border between East and West. It is hemmed in by dark forests, vast swamps, and jagged mountains. Violent death has long plagued its people, particularly those living in a remote Carpathian valley surrounding the ancient town of Dibrovno.

The valley has been populated since the time of the Scythians. Nevertheless, the town's history is shrouded in fearful superstition. Huns, Lithuanians, Poles, Russians, Tatars, and others have looted, plundered, and killed their way into Dibrovno; but no would be conqueror ever stays. Even the murderous Nazi and Soviet war machines swept around Dibrovno as quickly as possible, their legions refusing to seize and fortify what geography and military logic otherwise dictated was an impregnable bastion.

The people who live in and around Dibrovno know why history passes them by. They know why the tour buses never visit the town's well-maintained castle. They also know why visitors are warned not to linger, lest unspeakable things happen. Some laugh off or ignore those warnings. When they subsequently vanish, rumors as to their fate become grist to the kind of folklore that almost never spills out into the larger world.

Until now.

CHAPTER 1

October 2016 – Detroit's Western Suburbs

William Brody stood in the book shelf lined front room, staring outside. The gray sky unloaded in fat pounding drops, the booming echo of thunder reaching through the home's rattling picture window.

Two months ago he got what he asked for.

No, begged for.

He got the chance to do something big, something meaningful.

Did they ever give it to him. At least that was what he was made to believe when his boss was ladling heaping bellyfuls of it onto his plate. However, it wasn't what it seemed. Not much in life ever is, and it took him longer than most to figure that out. Luckily, one of the side effects of being hunted by a werewolf is that it tends to focus the mind.

He created his own assignment. One not built on a lie. One he believed could give him what he had sought his entire adult life. Nevertheless, they could never find out, though he was beyond caring about their hypocritical rules. Besides, the juicy possibility of a public flagellation was not posted anywhere near the top of his fuck-me-I'm-screwed list of the month.

Then again, upon realizing how insecure his place on the food chain had become embracing reality was not as confining as one would think. It opened up all sorts of possibilities. That is provided one attains a certain comfort with moral relativism applied writ large, and little in life greases that slippery slope like the threat of death.

There would be a price to pay for his decision.

He had not been willing to pay it before.

Now he was ready, even if there was a monster waiting at the end of it.

CHAPTER 2

August 2016 – Detroit, Michigan

The BMW roared out of the underground parking garage. Thousands of LED light tubes marched across the sixteen story casino rising above. They cast shimmering blues, reds, and greens across the fast moving car's crisp white exterior. The driver raced past a highway entrance ramp, swerving onto a side street swathed in shadows. Dubstep thumped from the speakers. The thrumming bass drowned out the sound of squealing tires ripping through one turn after another.

A doughy middle aged man squirmed in the passenger seat. An empty rocks glass dangled from his tingling fingers as he leered at the voluptuous driver's suicide-girl-hair, ivory skin, and plum-red lipstick. She glanced over as if reading his mind, eyes dancing with a wicked energy. The man reflexively grabbed at the bulge in his trim slacks, his lust volcanic. Her boyfriend passed out in the back seat long since forgotten. The car slewed even more violently around the next corner, braking to a screeching stop, driver side door swinging open.

"C'mon," The woman purred, face shining with sweat and need as she glided into the night.

The man staggered in his haste to follow, his head spinning. She took his hand and pulled him into an empty field overgrown with knee high weeds. Plastic bags and battered beer cans gleamed in the moonlight, marking their path. An abandoned house loomed to their right. A tremor tickled up the man's spine. He looked back at the pristinely polished sedan, engine running, high beams illuminating ghostly steam rising from a manhole cover in the otherwise deserted street—

The woman's vice-like grip jerked his wandering head around.

They neared the middle of the vacant lot, his hand falling from hers. He took a few more steps and then stumbled, falling behind the woman as he cast repeated glances over his shoulder. The car's speakers pumped out a frenetic beat, jangling the man's nerves.

He shivered, for the first time feeling fear. He faced the car's beckoning safety, staring at the open *rear* door, his alcohol dulled mind not quite comprehending what it implied - nor understanding the tingling warmth rippling through his body, prodding him to do something. He opened his mouth, ready to suggest—

A rumbling growl erupted from behind him.

Every hair on the man's body stiffened. The deep inhuman noise resonated through his chest, sounding like nothing he had ever heard in his life. He trembled, standing rooted in frozen horror for what seemed like forever.

The guttural breathing over the man's shoulder not once lessened in its homicidal intensity.

The man swallowed. Tongue thick.

He pivoted, feet shuffling in quicksand, craning his head up in disbelieving shock.

Pitiless yellow eyes swiveled down, rows of razor sharp teeth flashing from the elongated muzzle of what looked like the biggest wolf he had ever seen.

But wolves don't stand upright.

The creature growled.

The man's jugular vein throbbed under his starched shirt collar, his brain scarcely comprehending the signals racing to it from his palpitating optic nerves. He opened his mouth, but nothing came out. After a moment a whine escaped his lips. A whine that turned into a moan at the realization that the growl's coming from this *thing* sounded as much human as animal.

It snarled in response, an angry, vicious sound punctuated by black lips skinning back from fangs the size of knives.

The man's bladder emptied in a hot streaming burst down his pant leg, awakening in him a surge of energy. His Italian calfskin wingtips skidded in the trash strewn grass, stumbling steps backward leaving him agonizingly close to the creature until the double leather soles finally caught traction. He twisted into a flat out sprint.

The car. If I can just get to the car.

The man's breath came in ragged gasps; adrenaline charged legs propelling him faster than he thought possible toward the beckoning car door, his face brightening with hope—

Something slammed into the man's side. The brutal impact spun him to the ground, pain radiating from his shattered hip. Gasping, he trailed one hand down, following a jagged tear in his flesh to find something slimy and meaty bulging out. The man levered himself up, twisting to see a rope of intestine pulsing in the night air. He screamed in mindless terror—

A clawed hand grasped the man's throat, crushing his windpipe. The corded arm rose with the smooth strength of a pneumatically controlled steel lever, lifting the man up, body dangling, feet kicking weakly against the creature's knees.

The man floated on the edge of reality, perceiving a silvery full moon slipping free of the clouds. He felt his shirt torn away. Needle sharp pain lanced through his midsection as his organs spilled from his freshly opened abdominal cavity. Consciousness slipped into darkness, the jaws of something that shouldn't have been possible slicing into his softly palpitating throat.

Bestial grunting and crunching filled the air.

It was over in minutes.

Two yipping shadows streaked into the night.

Silence once more fell over the empty lot.

Within an hour the blood had congealed into a gelatinous puddle. Scraps of torn clothing once worth more than the idling BMW blanketed the matted grass. The occasional cloud scudded across the moon hovering above what had once been the country's greatest industrial city.

Sometime later a coyote appeared.

The swirling wind shifted.

The salivating coyote whimpered, staring longingly at the corpse. However, the breeze's threatening message sent her scampering away.

Nothing else approached the kill.

Hours passed.

The night faded from black to charcoal gray.

A naked man and woman emerged from an abandoned house. They jumped into the undisturbed vehicle as dawn broke in bright streamers of orange and yellow.

The BMW sped off into the lingering darkness to the West.

CHAPTER 3

August 2016 – The sky over Detroit, Michigan

"That's not exactly light reading."

Brody swiveled toward his seatmate; a well-dressed business-woman.

"How do civilizations fail?" The woman paraphrased the title of his book, the newspaper in her face since their flight departed from Washington D.C. had finally dropped away from her chest.

"Most have certain things in common," He said. She had shoulder length brown hair, and a tired demeanor that implied too many years of travel. Then again, her eyes sparkled with an inquisitiveness that he found attractive.

"Namely?" She let the crinkling newspaper slide into her lap.

A chill coursed through Brody. *Something about the way she held her head.* He pressed his lips tight in response, pushing back the painful memories and reverting to the guarded overly formal manner of speech he had adopted of late when speaking with the opposite sex. "The majority cedes limited power to a minority who directs society. In return, the masses enjoy basic comforts and happiness."

"So how does it get messed up?"

"The minority abuses its privilege and ignores the brewing hatreds and resentments until too late. Or they crack down hard, and fail miserably."

"Where do we fit in?"

"I haven't…ummm…read that far."

She sat back, smiling in a way that didn't reach her eyes.

He pinched the bridge of his nose at not only his inability to let go of his past but his cluelessness in the face of a question that in one way or another seemed to be defining the wreckage that was his career. Then again, nothing of late came easy for Special Agent William Brody, who a few weeks earlier celebrated his tenth and potentially last year in the FBI.

A newspaper rustled to his left. She had taken his silence as license to return to her perusal of current events. He winced at the screaming headline: *"CEO of America's Largest Bank Negotiating New Multi-Billion Dollar Settlement with Feds over Forged Mortgage Documents."*

"Can you believe this?" She said.

Brody's stomach knotted up. She must have caught him looking.

"Bankers are using fake paperwork to foreclose on homeowners, and nobody gets pinched." She lowered the paper's top corner, her sharp dark eyes settling on his, "Meanwhile, I'm busting my ass as a drug rep. And guess what? If I get even one DUI, my career is over."

He nodded his head sympathetically; too embarrassed to tell her what he did for a living.

She grunted and disappeared behind her newspaper.

Brody slumped as he turned back to the window. They had dipped below the billowy clouds breaking up under the mid-morning sun. Detroit smoldered below, a crumbling hole in a ring of decaying suburbs. The aircraft banked onto its final flight path west of the sprawling city. Countless streets radiated from Telegraph Road's north-south expanse like giant spokes linking the various stages of his life. Nearly forty years ago his family had moved from Dearborn to an exurban township once known as Michigan's corn capital - now overrun with subdivisions sprouting like weeds.

He sat back, absorbing the uneasy jolt when the big wheels skidded down. The engines roared as the pilot braked the aircraft. Meanwhile, Brody contemplated a life of failure weighing on him with the same crushing force that had buried Detroit's beleaguered residents.

CHAPTER 4

September 1969 – New York City, New York

"Thanks for letting us get out for the evening." She smiled, patting him on the shoulder.

Jimmy Donnelly beamed at his mother. The teenager's grin faded however when a plaintive whine from inside the townhouse carried to the front door.

His mom stiffened.

"Jimmy's got this," His father said, putting an arm around her.

One year ago Jimmy's parents had pulled him away from his baseball card collection to deliver the earth-shattering news that he would have a brother. He distinctly remembered the wispy sound made by his treasured Tom Seaver card as it floated to the floor from his trembling hand. In the ensuing weeks, his mother's swelling belly had loomed like a lengthening sword of Damocles. Then, almost three months ago baby Andrew arrived. From that moment on Jimmy's life had been an absolute hell. He despised every minute. Each gooey diaper; each delicately tilted bottle of milk perched between his brother's sucking lips; and the endlessly repeated stories that left him wanting to blow his brains out.

"Don't forget to change Andrew's diaper," Jimmy's mom said, the turquoise, lime green, and white swirls of her side pleated dress perfectly complementing her husband's striped mock turtleneck. "That butt rash of his isn't going away."

"Yes, mom," Jimmy said, waving goodbye as his parents bounced down the concrete front steps. Clicking the lock shut on the door he eyed the new 23-inch solid-state TV resting in its thick walnut cabinet. After several seconds, he reluctantly tore his gaze away and tiptoed up the stairs to peek into the nursery. Mercifully, Andrew had fallen back asleep. His chest rose and fell ever so slightly, tufts of wispy hair poking this way and that on his round head.

Jimmy stared. It was several moments before he noticed his clenched jaw and balled up fists. Exhaling, he forced himself to relax and backed away from the bedroom. He slipped down the stairs and curled up on the family room's olive green couch. *The Mod Squad's* latest episode was reaching its climax, his brother quickly forgotten.

Then it drifted down the stairs, a squeak almost inaudible.

The yap came next, questioning, searching to see if his call for help had been heard.

Jimmy grated his teeth, standing to crank the TV volume louder, his shoulders tensing.

Not thirty seconds later came the first yell, followed by a warbling murmur that sounded like a cat.

Jimmy slammed his fist into the couch and marched upstairs. He placed his palm on the bedroom door, easing it open. Through the crib's white slats he spied his brother's pudgy face, eyes open, lower lip quivering. Jimmy cursed. Andrew broke into a wailing call of need. The crying crested like breakers buffeting his parent's sail boat, before sliding into a trough of whimpers only to race back up the next wave into another high-pitched yowl louder than the last.

Jimmy rolled his eyes at first but then paused. Something about the crying sounded different; louder, more insistent. His lips curled up in a sneer.

Andrew's loudest scream cut off, and he began choking uncontrollably.

A residual feeling of nervous responsibility shot through Jimmy. Not so much fear that his brother was genuinely hurt, but terror at what his parents would do if his brother was injured on his watch. Panicking, he rushed forward, but feeling put off, almost jilted when the baby's response fell somewhat short of his usual cooing, grinning, and delightfully wringing hands. Had Jimmy glanced up he would have known why. In the wall mounted mirror glimmered Jimmy's eerie reflection; sharp overdeveloped teeth protruded from lips peeled back from his gums.

Jimmy didn't notice his appearance. Even if he had he wouldn't have cared. He delighted in who he was and what he was becoming. Now, however, he frowned as he focused in on the distended diaper filled with yellow stringy shit pooling up around his brother's marble sized balls. Jimmy's anger pushed harder, but before he hit his tipping point the spell that had come over him broke like a fever.

Jimmy felt his lips slide back down over his teeth. His fists opened, the tension draining from his joints. He took a deep breath and began to wipe clean his cooing little brother, being careful to avoid inflaming the reddened space between Andrew's butt cheeks.

Nonetheless, as Jimmy wrested control over the darkness, Andrew's tiny penis stiffened. Jimmy stepped back; his jaw clenched in disgust. Raw emotion boiled over, his pupils dialing down into pinpricks of laser-like anger as he caught sight of a cracked blister marking the epicenter of his brother's raging diaper rash. Hands trembling, he snatched up the rag; savagely pressing it into the baby's inflamed bottom.

A high-pitched scream cut through the darkening room.

Downstairs, the *ABC Movie of the Week* began, drowned out by Andrew's cries of pain as Jimmy swiped the rag back and forth. The blackness took over. A strange smile creased Jimmy's face. He stared off, open mouthed, eyes glazed over as he fell into a dazed hypnotic state equaling the numb pleasure he felt when beating off to the Penthouse magazine he had found in his dad's underwear drawer.

Andrew's stubby arms and legs flailed as Jimmy sanded at the baby's shiny cheeks as if trying to strip paint from a plank. Streaks of light zipped behind Jimmy's fluttering eyelids, lips drawn back so tight that his teeth ached, his brother's shrieks pushing him on. It was the first time he had experienced such a delicious energy. He didn't want to let it go. He couldn't—

The screaming cut off.

Jimmy jumped. Panting he caught his breath, the blood throbbing in his temples, his blurred vision only slowly coming back into focus. What he saw sent a bolt of terror slicing between his shoulder blades.

Andrew's eyes were closed.

Have I... What I have done?

The room swirled around him.

Then he noticed his brother's chest shallowly rising and falling. Jimmy exhaled in relief as he shook his sore wrist. He glanced at the clock on the top of the dresser. It had been fifteen minutes since he first set foot in the nursery. Silvery moonlight streamed in through the window. He flipped the switch on the wall, chasing away the darkness. Only then did he see the white cloth, pink streaks of blood smeared on it.

Oh, Jesus!

He bent to examine his brother, anxiety turning to relief as he saw that though fire-engine red, the sores appeared as they had before. He grabbed up gobs of Vaseline, shaky hands slathering it on, panicky at first, then with more assurance. He would get away with it.

He smiled a cruel thin lipped smile that just managed to cover his canines.

Life was good again for Jimmy Donnelly.

August 2016 – Detroit, Michigan

Brody's brain spun in a loop as he adjusted the rental car's seat. He cruised east on the highway, passing the landmark eight-story high Uniroyal Tire serving as the southwestern gateway to Detroit. Four days ago his bureau chief, an affable agent named Hiller had provided the first good news he had heard in ages; he was being transferred from exile in Cincinnati and back to the big leagues. Something was going down and the Bureau needed every agent they could get with Wall Street experience, including Brody.

Upon reporting to Quantico, Brody learned that a bank vice president had gone missing from his yacht while anchored off the Hamptons. That came from Brody's new boss, a slick looking man named Wilson who seemed even more put off by the fact the banker's savings and brokerage accounts had been drained and handed over to Occupy the SEC, Habitat for Humanity, and other such hippie organizations. The Bureau's first impulse was that the banker had been kidnapped and extorted.

Then a letter arrived at the missing banker's estate. It came in an unmarked envelope, weighty in the hand of the Guatemalan maid who found it. Inside nestled a single sheet of creamy archive quality paper, the page blank but for a single jarring question handwritten in pigment-based ink.

"Why no jail?"

One day later the CFO of another mega-bank vanished. His accounts also emptied. Another letter turned up. Delivered on the same old world stationary, in the same beautifully penned cursive, and asking once more: *Why no jail?* This time a deep red seal had been pressed into the paper. However, the seal's crest had not been inscribed from wax, clay, lead or any of the other traditional material used to authenticate a document. Forensic analysis subsequently determined it had been made from the missing CFO's blood—

The mind numbing voice coming from the car radio shifted in tone, shaking Brody from his reverie with the news that the world's biggest banks had colluded to fix yet another supposedly inviolate and trusted market, this time commodities. It would be one of many topics to be covered in today's anticipated hearing on Capitol Hill. He punched the radio off, staring out the window at the bankrupt city through which the highway ran. Six decades of population loss had been capped by a corrupt mayor who teamed up with the CEO of Wall Street's biggest bank to restructure the city's debts, a decision akin to getting sex advice from a pedophile.

The bank, while in the midst of conning the city into interest-rate swap deals, was also knee deep in handing out subprime loans to anyone who could fog a mirror. These loans were securitized and promoted to investors who, not knowing the rating agencies were in on the scam, believed in the triple-A seals of approval assigned to anything pushed by the banks. The bullshit stopped when Lehman became the sacrificial lamb and interest rates soared on the city's swaps. Detroit's emergency manager ended up asking big finance to take a haircut. All had refused, but for one intrepid hedge fund manager out of Connecticut.

Rutherford Cameron's lustrous G6 jetted into Detroit the day before Brody debouched from his coach class misery. He glanced toward the car's passenger seat. There, a manila envelope contained transcripts of Cameron's communications documenting his offer to take a hit on his investment in hopes of helping the city get back on its feet. To celebrate, Detroit's emergency manager had met Cameron in a downtown entertainment district known as "Greek town." Cameron's final call home to his wife and kids had described a lavish celebratory dinner, the thought of which made Brody's mouth water. Flaming cheese; olives soaked in citrus zest, garlic, and oregano; tangy barrel-aged feta; lamb; spinach pie; and a plethora of sides served with hot bread and washed down with bottles of Xinomavro, and Assyrtiko.

Dinner had rolled along a little too well for Cameron, however, dizzy from more than the praise bestowed upon him. He had been last seen chatting it up with a couple at a casino blackjack table; drink in hand, his silk tie hanging askew from his well-tanned neck; vicuña wool jacket sleeves rolled up, and having the time of his life.

Just after daybreak they found Cameron's body in an abandoned lot.

Brody grimaced, thinking of his first job with the Bureau. He had been assigned to one of the few task forces scrutinizing Wall Street. Then, America's biggest banks blew themselves up. He had hounded his department head to investigate, but was reassigned for his efforts.

At least this time he was finally searching for justice, albeit in a world that rendered the term meaningless for most. Nonetheless, cracking open this case could earn him another shot at the system and maybe chase away the depression that had settled over him like a heavy black cloud.

Chapter 5

August 2016 – London, England

Detective Inspector Desmond Cusick braced his body against the wind cutting across the rooftop. Honking drifted up from below; drivers stuck in London's rush hour gridlock. He turned to scowl at his new partner.

Ian Hume straightened at the sight of Cusick's craggy face.

"Come here!" Cusick roared. The wind tore the words from his throat.

Hume edged forward, stopping several feet behind Cusick's perch.

"Goddamn it, don't be such a wanker!" Cusick said. Why he had been given such a wet behind the ears partner had initially befuddled him. However, staring out over the towering building's cliff-like edge, it began to make sense.

Twenty floors below the ninth floor rooftop jutted out from the massive structure's side. There, the pancaked body of a Vice-president from America's biggest bank had been found one week before. The initial investigation chalked it up as a suicide. Even so, no note had been found from a man otherwise at the peak of his career. Nevertheless, the authorities had closed the case. Then another senior banker took a dive, this time plunging off the roof of the same American bank's Hong Kong offices. The Mayor of London, recognizing he had a bloody cock-up on his hands, demanded they reopen the VP's file. Scotland Yard sent in Cusick.

His preliminary investigation showed nothing supposedly understood about the VP's death proved accurate. The initial Metropolitan Police report had been the dodgiest document he ever saw. Only because of a local reporter's work had Cusick discovered that three of the jumper's immediate co-workers were under investigation for rigging commodities markets. However, no one from the police had questioned them. Movement below interrupted his musing.

A bearded man shuffled through the alley's trash cans, one of the unfortunates left behind by the waves of globalization and financial innovation that had made London the richest city in the world. The homeless chap balanced a paper plate in his left hand. His right hand combed through the refuse picking out food scraps. Not fifty meters away the dark alley emptied into the bright, spotless street. Fresh faced junior bankers in tailored Saville Row suits hurried past, oblivious to the underworld a stone's throw away.

Meanwhile, a tentative presence inched closer on the rooftop's narrow edge.

"Look down," Cusick said. "Anything funny strike you about where our jumper landed?"

Hume eyed the chasm. His face pale, he glanced back to the sheltering rooftop door and then peeked again over the building's side. "How did that guy end up here," He jerked his thumb behind them, "and then down there?"

Cusick smiled for the first time all morning. Maybe young Hume wasn't as daft as he had suspected. No one other than senior security and maintenance personnel could access the roof. Immensely bulky and massive cooling machinery virtually blocked off this side of the building. Only after much effort had they figured out how to reach where they stood. In contrast, the roof's open opposite side featured a helicopter landing pad conveniently jutting out over the abyss.

"Either our banker wormed his way through the mess behind us to avoid being seen when he plummeted arse over tit," Cusick said, walking through it, "making sure to land on the projecting part of the roof below and guarantee that not until the next morning at the earliest would he be found or—"

"Somebody bloody well helped him along."

"It's that simple?"

"It's that simple," Hume responded.

Cusick frowned as he peered into the darkness below.

Nothing was ever that simple.

CHAPTER 6

February 1973 – New York City, New York

Jimmy glanced at the clock for the tenth time in the last two minutes. *What was going on in there?*

He sat on a hard plastic chair in the vice-principal's outer office. The gray-haired secretary pounded away on a typewriter, oblivious to the teenager wringing his hands.

He had started the fight. No doubt about that. The only question was how long would he be suspended?

The vice-principal's door opened. A red faced student stepped out, one hand pressing a bag of ice up to a swollen lip. The teenager, named McHenry, glared at Jimmy as a heavy set security guard pushed him forward.

"It's your turn Donnelly."

Jimmy jumped at the sound of vice-principal Fitzpatrick's voice. With a shock of red hair, and tired green eyes "Fitz" as everybody knew him, was a walking Irish stereotype in more ways than one, including his temper. Jimmy squeezed into Fitz's claustrophobically small office, the vice-principal waving him into a rickety chair in front of the comically large hickory desk taking up virtually the entire room.

Fitz fell into a plush leather chair opposite Jimmy.

An envelope sat open on the desk. Jimmy gulped when he saw his name affixed to the protruding tab.

"I cannot figure this out," Fitz said, leaning forward, his suit jacket bunching up around his shoulders. "McHenry told me that one of your buddies hit him in the head with a French fry at lunch. He says that when he complained about it, you sucker punched him. Here's the thing…"

Fitz's hand drifted over to rest on a fat file emblazoned with McHenry's name. He paused, making sure Jimmy watched.

Jimmy stared, his mouth dry. *I'm so fucked. That's exactly how it went down.*

"McHenry is a jackass," Fitz announced. "If it weren't for his father's donations, he would have been kicked out of school years ago. On the other hand, you've never been in trouble. Though I'm not surprised, bet you didn't know that I used to work with your dad. How is he? Still holding down the fort at Salomon Brothers?"

Fitz waved off Jimmy's attempt to reply, "Why don't you tell me what *really* happened in that lunch room today."

Jimmy froze, his mouth open in an 'o' for one painfully long second before he realized what was happening. He tried his hardest to look earnest as the lies spilled from his mouth. "Yes sir. McHenry swung at me first…"

Thirty minutes later Jimmy strolled out of the office, a smile creasing his face. He wasn't getting suspended. His father wouldn't be called. What's more, and courtesy of Fitz's orders, McHenry was taking the rap for everything.

Jimmy Donnelly had learned much about how justice worked in *his* world.

Life was good.

August 2016 – London, England

Cusick and Hume hustled into the skyscraper's interior, winding their way to the elevator. At Cusick's request their escort, a powerfully built Pakistani security guard, marched them to the exit into the alley. There the detectives plunged outside, the alley's rank smell slapping them in the face. As a teenager working in a restaurant, Cusick remembered the godawful task of taking the fryer's rancid oil out for disposal. Combine that with the dead air hanging heavy between the huge buildings, the grime and human waste permeating the dark, narrow alleyway, and—

"C'mon man. What're we doing out here." Hume muttered through his right arm mashed up across his mouth and nose.

"There," Cusick pointed up the alley. Derby shoes splashed through puddles of filth as he headed for a homeless man digging through a trash can—the same man he had seen from the roof. Badge flipped open Cusick stopped in front of his fragrant target, careful not to stand too close.

"We're not here to harass you. Just a few questions okay?"

The man's eyes showed white in his dirt streaked face. He nodded, crumbs scattered through his beard.

"You got a name?"

"Patrick."

"This your regular hunting grounds?"

Patrick cleared his throat, a death grip on the paper plate's bread crusts, half eaten chicken wings, and rotting celery. "As soon as it gets light and until they," He jerked his head toward the bustling street outside the alley, "are out."

"Ever miss a day?"

"You kidding? This's one of the best alley's around. You wouldn't believe what gets thrown away."

"Notice anything strange lately? Maybe in the middle of the night? A few weeks back?"

"Piss off."

"It'd be a shame if someone else jumped your claim."

Patrick met Cusick's stare, saying nothing. A sharp intelligence danced behind his soft eyes.

After several seconds he gave in with a sigh, "You mean the jumper."

"Anybody come talk to you?"

"I heard a thump one night. The next day they pulled a body off that lower roof," Patrick said, pointing. "That's all I know."

Cusick frowned. Patrick's jumpy eyes far from jived with his words.

"How'd you end up here?"

"I worked as a consultant for fifteen years." A weary smile tugged at the corners of Patrick's mouth. "Then I got me P45." He eyed Cusick's hand as it flipped open a billfold. "Couldn't find work, ran down my accounts. Hit the bottle."

Cusick held up a ten pound note.

Patrick's pupils dilated, but he paused as if he faced a real decision.

Cusick dug a few more pence from his pocket. "You got three seconds or—"

"You bloody well better know what you're doing," Patrick said, snatching the proffered money. "I heard a weird sound right after the jumper fell. It came from up there." He pointed toward the rooftop. "Before I say anything else – I'm not crazy. I used to bring home a regular paycheck before the troubles hit."

Cusick didn't know what to believe. He lived in a society built on lies. Even so, once in a while the ugly truth of what London had become slithered free. He liked being there when it did.

"About that sound…"

"It damned near scared me to death," Patrick said, coughing and glancing down.

Cusick waited, a strange feeling life was about to change teasing a dark corner of his mind.

Finally, Patrick spoke in a voice barely more than a whisper. "It was something howling."

CHAPTER 7

August 2016 – Detroit, Michigan

Brody merged onto the trash strewn highway off ramp. A red traffic light hung listlessly above the potholed service drive. Shattered shells of old buildings, once housing bustling stores, formed a lifeless concrete canyon.

To his left a beggar slouched against a torn chain link fence. His tattered t-shirt read: "US Third Infantry Division." Dirty fingers gripped a cardboard sign: "Iraq War Veteran. Please Help." The grimy McDonald's coffee cup in front of him was empty.

Brody fished in his pocket and tossed a couple of wadded up dollars out of the window.

The man scrambled to life, waving his thanks.

The light turned green.

Brody wound his way into a labyrinth of side streets marking Detroit's east side; meaning everything east of Woodward Avenue. A one-time symbol of technological progress, Woodward featured the first mile of paved concrete laid down in the United States. Now it drove like a dirt road after a hard rain.

He turned the corner. Where homes once stood weeds swayed waist high in the hot breeze. Jarringly tilted telephone poles resembled old pictures of Nazi obstacles guarding the D-Day invasion beaches. Burned out buildings punctuated most blocks, the carcasses of torched cars blighted the worst streets. In the few occupied homes faces appeared between narrow gaps in shades otherwise drawn tight. His vehicle, a Chevy, a symbol of everything the people once had. In the street, the occasional piece of paper blowing in the random wind came up haltingly as if it were too much effort in the summer's heat. Not a single kid played on the sidewalks.

He cruised by the low slung wreck of an elementary school. Chain link fence posts stood forlorn guard around the building, the fencing long since torn out by scavengers trying to survive in a twenty first century America fast becoming a nation of Jawas. Next to the school wispy strands of black smoke reached skyward as crackling flames licked along the shattered roof of a century old Craftsman house - the fire department nowhere to be seen.

On the opposite side of the street, a Rottweiler ambled along a buckled sidewalk. A massive scar ran down its muscular shoulder. Without breaking stride, the dog turned its head, locked eyes with Brody, and veered behind another abandoned home. Brody gripped the leather wrapped steering wheel, unable to shake the feeling the country stood on the precipice of a dark inflection point.

He rounded the next corner and was there.

A field took up most of the block, a smattering of homes in various states of abandonment or occupation clustered on the far end. He cruised up to where yellow tape marked a portion of the clearing. Nearby a couch squatted in front of a wrecked house, coil springs showing through ripped cushions. A couple of beat up squad cars, a work van, and an unmarked police car blocked the street. Brody parked and stepped out of the rental, the desolate cityscape bleached white by the late morning sun. In the distance gleamed the silver shining towers of General Motors world headquarters, thrusting into the sky like so many silos.

A beat cop leaning on a squad car eyed him as he stepped by, Brody's shoes crunching in the dry grass. The sickly vinegar smell of piss and decay filled the heavy air. He dodged empty liquor bottles scattered in the weeds, eying the decrepit house to his right. A graffiti covered plywood sheet hung diagonally over what had been the abandoned home's front door. The bottom corner had been ripped apart as if something had clawed through it. Brody walked around the house in a big arc. His eyes never quite left the empty window frames, the hot air pushing strips of washed-out wallpaper hanging inside, blackness beyond, more darkness under the porch. He came around the house thankful to see other people.

A short beer keg of a man picked at an object in the tall grass.

Beyond him stood what had to be the local Bureau agent.

To the agent's left a grizzled street cop argued with a civilian as another cop observed.

"Ok, Ray that's enough." The officer held his hands up to calm down a caramel colored older man, big ears projecting from his round head. The FBI agent watched. He was a rangy fellow that looked at least a decade older than Brody, hands on his hips, his eyes concealed behind *Top Gun* style aviator sunglasses.

"I hear *sounds* at night. They ain't normal, man." Ray's girlish voice carried across the field, sweat shining on his bald pate.

A young cop lingering on the fringe of the conversation offered his two cents, "Look Bi—"

Ray's eyes narrowed.

"Sorry..." The second cop stammered, "It's probably just a pack of dogs."

The senior officer, a sergeant, glared at his partner. Everybody around here referred to Ray as "The Bitch" in part because of his high-pitched voice, but mostly because his ex-wife had cuckolded him with every swinging dick around. The sergeant sighed and directed the younger cop to get a statement. He could care less about Ray, but the dogs were an issue. The other day a pack of pit bulls took the hands and feet off some poor bastard.

"You've got a bigger problem than dogs," The man poking around the field said, standing up, brow furrowed, deep lines creasing his forehead.

Brody sneezed.

The sergeant nearly jumped out of his skin.

"Jim Vance," The FBI agent said, right hand extended in greeting, pointing with his left. "This here's Sergeant Jefferson. And that's the medical examiner, Dr. Elliot."

They strode toward Elliot, careful to avoid stepping on anything passable as evidence, the ripe odor of putrid flesh permeating the air.

"Jesus Christ," Brody gasped as he got his first glance at the remains. Even Jefferson, who had doubtlessly worked numerous homicides, breathed shallowly.

"Not exactly," Elliot said to Brody as he snapped on a fresh pair of surgical gloves, "but there's a certain 'quality' to the scale of dismemberment."

Bile rose in Brody's throat. He swallowed it back, fighting to hold his composure.

"The head is nowhere to be found. A leg is over there," Elliot said, gesturing toward a fly covered lump.

Brody didn't look, thinking of Cameron's watch and the customized inscription that had proved key to the body's early identification. It was a *Panerai Luminor 1950 3 Days GMT* worth as much as Brody's rental car. Yet, it had been discovered out in the open and untouched. *Even the scavengers had avoided what went down.* In spite of the nausea roiling his stomach Brody willed himself to analyze the body, noticing the long hairs stuck in the bloody grass underneath the wrecked torso.

"Cause of death?" Vance said.

"Claws and teeth," Elliot replied.

"You sure about that?" Vance said. "Maybe he was killed somewhere else, dumped here, and then a pack of dogs got to him?"

"The victim was alive when he entered this field," Elliot said, his voice insistent. "There are no signs of man-made trauma such as that inflicted by a knife, gun, baseball bat, garrote, you name it."

Brody gritted his teeth. The mob had once used garrotes, but that had been years ago. Furthermore, they had nothing to link Cameron to any non-Wall Street initiated organized crime.

"See how the skin's been shredded?" Elliot said, driving home his point.

Most of the flesh had been removed from the hipbone; cracks spider webbed across the abraded surface. In addition, a line of deep punctures ran in a semicircular row across the outside of the hip. Brody felt weak and small in the face of the carnage, clinging to the hope that the damage was man made.

"These wounds are from teeth, big ones. They shattered the Iliac Crest," Elliot said. "No dog can splinter a bone like that. Nor have I ever heard of a dog with teeth like this." He pulled a plastic baggy out of his pocket; the curved cutting end of what must have been a six-inch long fang in the otherwise incongruous container.

Elliot turned their attention back to the body, "Notice anything about the hole on the victim's hip."

"It's larger than the others," Brody said.

"That's because this tooth was ripped free by our victim twisting away from whatever sought to disembowel him."

Vance snorted, running a hand across his close-cropped hair.

"I sent samples to the lab at Michigan State University," Elliot said, stretching his lower back. "You can expect the results back quick, maybe later today."

"Keep me in the loop Doc," Brody said, nodding his approval as he strode off.

"Christ, what a mess," Vance said, falling in beside him.

"That mess had a wife and two kids," Brody said as he opened his car door, his skin crawling with nerves, eyes drawn to the derelict house and its shadowy interior. An irrational part of him wondered if Cameron's killer was still around.

"I ordered a review of local flights to see if the victim's casino companions arrived in town recently," Vance said.

Brody nodded to indicate his approval. Procedure dictated waiting on the agent in charge but he wasn't one to pull rank even on the rare instances he had it. A breeze kicked up, the plywood sheet over the abandoned home's front doorway banging open and closed. He tensed, sensing something moving inside.

"I also assigned someone to review the security camera footage from the casino."

"Good," Brody said, eyeing the house.

"Hopefully, we'll get a better look at the suspects."

Brody stared at the house, sure he saw a shadow within a busted out window.

"They got cameras in the parking garage. Maybe we can get a plate number on the perp's car."

"Uh huh," Brody said, craning his neck. There was no angle to the sunlight, leaving the home's interior swathed in darkness.

Vance drawled on. The beat cop appeared, shuffling through the grass next to the house, eyes glued to his smart phone, smiling as his fingers texted in a rhythmic pattern. The shadow *moved* in response to the approaching cop—

"Look out!" Brody shouted, ripping his .45 free of its holster.

The cop's smart phone fell into the grass, his hand dropping to the Glock on his hip as Brody targeted *something* inside.

"Stand down," Vance yelled. "Stand down for chrissakes, it's just a cabinet."

The light shifted. Then Brody saw it. A hutch in what must have been the dining room.

He paused, and then holstered his pistol, an old Model 1911 semi-automatic.

The beat cop glared at him as if he were out of his mind.

Vance's hand gripped Brody's shoulder.

He turned, seeing the agent's lips moving, hearing nothing. After another moment Vance's voice penetrated past the ringing in his ears, "Take it easy, Brody. Calm down."

Brody fell into the car's driver's seat, the door thunking shut after him. Confusion replaced by embarrassment.

"With what happened in Dallas and Baton Rouge I get it," Vance said as he squatted, head level with the open window. "We're all on edge. But still, what the fuck was that about?"

"Instincts a little off, I guess."

"You *guess?*" Vance said. "We've got a hedge fund manager gutted by an animal of some sort, and now you're acting like this?"

"I don't know much more than you," Brody said, "and not enough for that stunt I just pulled."

"Look, son. I've been playing this game a long time," Vance said. "So don't piss down my leg and tell me it's raining."

Brody paused, sizing up his colleague. Vance couldn't have been more than fifty-five, but he looked older, his face leathery in the way of certain folks that had spent a lifetime in the sun.

"Fair enough," Brody finally responded. "Now, if you don't mind I'm gonna pay a visit to that blackjack dealer that last saw Cameron alive." He shifted in the leather seat's hot grip. Needing a distraction he turned on the radio.

"I heard this ain't the only banker that's run into some misfortune," Vance said

"Forget that. If word gets out, it'll turn into a clown show," Brody said. He clicked on his seatbelt, stiffening at the news coming in over the radio: *"The embattled CEO of Wall Street's Biggest Bank, testifying today on Capitol Hill, to receive a 75 percent raise—"*

"DOJ hit Donnelly's bank with $20 billion in fines, and now this?" Vance said.

"You're preachin' to the choir," Brody said, suppressing a flash of hatred at the mention of Donnelly's name.

"That may be, but the people aren't stupid," Vance said, stretching to his full height. "They see us looking the other way every time these guys ignore the law. You tell me breaking bad doesn't seem like a good idea when you're the one waking up to the fact hope ain't change."

"That's the catch, isn't it?" Brody said. "Our job isn't about to get any easier, is it?"

"That's where you're wrong, friend. It's more than our problem," Vance said, glancing at the downtown skyline less than a mile away. "I didn't take to Detroit at first. However, the city's grown on me. Though, I'll tell you something that hasn't. There's this ring of prosperity around the business district that's nicer than ever. Surrounding it is a hundred square miles of misery. What happened to Cameron, part of me thinks it's just the beginning."

Brody stared up at Vance.

Seconds ticked by under the hot sun.

Vance bit his tongue, sensing Brody was chewing on something good.

"I had been looking into mortgage and securities fraud on Wall Street," Brody finally said, a voice inside telling him he could trust Vance. "I compiled enough evidence to go after Donnelly. The Attorney General's office shut me down. I pushed harder. They pushed back. I lost."

Vance's eyes opened wider, drilling into Brody.

"We had one of Donnelly's underlings on the hook," Brody said. "I was sure he would roll over."

"That's right," Vance said. "Sweat him and see what he gives up."

"The AG's office and the SEC Chief of Enforcement claimed lack of evidence." A bitter smile played across Brody's lips, "Apparently the SEC Chief once worked with Donnelly."

"But how did you end up—"

"If I screw this up that's it." Brody didn't want to discuss the possibility that his life's goals were slipping away.

Vance's right eye twitched. His new partner hadn't told him everything but he had told him enough.

"Thanks for listening," Brody said. "I appreciate it, but I gotta skate."

"It's your show," Vance said.

Brody pulled away, trying to ignore the sick dread eating at him. The blackjack dealer lived in Brody's hometown. He felt a sudden need to check in on his parents. He didn't have the time, but he didn't know when he would be home again.

He flipped the radio on: "*The country's biggest bank is the subject of at least six major federal investigations, and today's testimony by its CEO is meant—*" He punched the radio off, exiting the highway after thirty minutes of driving in silence. He cruised west into the heart of the township and the subdivision where the blackjack dealer lived. A half hour later he jumped back on the road.

The dealer hadn't helped. She claimed she hardly remembered Cameron, no less the couple chatting it up with him.

He didn't buy it. She was lying.

The look in her eyes also told him something else.

She was scared.

Brody pulled onto a north-south running side street, leaving his hometown's depressing main drag behind, a choked parking lot of congestion boasting three of the most dangerous intersections in the state. Meanwhile, the refugees from Detroit flowed in on the strength of the community and school district's reputation, both now ghosts of their former selves, the once promising township lacking a downtown, an identity, and a soul.

CHAPTER 8

September 1977 – New Haven, Connecticut

Jimmy Donnelly stopped midstride, cocking his head at the tantalizing sound of jiggling ice cubes and the chance to alleviate the frustration that had been plaguing him all week. The pledges had been depressingly perfect. Even when ordered to burn one hundred dollar bills in front of a homeless woman, not a single one of them had protested, no less blanched. That meant no one needed to be punished.

Until now.

Donnelly tried hard not to smile, his face screwed into an appropriate mask of rage as he adjusted the cuff of his navy blue blazer and spun on his heels. His immaculately shined loafers clicked across the hardwood floor, reflecting the subdued light from dozens of candles holding at bay the dark shadows enveloping the great room's edges. He marched down the line of ten pledges, each stripped naked and sucking their thumbs while standing in a metal bucket of ice water.

Donnelly's eyes settled on his target, Herbert Rasher. Herbert's double chin and narrow shoulders gave way to pepperoni-sized nipples protruding from the pledge's pale shivering skin. Donnelly's eyes scanned down further, before forcing himself to look away from Herbert's feminine pear shaped lower body. The corner of Donnelly's lip curled, the fat but oh so ambitious pledge was on his way to becoming a congressman every bit as venal as his dear old dad, a former chapter president. First however, Herbert would learn a lesson in power.

"Explain that noise I heard," Donnelly said.

"What noise, sir?"

Donnelly's hands curled into fists, Herbert's lie a colossal mistake.

"Mister Fitch," Donnelly said, smiling cruelly.

Fitch, the house treasurer, stepped forward from the line of brothers standing at heightened attention opposite the pledges.

"Is Herbert being appropriately forthcoming?" Donnelly said, never taking his eyes off the pledge.

"No, sir. Everybody heard the ice slosh in the bucket, sir." Fitch's voice rang clearly in the wood paneled room.

"Thank you, Mister Fitch. What's the penalty for failure?"

"I'll retrieve the paddle, sir." Fitch said, hardly needing to remind anyone that the hazing ritual required the pledges to stand perfectly motionless in the frigid water for twenty minutes straight.

"No," Donnelly said, licking his lips. "Herbert lied to his president in front of the entire chapter. Bring out 'Old Jake.'"

A collective gasp swept through the room. The pledges eyes widened, not knowing what was coming but frightened by the stunned reaction of the upperclassmen.

"But sir!" Fitch cried.

"If you can't perform your duties I'll find someone that will."

"No, sir. I mean I will grab it right away sir," Fitch said, hands shaking as he ran for the basement stairs.

"Mister Cardle," Donnelly barked.

"Yes, sir."

"Take away all the pledges away, except Herbert. They've passed."

"Sir."

The freezing teenagers slipped away across the hardwood floors, casting terrified glances back. The double doors boomed shut behind them. The room fell silent, except for Herbert's wheezing through his quivering lips.

The seventeen remaining fraternity brothers nervously awaited Fitch's return. The entire time Donnelly stared down the shivering pledge, Donnelly's mouth slightly open as he breathed harder in anticipation, sharp canines protruding.

Herbert stared at Donnelly's big teeth, fighting against the pressure in his rapidly filling bladder.

After several moments dimly heard footsteps gave way to Fitch marching into view, a foot-long wooden box in his shaking hand.

"Sir I—" Fitch began.

"I'll do it, you pussy."

Fitch handed off the box. A shiver of fear danced along his scalp at the sight of his chapter president's dilated pupils. They were black, inhuman. Fitch stepped back.

"Turn around, and bend over," Donnelly said to Herbert while rolling up his sleeves.

Herbert complied.

Murmurs swept through the room. Fraternity brothers glanced to their left and right, furtively making eye contact with each other, wondering when Donnelly would stop.

Struggling not to stare too hard at Herbert's wide swept hips and fleshy white backside, Donnelly opened the box. The fraternity brothers fell into a silenced shock, staring at the object Donnelly removed and held in his hand.

It was a long Coco-Cola bottle thick dildo.

Fitch gasped, breathing heavily. The look on Donnelly's face was sickening. His lips had skinned back from his teeth, making them look bigger than he remembered. Even worse, Donnelly was leering at Herbert's quaking body. Each time Fitch looked at Donnelly a feeling of something slithering along his skin prodded him to back away further.

Donnelly held the rubbery dildo up like a long lost artifact, barely controlling his volcanically broiling excitement. Though many of the watching fraternity brothers appeared anguished, several of their peers leaned forward excitedly.

Herbert risked a glance over his shoulder, shock registering on his face.

Donnelly's onrushing tunnel vision focused in on Herbert, a long suppressed memory of his screaming baby brother momentarily sending exploding lights dancing behind his eyes. He felt impossibly powerful, his consciousness straddling two worlds, senses alive. Then the darkness swept in. Donnelly's arm thrust forward violently, eyes dulling over as a jolt of pleasure shot from his toes to his balls.

Herbert's first bleating screams pierced the room.

Outside the old Victorian fraternity house, a blood moon hung low and orange in the night sky.

August 2016 – Detroit's Western Suburbs

Brody turned into his old neighborhood, feeling a twinge of anxiety. He was wasting time and knew it. Even so, just being there made him feel safe, reminding him of a pleasant childhood before he discovered the awful truth of what the world—

His sentimental journey hit the brick wall of reality, a foreclosure notice fluttering on the front door of the third home he drove past. On the driveway, a woman in a tank top filled an aluminum framed lawn chair. It's frayed green, white, and blue webbing barely supported her prodigious weight. Two children played in a sprinkler on a patchy front lawn dotted with dandelions.

He guided the car down the street and around the bend where his childhood best friend, Chris Granger, had been raised. Chris' parents, retired school teachers, had lived there since 1977 when it had been built. Past their house loomed his first girlfriend's old place. A leggy brunette who loved alternative music, she had taken his virginity and provided him a four year relationship that lasted two year's too long.

Brody braked and pulled into the next home's sloping driveway. A flat expanse of garage door took up half its brown bricked width. He stepped from his car, peeking over his shoulder. Across the street and behind a single row of houses a quarter mile strip of woodland and parks separated his neighborhood from the next one to the west. His mostly joyful youth had included endless hours in the wilderness playground that on only three occasions ever caused him to feel frightened.

The first time he discovered the world might not be as safe as he thought had been when he and Chris swore they found Bigfoot footprints. In the late 1970s, it seemed to any sensible kid the beast was genuine. Leonard Nimoy's tense, creepy *In Search Of* spoke of it while the next night the *Six Million Dollar Man* battled the creature. Meanwhile, the Saturday afternoon horror movie of the week's eerie Led Zeppelin scored intro all too often led into another TV showing of the *Legend of Boggy Creek*. Brody's smile turned down as he remembered the second time the forest put a shock into him...

By nine years of age, he knew every trail, creek, and gulley crisscrossing the woods. Not coincidentally, one cold winter day he and

Chris discovered a fort. But it wasn't just any fort. It belonged to Frank Castro. Every kid feared the big teenager and his gang. Sundry humiliations, scams, petty robberies; Frank and his buddies loved shaking down weaker kids. They always got away with it.

Brody's anger at the injustice of Frank's predations had resurfaced that day they found the ground level fort. An anger usurped by the opportunity posed from Frank's arrogant decision to secure the padlocked door with outside hinges. Wielding the matching Swiss Army knives he and Chris had received from their parents for Christmas, they unfolded the screwdriver attachments and methodically dismantled the door. Inside they found a treasure trove of early 1980s burnout paraphernalia - candles, incense, Heavy Metal music, and weirdly decorated pipes nothing like what his dad stuffed with sweet tobacco for an evening smoke.

Brody harbored no illusions as to how Frank's crew stocked their funky fort. Their parents gave them whatever they wanted. If that wasn't enough they used the money they stole to buy up everything else. It was payback time. He and Chris helped themselves; cassette tapes, matches, lighters, and a switchblade. With their coats stuffed, they had headed home. However, not two minutes later they ran into trouble - three ugly teenagers led by Frank Castro brandishing a pellet gun. To the quaking kids, the teenagers seemed gigantic.

"You see anybody out here?" Frank said, his friend's Todd and Craig glowering around his shoulders. Todd's beady eyes stared out of his porcine face with a creepy intensity that had caused Chris to turn paler than the back of his grandma's arms.

"Back that way," Brody said as he pointed over his shoulder. "Two guys in a hurry and headed toward the other sub-division." Had he left it at that it might have been enough, but he couldn't be sure, especially with Chris looking like this was all news to him. He threw in the kicker, "We can help you find 'em if you want."

Chris nearly fainted.

"Alright," Frank's accusatory glare disappeared. "Holler if you see anything."

Brody nodded, needing to pee.

The big teenager's gang plunged down the trail.

"Let's go," Chris said.

"Are you kidding me?" Brody shot back. "If we don't do this right, we'll pay."

In retrospect, their outfits had probably saved them, the winter jackets matched in their bulk by coordinating ski pants. The combined effect not only hid their bulging pockets underneath but may have thrown off Frank's crew when they confronted the clammy faced boys. Brody moved off a few steps into the forest. Reaching into his pocket he pulled out a pipe and tossed it down. Brody glanced at Chris, who nodded his understanding and dropped the best prize of the day - the knife.

"We found something!" Brody yelled, cupping his hands to his mouth.

Within moments Frank and his toadies appeared, Frank swiping the pipe off the ground, eyes wide in recognition.

"Holy shit, look at this!" Chris said from down the path, his voice sounding convincingly surprised.

"Hey, it's my switchblade," Frank snarled as he shouldered past Brody.

Brody couldn't believe their luck. But then, and to his horror, he realized the path also showed the tracks they had left an hour prior in the fresh snow, footprints moving toward the fort.

He gulped.

They were pinched.

Instead, Frank took one glimpse at the tracks and lumbered off, "C'mon. They might be headed back."

Frank's cronies tore after their leader, as Brody and Chris used the distraction to make good on their escape...

Brody's frown deepened as he thought of the third time his woods had put the fear of God into him.

Not now.

CHAPTER 9

August 2016 – Detroit's Western Suburbs

A door slammed. Brody turned toward the white and gray split level across the street. A For Sale sign listed forlornly on the front lawn.

"Lookie, here," The owner, a burly man named Matt Potter, said as he marched down his driveway.

Brody smiled but he didn't have time for small talk. However, as Matt's ruddy face broke into a grin Brody relaxed a bit, gesturing at the sign, "Retiring already?"

"I lost my job," Matt said, his smile disappearing. "Ford is moving the plant to Mexico."

A breeze kicked up like a blast furnace had opened in Brody's face. Sweat trickled down the small of his back.

"It doesn't make sense, does it? The cost of moving the machinery alone is insane..."

Brody listened. *What could he say? That guys like Matt didn't have a chance unless they put it all on the line? Nobody wanted to hear that.*

Shadows flitted across the road.

"My former supervisor told me I should go back to school," Matt said. "What does he expect? People don't just change who they are."

Brody nodded empathetically but distracted by the shadows, glanced up. Two hawks wheeled high above.

"I'll tell you something. Karma is a bitch. What goes around comes around." Matt brought Brody back to ground level.

"Yea, well," Brody sighed. "I've seen plenty of bad people do what they want, and get away with it."

An awkward silence followed.

"I got an appointment with the realtor," Matt said, sticking out his hand.

Brody took it, Matt's grip tight.

"I hope you remember what it's like to not only give a shit, but to do something about it before it's too late," Matt said, releasing Brody's hand and marching off.

After a long moment, Brody turned and walked up his parent's driveway. Having called ahead, he yanked open the screeching screen door without knocking. His dad was a spry seventy-five but his mom had been battling rheumatoid arthritis for decades. Brody greeted his parents and followed them into the kitchen where the TV caught his attention: *"Jimmy Donnelly is testifying on Capitol Hill in conjunction with yesterday's announcement that his bank has agreed to a $1.92 billion settlement with the U.S. Department of Justice. The bank had been fighting against claims that it laundered billions of dollars for Mexican drug cartels."* The screen cut to a live feed of a congressman pontificating for the cameras: *"Your latest settlement is in response to at least the third felony admitted to by your bank in the past four years—"* Another voice cut in, *"Let me explain something you're missing."* The screen switched to the smiling face of Jimmy Donnelly.

"Could you please turn that off?" Brody said as he sat down at the kitchen table.

"Sure, hun," His mother said. Her once dainty hands were curled into gnarled hooks. Even so, she managed to not only get the right button on the remote, but quicker than one would have thought possible threw together a bologna sandwich and fizzing glass of Vernors ginger ale.

"Anything new to report?" She asked, shoveling some chips on the plate, nearly dropping it as she set it in front of Brody, "Maybe you've got someone new? Like that nice girl you brought over for Christmas that one time? Any fool could see—"

"Enough mom," Brody said with a sigh as a long suppressed memory jogged loose... He was in Vermont, riding up a chairlift. The woman pressed in next to him gleefully kicked her boots over the thirty-plus foot drop to the snow below. He had always been nervous about heights, but something about being with *her* made him confident. He remembered how he had leaned in, her hair cool, smelling crisply of the outdoors, the blood pounding in his heart—

"You hear about the Grangers?" His dad said, waving the cat off the table.

Brody tore off a corner of his sandwich and tossed the prize in a soft arc. The agile feline caught it with ease as Brody shook his head 'no' in response to his father's question. The Grangers had always treated him like a second son. For that, and innumerable other reasons, he would forever be grateful.

"They're losing their house," Brody's Dad said. "They were cooking dinner. A grease fire started. The fire department ended up hosing the place down like it was the *Towering Inferno.*"

"They didn't have insurance?"

His dad told him how the insurance company rebuilt the house. Meanwhile, the Grangers and their insurer had requested a ten day payoff from the bank servicing the loan. The bank said to suspend the monthly auto withdrawal. Then the insurer sent the bank a check along with a letter requesting they pay off the mortgage. The bank cashed the check upon receipt and put the money in a suspense account. The Grangers, having always been financially prudent, discovered the mortgage still in effect. The collectors wouldn't leave them alone, calling day and night. Then the bank asked if the Grangers could fax them another payoff request. The Grangers did. The bank said they never received it. The Grangers faxed them again and emailed a scanned copy to be sure. It didn't matter. The bank collectors wanted nine grand in fees plus the monies they claimed past due, even though the bank had cashed the insurance company's check.

Brody listened, knowing *whose* bank not only held the Granger's mortgage but had decided to strong-arm certain people into paying more fees. People that he had let down all because—

"Tell me someone is investigating this?"

"It's complicated," Brody responded, fidgeting in his seat.

"Fraud is just lying to steal. How complicated is that? It's the same as if someone broke into their house with a gun. If that happens then you've got every right to—"

Brody's ringing smart phone saved him from the lecture. He jumped up from his chair and stepped outside onto the concrete patio leading to the swimming pool. At one time at least a third of the neighbors had pools. Now most couldn't afford it. He answered the call.

"Doctor Timothy Martin speaking, the Detroit medical examiner told me to get ahold of you. I'm head of the Diagnostic Center for

Population and Animal Health at Michigan State University. I've finished my analysis of the sample that was sent."

"So whaddya have for me, Doc? Rottweiler, Pit Bull, or what?"

"Uhhh, no," Martin cleared his throat.

"Come again," Brody said. The smart phone felt hot against his ear, a sickening buzzing feeling making him feel queasy.

"Maybe we could discuss this in person?"

"Ok, let's meet out in Brighton," Brody said. "It's halfway, and there's a little pub downtown, a bit of a dive but known for its hamburgers—"

"I know the place," Martin said. "I'm on my way."

July 1988 – New York City, New York

Mary Jackson's world crumbled as her husband Dan raged at the young bank manager.

The banker sat behind his desk, a degree from Yale framed on the wall behind his impassive head. A plastic name plate shined under the ceiling's harsh fluorescent lighting. The manager's name "Jim Donnelly" embossed in white lettering. At initial glance it all checked out. Yet, something about him seemed *off*.

Mary was trying to place the source of her discomfort when Donnelly's gaze flickered across her ample cleavage. At the same time his lips parted to reveal unusually large teeth. A long, lolling tongue slipped past those teeth. The tip pointed toward Mary for just a moment before it slithered back inside as the right side of Donnelly's mouth curled up in a sneer, his eyes glittering with hunger.

Dan didn't see any of it, though he wouldn't have noticed a meteor hitting her on the head. That was because Donnelly had denied their request for a loan they desperately needed to expand their newly thriving auto garage, and a loan that represented perhaps their one chance to make something better of their lives. Donnelly had responded to Dan's hostility with a maddeningly paternal tone, calmly explaining that without a regular verifiable income, or without putting their house up as collateral it wouldn't work out.

"I'm done with this asshole," Dan said, jumping to his feet as he waved his hand at Mary. "I'll see you in the car."

He slammed the door behind him, the office walls rattling.

Mary, a cocktail waitress at a sports bar, knew she had to do something. She hesitated, the office feeling that much smaller with Dan's protective presence gone. Donnelly's ogling gaze devoured her chest once more. Mary shook off her fears, knowing how important this was and responding as she had with other men easily manipulated by her physical charms. Nevertheless, she overlooked one important fact. Donnelly wasn't like most other men.

"Gee, Mister Donnelly. I'm awfully sorry about my husband," Mary said, cautiously smiling. "It's just that this loan is so important." She leaned forward as she spoke, her breasts practically spilling from her form-fitting dress.

"Loans are complicated things, Mrs. Jackson. There's risk and not much upside." Donnelly stood, his smile becoming even more wolfish. Trying to control his dizzying emotions he hurried to the door, clicking it locked. An electric energy pulsed within him as his lips pulled back from his teeth, "On the other hand, I'm finding myself open to a change of mind."

Mary, who had brightened with the thought Donnelly might be an easy play, quivered anew at the sight of his teeth. His expression more frightening than similar stares she had seen before from men like him. Most typically at work, when a certain type of guy would walk into the bar and offer her fifty bucks for the panties she had been wearing throughout a grimy eight hour shift. The kind of guy that when she said no upped the ante to one hundred bucks if she would let him smell her pussy. As bad as those guys were, however, Donnelly exuded danger in a way every day perverts could never hope to match. Yet, Mary suppressed her instincts.

They needed that loan worse than anything.

She choked back her unease, smiling sweetly.

Donnelly walked up in front of Mary. A familiar and delicious darkness rushed through his body, the tingling feeling in his legs tickling his awakening crotch.

Mary glanced up, the man's eyes dancing wildly behind fluttering eyelids. *Why was he getting so close? Normal creeps just wanted a look down her top.* A sickening dread shot through her lurching stomach as she finally understood Donnelly expected more than she had ever before been prepared to offer. Unfortunately for Mary, that realization came too late to matter.

Donnelly stepped between her legs, midsection pressing toward her face. She twisted away. His right hand shot out and grasped the back of her head, fingers digging painfully into her scalp, the fight draining from her muscles. She fell back into the chair, tears shimmering in her eyes. "Oh God, please no!" she heard herself begging, regretting it as soon as the words escaped her lips, seeing Donnelly's slacks lewdly tenting in response.

Donnelly panted at the sight of her deliciously trembling figure. Fumbling with his fly, his left hand fished inside. His right hand released her sobbing head, and roughly ripped down the top of her dress. Saliva flooded his mouth at the sight of her lush breasts spilling free. A barely repressed urge to taste her nearly overpowered his dwindling self-control. His last thought before he pulled her whimpering mouth to him was that *life was awesome.*

CHAPTER 10

August 2016 – London, England

Detective Ian Cusick finished the report and eased back in his chair. His desk lamp battled against the empty office's darkness. Even Hume had gone home. He stared at the glowing computer screen. The grand reopening of the file had been for show. When he refused to play along, his boss had buried him in menial work, a big chunk of it he was finally wrapping up. In the meantime, he had hedged his bets and given Patrick a cheap disposable phone and his number. That had been two weeks prior. He had heard nothing since.

Still, it had only been in the past few days that he had been able to sleep through the night again. He shook his head, a wry smile crossing his lips…*the howling. That Patrick was a cheeky bastard - probably enjoyed sending the cops on a wild goose chase after the werewolves of London. Well played friend, well played indeed.*

Cusick hit send and stood, taking one last glance at a picture on his desk of his wife and three kids. He glided through the ghostly quiet of the empty cubicles. The huge room bustled with a sea of activity on most days. Even so, this late on a Friday night not even a janitor could be found.

He hit the down elevator button just as his phone buzzed with a text message. He glanced at the phone's screen, his eyes widening.

"It's Patrick. It's happening again. Please hurry!"

August 2016 – Southeast Michigan

Brody squinted as he stepped inside the pub. It was dark inside in spite of the mid-day sun. The smell of fried onion rings and grilled meat hung in the stale air. A wall-mounted TV broadcast the latest news about Donnelly's testimony before Congress. Brody spotted a trim older man sitting in a low slung booth. The man played with his smart phone while nursing a gin and tonic, ice cubes clinking in the sweating glass.

Brody strolled over, hand extended, "Good afternoon Doc, Special Agent Will Brody."

"How did you—"

"I pulled your file."

Martin's face reddened. "Why would—"

"Take it easy, I'm just kidding."

"Oh," Martin relaxed. "Of course, I just meant with all the NSA stuff—"

"Lousy joke," Brody said, the back of his neck tightening into a knot. *The Goddamn NSA had everybody with a badge looking like the fucking Gestapo.*

"What's so hot you couldn't discuss it over the phone?" Brody said, sliding into the opposite side of the booth.

Martin drained his drink in one gulp.

The waitress sashayed over. She looked as if she had been ridden hard and put away wet.

The Doc rang up another high ball. Brody ordered a root beer, watching Martin fumble with a brown messenger shoulder bag. After the waitress wandered off Martin finally pulled from the bag a clear zip-locked specimen pouch. It was holding a tooth remnant that looked like the exact twin to the one Elliot had been waving around at the crime scene.

"I'm just going to say it," Martin said. "This tooth is human."

Brody pressed his fingers into the corners of his eyes, grinding at the ever present headache that had taken a quantum leap in intensity. The waitress came back. She had hardly served their drinks when Martin pounded down half of his. Brody's hands fell from his face, his mouth hanging open. *Catching flies, grandma would have said had she been still alive.* He stared out the pub's plate glass front windows. The shadows lengthened on the sidewalk. The feeling something was wrong in the world bearing on him stronger than ever.

"On the other hand, the hairs recovered from the crime scene are canine," Martin said, depositing a second specimen bag on the table, "though not from a dog."

"A wolf?" Brody said, his voice ragged.

"I don't know," Martin said, shaking his head in confusion.

A thought hit Brody, his stomach contracting in a way that was telling him not to say what he was thinking, but he couldn't stop himself. He had to *ask*.

"We have canine hair and a tooth that looks like it came from some animal, but your tests are showing it to be human," Brody said. "I'm not one to question science just because it doesn't fit my notion of how things should be. So in the spirit of keeping our options open…" Brody began to stammer. "You know, for shits and giggles. I'm just gonna throw this idea out there. What about a were—"

"A hoax?" Martin interjected. "You were going to ask how hard it would be for a prankster to make this look like some kind of monster was involved, right?"

"Of course," Brody said, flushing as he pulled his ringing smart phone from his pocket. He motioned for Martin to stay and headed for the door. Though he hadn't been allowed to finish, he was damned if he would now. The man had not only cut him off quick, but he looked like he was about to crap his pants.

August 2016 – London, England

Patrick peeked out from where he hid, wedged behind a dumpster. He had been scrounging for a snack when a sudden gash of light had sent him scurrying for cover.

Almost immediately he had realized a Friday night party was rocking the offices high above. The pattern was always the same. A younger toff from the trading desk would meet the supplier in the alley, pick up the goods, the high-end hookers would show, and everybody is happy. This time however, the young trader had been accompanied by a distinguished looking older fellow in a double breasted suit.

"You sure you wanna do this, Neil? It's a simple transaction," said the younger man.

"Everyone needs to live a little," Neil said, his voice sounding slurred in the eerily silent night.

Patrick couldn't believe his eyes. *It couldn't have been a coincidence that 'Neil' was there. Yet these muppets couldn't imagine that the cops would target them for a sting operation. What had 'Neil' done to warrant this? Stolen from one of the big dogs?*

A muffled thump echoed from down the alley.

"C'mon. He's here," The young trader said, grabbing Neil by the arm as he tore off into the darkness.

Patrick eased out from behind his hiding place to watch—

An enormous shape loomed over the two men. They slid to a sudden stop on the gravelly concrete, the young trader bleating out, "Holy Mary Mother of God" as he pivoted to run. He never completed his turn.

It was already moving, so fast it hardly registered on Patrick's eyeballs.

A stunned oomph escaped the young man's lips as his skull was whipped into a brick wall with a nauseating crack. His lifeless body held for a moment and then sagged to the ground like a sack of wet meat. Neil dropped to his knees and begged for his life; all dignity, breeding, and upper-class bearing gone in a miasma of bowel shaking terror.

Piss shot down Patrick's leg as more screams and snarls rent the night. A voice inside yelled at him to flee. That if he moved now while *it* was distracted he could make it to the street. Then again, he had spent years doing little more than boozing, eating, and sleeping. That *thing* would be on him before he took a few steps.

The shrieking reached a high pitched crescendo, and then abruptly cut off. A sickening snapping of something chewing through bone carried toward Patrick like the sound of a man crunching through a bag of crisps. He contorted his body as far behind the pungent dumpster as he could get, his head pressed to the cold, gritty asphalt. Tears streaked down his face at the thought of whatever was out there. Nevertheless, survival instincts kicked in, his trembling fingers fishing the phone from his pocket, punching at the tiny keyboard. It had been years since he owned one of these maddening devices and the infuriating autocorrect more than once left his heart hammering, but he finally hit send. Only then did he realize just how much the phone's screen lit up his hiding place. He snapped the device shut, working to still his labored breathing.

Total silence enveloped the alley.

Maybe it was gone?

He dipped his head under the dumpster, trying to ignore the sour vinegary smell of his fright. He didn't see a thing, but paused another moment. Listening, and hearing nothing.

Maybe it ran off.

He made his move, pushing backward. His feet and legs inched wormlike, shoulders and arms hunching as he leveraged himself out from behind the dumpster. He brightened at the thought he might get out from—

His legs buckled.

Confused, he pushed again. *He didn't remember a wall being there.* He rolled over on his back and lifted his head to see his feet pushed up against a set of fur covered legs. From high above, saliva and blood splattered down onto his ankles like paint droplets from a carelessly wielded brush.

Patrick's panic struck eyes panned up.

The moon hung fat in the night sky.

An immense presence blotted out everything else, the savagely grinning face of hell itself leaning down, dripping jaws opening wide.

August 2016 – Southeast Michigan

Brody stepped outside the bar, wrinkling his nose at a pungent odor. He turned to see a rabbit twisted in the street, mouth open in a silent scream. Frowning at the sight of the dead animal, he answered his phone.

It was Vance. One of Cameron's casino companions matched up with the description of a man travelling out of the Ukraine. As Brody listened he couldn't help but notice the edge to Vance's voice, "You holding out on me?"

Silence greeted Brody's entreaty.

For a second, he thought Vance had hung up on him, but then the agent responded, "I have a friend at Scotland Yard."

"Go on." Brody gritted his teeth.

"Several bankers in London have offed themselves. At least that's what the British press is reporting, though nobody is mentioning that they all worked for Donnelly's bank. In addition, my contact thinks that these so-called suicides were helped along."

Christ, he could use a beer.

"Here's the kicker, the jumper's co-workers were being investigated for rigging commodities markets. The other night my guy got tipped off. He went in by himself, said it looked like a slaughterhouse, blood everywhere. He lost his cool. By the time he returned with back up all they found was what remained of some homeless dude. My guy said there was no way just one person got whacked, says he's never been on a crime scene like it, says he's done with this, has a wife and kids."

Brody's heart raced.

"That's not all," Vance said. "Our New York office is investigating the disappearance of a trader from Donnelly's bank. He went for a walk and never came back. Check this out. He specialized in oil markets - one of the commodities allegedly rigged by the same bankers in London."

"We're missing something," Brody said. "It doesn't feel right."

"That may be, but justice's big wheel stopped spinning a long time ago," Vance said. "Right or wrong, you don't come up with something good and *they* will pound you into the dirt."

Brody hung up, his hands shaking as he headed back inside.

A fresh drink sat in front of Martin.

"Keep that up Doc, and you're gonna be higher than a white pine."

"Piss off," Martin said.

"We really gonna do this?"

"There's something else," Martin said.

Brody eased into the booth.

"Before I got your samples I had received another tooth fragment. It came from a Second World War mass grave being investigated by some professors from the University of Michigan," Martin said. "This dig they're working is located in the Ukraine. You're not going to believe this but the DNA test for their tooth fragment *matched* that of yours."

Not two minutes later Brody was sprinting to his car, phone to his ear and Wilson on the other end.

"Guess what?" Wilson said.

"Try me."

"Cameron's wife found a letter. The envelope contained a finger."

"I take it once the lab runs the tests it will match Cameron's DNA."

"The Bureau jet is at Detroit Metro," Wilson said. "We tracked our suspect on a flight from Kiev to LaGuardia just before the Hampton's disappearances. We think he followed Cameron out to Detroit and then went back to the Ukraine. The MVS has been alerted you're coming."

Brody winced. Ukraine's Ministry of Internal Affairs, or MVS, had participated in the rendition of the CIA's captured prizes during the previous decade. *If there was one part of the U.S. Government not associated with the AG's office that he despised the cowboys from the CIA were it.* He filled in Wilson on his meeting with Martin.

Wilson exploded in anger, "Goddammit, Brody. Don't give me any weird shit. Find me something we can work with, and now."

Brody tried to respond, but Wilson raged on about how he'd be damned if he would even think of launching an investigation into whether a fucking animal was responsible for a hedge fund manager's death. Brody waited patiently. Before Wilson hung up he won permissions to visit the professors working the Ukrainian mass grave. However, as Brody drove to the airport he knew he would need a ton of evidence before jumping to any conclusions that could land him permanently on the bench. He mulled it over for a minute or two before deciding he wasn't going to trust Wilson or the AG.

He called Vance.

"You got a minute?" Brody asked.

"More like a second," The older man said. "Right now, I'm busier than a cucumber in a women's prison."

Brody paused at his partner's choice of phrasing then explained what he needed. While in the Ukraine he would lose the MVS and visit the professors without having to worry about any unwanted meddling from the Ukrainian authorities. Vance agreed to help run interference in case Wilson got jumpy about it. Brody hung up feeling better.

Within minutes of arriving at the airport he settled into the plush Gulfstream, though the plane's slick comfort couldn't take his larger headaches away. He fumbled yet again with his ringing smart phone.

"We have a bigger problem than I thought."

It was Elliot.

Brody stared at the screen for several seconds before finally answering the medical examiner, "Yes..."

"We still can't get any clarification on the irregularities in the DNA. Not to take away from that issue but the bigger problem goes to the core of what we think the evidence is telling us."

"Which is?"

"We have DNA sets that match up with a human, and or animal as responsible for the victim's death. However, the measurement of the distance between each tooth impression in the bone and the indicator of the larger mouth they came from matches no known land predator I know of, minus maybe a tiger."

Brody sighed.

Elliot heard him, "Look, I know how ridiculous this sounds. There has to be an answer that makes sense. In the meantime I'll—"

"Ok, Doc. I get it," Brody said. "However, what if were not being open-minded enough? What if—"

"If I were you I wouldn't get too far out over my skies on this one," Elliot said. "I've seen all kinds of crazy stuff. If there's one thing I've learned however, it's that sometimes the right answer isn't the one best supported by the evidence. Sometimes it's the most acceptable answer. Even if you're wrong it won't matter compared to what happens if you give your boss something he isn't prepared to believe."

In spite of his mounting frustration Brody thanked Elliot for his input, and thumbed off the smart phone.

The sky darkened as the powerful aircraft banked east.

Chapter 11

August 2016 – Dibrovno, Western Ukraine

Professor Owen Shaw kneeled in a large earthen pit, an ox-hair artist's brush in hand as he worked at the fine peppery soil, feathering free a human femur's distinctive curving expanse. Likely the final such remnant this mass grave was going to give up, and, as he hoped, perhaps the possible key to cracking its puzzle.

Owen eased back from his discovery and stood, taking a pull of hot water from his translucent red water pouch, glancing around as he drank. The pit in which he worked had been dug into a clearing in the Ukrainian foothills of the Carpathian Mountains. Covered in grasses and wildflowers when they arrived, most of the glade had since been cleared in a dusty hive of activity. Workers rushed around heavy canvas tents in what had been the front yard of an abandoned farmhouse offering a spectacular view of the tree covered valley floor below. For the umpteenth time, Owen couldn't help but wonder what had caused its inhabitants to leave.

"Union break's over." Ernie's voice boomed as he strode by, munching on a chocolate bar. In spite of his sweet tooth Doctor Ernst Beck, or as his friends knew him – Ernie, kept in shape. A shock of gray hair added to the physical bearing of one of the world's leading scholars in Holocaust studies, the team leader, and Owen's best friend. Nonetheless, even after a full month's work under Ernie's tireless direction the research team was hardly closer to figuring out how or why what appeared to be a squad of German soldiers had ended up in a mass grave dozens of miles from the nearest known Second World War battlefields.

Owen clambered from the pit, cradling his find. The late afternoon sun baked through his sweat stained Detroit Tigers ball cap as he carried the femur over to be tagged, cleaned, and processed at the field laboratory set up by Doctor Cynthia Davila of UC Davis. Every bit as unpretentious as Ernie, Cindy ranked as one of the top forensic biologists in the U.S.

Cindy darted into view. Her shoulder length hair had been drawn back in a ponytail that whipped after her head, mind and body brimming with the vitality of a woman half her age. Owen had once joked to Ernie that being around Cindy was like being trapped in a closet with a ferret. Ernie had smiled, and then warned him against repeating his observation. Owen's eyes sparkled, watching her casting about, a cup of yogurt in hand, searching for a spoon.

"You can try tonguing it," Owen said, grinning as he needled his notoriously straitlaced colleague and friend.

Cindy spun on her heels, the back of her hand wiping a bead of sweat from her bronze skin as she disappeared into her lab. She liked Owen, but often wondered when he was going to start acting like a thirty year old man and not one of her students.

An acrid antiseptic smell assaulted Owen's nostrils as he followed Cindy inside, the door hissing closed behind. A grad student poured a powder into a sterile 15-mL conical polypropylene tube. On the stainless steel table, next to him was a significant part of a reconstructed human rib cage. Just past the remains sat an expensive Dremel multi-function rotary tool. Labeled pans marched across another table's surface; detergent, five percent bleach, sterile distilled water, and one hundred percent ethanol. Beyond that table was yet another with a large drying rack. In the far corner of the room, a custom deep freezer hummed, quietly awaiting its latest addition.

Owen hefted the thigh bone.

Cindy pointed at a table.

Owen set it down, and turned to leave, pushing outside before the burnished door finished pneumatically opening; nearly running into Ernie striding by deep in conversation with a Polish graduate student named Anna.

"I'm telling you they're coming back. Someone in the Netherlands even got a picture."

"Picture of what?" Owen interrupted.

"Wolves," Anna responded without breaking stride.

"Pack it up people." Ernie's voice thundered across the work site, "Ten minutes."

Owen eyed the path leading into the forest and down to their base of operations. The town of Dibrovno sat at the bottom of the isolated valley, squeezed into a horseshoe shaped bend alongside the western bank of a sparkling blue river. A single rutted and potholed dirt road ran out from the town and to the main highway fifteen miles away. Nevertheless, in spite of its remoteness it had appealed to Owen from the start. One reason being the immense twelfth century castle located on the river's east bank. The citadel's highest spires overlooked red and brown roofed buildings erected on the west bank during the centuries following the castle's construction. Stone pilings sunk in the soft river-banks had created a labyrinthine network of basements, wine cellars, and tunnels. Cobblestoned stone steps thrust upward from countless alley ways, past intricately carved wooden doors to constricted streets.

To Owen's continued delight, the people had proved every bit as authentic as their town. Each day, heavy set women wearing triangu-lar babushkas and flowered aprons displayed their wares at roughhewn wooden booths set up on the main square. One could buy anything from delicate hand woven table runners and intricately patterned scarfs to blown glass vases and distinctively colored pottery. Rich and var-ied scents wafted across the square from any number of street vendors selling a variety of fried cheeses, steaming soups, crocks of lard filled with bacon or onions, freshly baked breads, hot doughnuts topped with crème or a choice of jams, plus endless varieties of fresh, smoked, or blood sausages.

Dibrovno should have made a hell of a tourist destination. Even so, he hadn't seen a single tour bus or hiker since they arrived.

At that thought Owen scowled, remembering when they had arrived several weeks ago and the mayor's strange statement that a wolf pack made it unsafe to work outside after nightfall. Owen had nearly laughed aloud but for Ernie hustling him from the mayor's office while reminding him, "Until recently wolf attacks were not uncommon in these parts. Where do you think the legends come from?"

Owen shook his head at Ernie's willing acceptance of the mayor's subsequent demand that they return to town each evening before nightfall. He and Ernie had been friends for nearly a decade. At first Owen had thought their relationship was in part a reaction to the fact Ernie and his wife couldn't have children of their own. Over the years, however, Owen realized what he had with Ernie was special. They had countless shared interests; from attending baseball games to spending afternoons playing board games like *Axis & Allies* to evenings discussing the world's problems over pints of beer. So the strange look that had creased Ernie's face that day—

Owen shook off his daydreaming as a chill passed through him. Noticing he was alone, he packed up his tools with more urgency, glancing up now and again at the overnight observation platform they had built to the mayor's specifications, twenty-five feet off the ground and jutting out from a huge old oak tree. As Owen eyed the platform, his remembrance of the mayor's comments made him shiver once more; even the word *wolf* seemed laden with an undefined if irrationally felt menace.

A loud bang caused him to jump.

He cast about, the farm house's front door swinging back and forth, a strange feeling crawling across his skin. He stared into the home's dark shadows, the feeling of being watched inescapable. His heart was hammering away in his chest when a pinching sensation caused him to look down to see his hands jammed hard into his jeans pockets. He pulled them free, eyes creeping back up.

An empty farmhouse stood before him, the feeling of being watched inexplicably gone.

He smiled and exhaled, feeling stupid as he grabbed his equipment and broke into a jog; anxious to catch up with everybody else.

CHAPTER 12

August 2016 – Eastern Ukraine

Brody swiveled in his seat, awestruck. As far as the eye could see were buildings torn apart by artillery, bombing, and missiles. Refugees, their belongings piled high on rickety pull carts or sputtering cars belching clouds of bitter black exhaust, trundled along the crumbling road's edge.

Brody's suspect, travelling under the name Karlovic, had been tracked to two villages. One was in the western part of the country, but the other was near the Russian border of all fucking places. After landing in Kiev Brody had been taken by helicopter to an airfield west of Donetsk. There the CIA had provided him a fake ID showing him to be a newspaper reporter and hooked him up with two reluctant but compliant reporters from the Washington Post. Brody's handler, a veteran CIA field officer going by the name Brandner, had proved far from comforting.

"There's something *you* should know," Brandner had said. "This isn't to get back to anybody else. You read me?"

Brody had nodded once in the affirmative. *Go figure, the CIA holding back Intel from the Bureau.*

"This guy you're after. Karlovic. We think he's a mercenary, but we aren't sure. All we know is that when things get hot, he turns up. On the off chance you find him call as much back-up as you've got. Don't even think about hot-dogging this one. Both times my best operators have come close to him it has gotten ugly."

"How ugly?" Brody took a chance, "Anything strange? Maybe bodies ripped up like an animal got to 'em?"

"Yea right," Brandner said, his eyes widening ever so slightly in response. "I said Karlovic is a pro. That doesn't mean he's a monster."

"How long have you guys been after him?" Brody said.

"Since the 70s."

"Why are you telling me this?"

"Because you won't find him."

"Thanks," Brody said, not at all trying to hide his dripping sarcasm.

"One more thing," Brandner said.

"I can hardly wait."

"Help never comes for free in this line of work. Don't trust anyone."

Brody scowled at the memory, and what had subsequently occurred. Following a bone jarring ride over roads destroyed by weeks of fighting he had reached the town where Karlovic may have gone to ground. It was a dead end.

Brody fingered his press pass, thinking again of the CIA agent's warning as the rented van swayed back and forth, the crump of big guns rumbling in the distance. He and his new colleagues, a bearded young correspondent named Simon and his partner Ryan; an easygoing fellow of twenty-five, were trying to get back to the airfield that would take them safely away from the Eastern Ukraine even as Ryan recorded every which way he could turn his camera.

The wrecks of knocked out tanks, armored personnel carriers, and trucks lined the road in a ragged column of spiraling smoke and dead bodies. Clouds of flies buzzed over scorched human remains belching foul sulfurous gasses in the oppressively humid air. They approached a checkpoint along the river where hundreds of people streamed across a pedestrian bridge that had survived the fighting. Big military trucks thumped across wooden slats spanning pontoon floats forming a temporary vehicle crossing. Artillery fire and god knows what else had twisted the main bridge into a mangled mess, the setting sun starkly illuminating its steel girders poking haphazardly into the sky. The van braked to a halt in the heavy traffic.

Brody gazed at a woman shambling along next to the idling vehicles, her skinny arms pulling a cart piled high with her meagre possessions. Behind the cart trailed two children; a girl of about five and a boy maybe a year younger. It was the girl that had caught his attention, for whatever reason she had waved at him.

He waved back.

She smiled.

A lump formed in Brody's throat. She had bright eyes and a blue dress once undoubtedly pretty, but soiled with dirt. He forced himself to smile back, knowing she would never come close to experiencing the sheltered upbringing he had enjoyed. At that thought, he reached into his travel bag. In spite of being a gym rat he just about never went anywhere without a treat. In this case he had picked up a roll of Lifesavers and bag of Sour Patch Kids just before leaving Detroit Metro Airport. Waving the kids over, he deposited the candy into their grateful hands. Their mother nodded her thanks.

Brody stared back, lips pressed tight, watching as they disappeared into the sea of humanity. Meanwhile, Simon was leaning out the window trying to interview the dazed combat survivors staggering along on foot. The men came from the Ukrainian army and militia, many of the latter wearing the Azov Battalion's *wolfsangel* insignia. Word was the unit's emblem was based on the badge of the former Nazi SS Panzer Division *Das Reich*. Though beaten, some of the men seemed hopeful; elements of a U.S. Airborne Brigade had reportedly arrived in the Western Ukraine to rebuild their ranks. Others could care less, ears bleeding from the massive concussive blasts caused by the heavy weapons that destroyed their vehicles. Brody looked past the men and into a large field next to the road, eyes settling on the carcass of a T-64 main battle tank. Despite weighing as much as a tractor-trailer the tank's turret laid on the ground, upended and at least a hundred feet away from the burned out chassis. He willed the van onward.

Time to find the professors, with any luck he could be at their location by nightfall.

Anywhere would be safer than here.

It had to be.

CHAPTER 13

August 2016 – Dibrovno, Western Ukraine

The winding path sloped downhill, the team of researchers stretched out in a shambling column. The deep greens and soft brown tones of the imposing old growth canopy cooled the air, sunlight fragmenting and streaming down like laser beams to dapple across the team's route. As they moved deeper into the valley however, the suns reach lessened and the path narrowed. The region's population, once booming, had fallen.

On the valley floor, wild boars roamed about an abandoned homestead, gorging on cabbage and potatoes planted by a former home owner that had given up, gone elsewhere or just disappeared. After another ten minutes marching, they came upon the remaining farms clustered just outside of town. Rows of sunflowers, rapeseeds, and well-maintained fields supported modest numbers of sheep, cows, and goats munching away at the rich grasses underneath. The path opened up into a rutted trail. They passed an old man walking next to a creaking horse drawn wagon. The man's wizened face stooped forward from a vulture thin neck and shoulders beat down by decades of back breaking manual labor. In front of another farmhouse, Owen, who had caught up with his colleagues, spotted a middle-aged woman gesticulating, sweat glistening on her flushed cheeks. Ravens circled above a large heap in the yard.

Owen sidled up next to Peter, one of the team's helpers, "What's she saying?"

Peter rolled his eyes and shook his head 'no' as he picked his way over a downed tree branch.

"Oh c'mon man," Owen said, upping his pace to match Peter's.

"She's sick of *it*." Peter finally responded. "*Something* gutted one of her pigs last night. Paw prints everywhere, big ones." An edge creased Peter's voice, belying his attempt to seem above the peasant woman's old world lamentations.

Owen surveyed the exposed stone foundation and low windows. Then he turned his attention back to Peter, noticing for the first time the man's air of semi-sophisticated weariness. "You're not from around here?"

"I came for the work," Peter said, tipping his blue cap up. "I ended up staying. Besides, once you ignore the rumors the town's people are pretty friendly."

"*Rumors?*"

"When I left Kiev I got ribbing from my friends," Peter said. "This area has a bit of a history."

"How so?"

"Silly stuff, like what a drunken uncle might say to tease a child." He marched off, ignoring Owen's upraised eyebrows.

A few minutes later they reached Dibrovno. Sturdy homes crowded close to the street, bright-colored perennials in wooden window boxes gamely holding their own against the heat. The river gurgled over rocks polished smooth by its relentless waters. The team split up in one's and two's, heading off to their rented rooms, or maybe for a drink and bite to eat. Owen's stomach growled. He yelled over his shoulder toward where Ernie had been lagging behind, "How about dinner after we drop off our stuff?"

Nobody replied.

"Ernie?" Owen turned.

His friend stood in the middle of the street, hands resting on canted hips as he stared at one of Dibrovno's foremost landmarks. The Church of the Holy Cross was a Romanesque stone building dating back to the town's earliest days. Ernie, a monthly parishioner when at home, had been visiting every morning before work. When Owen had inquired about Ernie's renewed piousness he had demurred. Owen, not being one to push things, let it go. Nevertheless, Ernie's peculiar behavior was getting wearisome. Owen walked toward his friend as he eyed a richly painted fresco where the outer wall's moss was studiously kept at bay. He reached out his hand and grasped Ernie's shoulder.

Ernie jumped, but recovered quickly, "Did you know that a Cossack raiding party burned this church down 700 years ago?"

"We've discussed that siege," Owen said. "Something on your mind?"

"You ever wonder if we're it?"

"*It?*"

"Yea, the end of the evolutionary line," Ernie said. "As good as it gets."

"Compared to what?"

"I don't know," Ernie said. "Maybe people are holding some assumptions that might not be true. For instance, what do you think happened to those German soldiers?"

"Who knows," Owen said. "Besides, that's Cindy's job. Our job is to identify *who* they were."

"Grow up. Cindy's under a ton of pressure, and in case you forgot we're a team."

Owen flushed red, but before he could apologize Ernie walked off.

Owen skulked after him. The sound of up tempo folk music and voices filtered toward him from the main street ahead.

Rounding a corner Owen shouldered his way to the front of a decent-sized crowd, slipping past grinning men in black vests and laughing women in flowered skirts watching a group of people dancing down the middle of the street. In the midst of it all, a reed-thin man with a mane of silver streaked hair hopped about and laughed as he energetically sawed back and forth on a violin. Next to him a teenager played a pan flute. Another carried a black accordion, his fingers dancing back and forth on the white keys flashing in the diminishing sunlight. Farther back a middle-aged man meandered through the edge of the crowd, strumming a guitar like instrument. Amidst the band dancers swirled, women and men smiling and perspiring as their feet skipped to the music's rhythm. Owen gestured at the last man, a questioning look on his face as he made eye contact with Ernie.

"The instrument he's playing is a *cobza*," Ernie said. "These men are *lăutari* - Romani musicians. They are often hired for wedding celebrations. The first of their kind came from Wallachia during the late eighteenth century."

"Isn't Wallachia—"

"Yes Owen, its Vlad the Impaler's homeland," Ernie said.

They watched the band dance by, the music diminishing in volume if not intensity as what appeared to be a Roma bride and groom followed along. The willowy bride's cinnamon-gold skin glowed in the dimming light. She appeared incredibly *young*.

"You sure this is a wedding?" Owen said.

Ernie didn't answer.

"Maybe it's a school play?" Owen mumbled.

"Your friend is correct, Mr. Historian. It's a Gypsy wedding."

The woman's voice came from Owen's left, speaking fluent American English but with a husky note that caught his ear. He didn't bother questioning that the interloper knew his identity. Every local not living under a rock would have known by now the particulars of a team of roughly twenty foreign professors and graduate students. "Whatever, lady. That girl can't be older than fifteen. The boy looks like he's still in middle school."

"Middle school," the woman laughed mockingly at his term for describing an age at which many of the Romani children had become adults in responsibilities if not name. "For someone interested in this region's past you don't seem to know much. Then again, you Americans have no real history. My village is older than your country, is it not?"

Owen turned, his pupils widening in surprise. A perceptible wrinkling of the skin framed emerald eyes sparkling with life. A playful smile crossed her ruby red lips, exposing polished white teeth. Raven black hair cascaded down the woman's shoulders, providing a stunning contrast to her alabaster white skin.

Ernie looked over and sighed; taking in both the woman's exquisite Slavic features as well as his friend's Pavlovian reaction. *In retrospect, Owen had been too young when he married. On the other hand, he had matured since his wife had left him. But now this...* Ernie hoped to God the expression on Owen's face came across as mere interest, and not the hungering look of a man eyeing this woman like she was a Five Guys hamburger.

They introduced themselves. Tanya Alexeevna Volchitsa smiled in response, her eyes lingering on the young American. *He had a curious air about him, his soft brown eyes brimming with intelligence and innocence.*

"Quite the beauty," Tanya stated, purposefully vague about whom she was speaking of as her tongue slid across her full lips.

Owen returned his gaze to the wedding party. It picked up energy as the older women swirled about in their multi-colored dresses. Even the men sang more zestfully. An incredible sense of awkwardness buffeted Owen as his hormones kicked into another gear, "Why the hurry?"

"Her family wants to marry her off before how you Americans say?" Tanya pointed, feigning a lack of familiarity with her grasp of English slang, "She begins messing around?"

Owen's eyes tracked along Tanya's extended finger, pointing to a white towel clutched in the bride's delicate hand but stained red with—

"It's proof that her hymen has been broken, a traditional part of the Gypsy wedding."

Tanya's matter of fact voice hardly belied Owen's uneasiness. He couldn't believe he was witnessing a teenage girl parading down the street with the bloody evidence of her deflowering brazenly displayed like the geek Ted showing off Samantha Baker's panties in *Sixteen Candles*.

"You Americans love your violence," Tanya said, observing Owen's reaction. "But if it's natural you get so uncomfortable."

"Where are they going?" Ernie said, speaking past Owen.

"Inside, as they should. Come." Tanya's voice tightened, "My country is full of legends. I am interested to hear what you have found."

The sky had shifted from blue to a dark purple. A brief tremor when she spoke suggested an acknowledgement of something more, but Owen chalked it up to the evening's drop in temperature.

Tanya stepped away, her rounded ass swaying in her tight jeans.

"Really?" Ernie gripped Owen's shoulder as he turned to follow. "This Tanya is a walking stereotype. For that matter, she looks to be maybe ten years older than you."

"What are you, my mother? Besides, a woman older than me can't be intelligent *and* hot?"

"Look, there are plenty of women like Tanya in big Eastern European cities, no matter what their age. But *that* kind of women doesn't just hang out in backwater towns like Dibrovno."

Owen laughed.

"Open your eyes, lad. There's something more to her than she's letting on."

"I hope so," Owen said with a smile. "It's been a long time since I've had something more of anything. Stop worrying, I got it under control."

"Just watch yourself," Ernie said. "Because sometimes it seems to me as if the milk has slipped right out from your cereal bowl."

"Is there a problem?" Tanya stood in the middle of the street, looking back.

The two men stopped arguing. Owen shook his head no as she pivoted and led them into a labyrinthine maze of side streets. Their footsteps echoed loudly on the mostly deserted cobblestone, the gloom deepening as they neared the tavern near the town center. The three story building huddled up to a squat bridge that crossed the river, the castle dominating the opposite bank.

Ernie held the door open as Owen and Tanya plunged inside, pausing before following. He mentally circled back to the demons stalking his thoughts, his eyes settling on a thicket of cattails sprouting from the river's broodingly dark waters. The castle's immense walls dwarfed it all, rising gray and stout from the water's edge. It was a view he had seen many times before. Nonetheless, for some reason his skin crawled. He craned his head up, trying to find the source of his anxiety. The gloaming couldn't conceal someone watching from a castle window; a tall, bulky figure, his head unusually large and misshapen.

Ernie blinked in confusion.

However, when his vision came back into focus the figure had vanished.

He shot another look at the castle. Seeing nothing he shook it off as a product of his imagination, stooping to pass under the tavern's doorway. Inside, dark wooden paneling evoked the feeling of being in an old English pub. However, and as he knew from past visits, this tavern had a local twist. Each of the three cozy floors displayed the mounted head of an animal prodigious in size for its species. A boar's head hung near the front door, its five inch tusks protruding from its snarling mouth. The second floor exhibited an imposing antlered red stag. On the top floor, the bar owner had mounted the immense shaggy skull of a *wisent*, or European wood bison; an animal that could weigh over a ton. In the weeks since the team had arrived no one had offered the slightest help in identifying the hunter who had killed these magnificent beasts. Any questions about it had always been met with a shrug, invariably followed by a round of shots and conservation about their progress on the dig.

Ernie glanced up at the boar's head and then wound his way through the packed wooden tables greeting him with the rapid fire sound of the local dialect, laughter, and silverware clinking on plates. The air was redolent of cigarette smoke and boiled sausage. A darkly stained wooden bar ran along one wall. Behind it a well-polished mirror had been lined with a collection of vodkas, various brandies, locally made *medovuha,* as golden sweet as the honey it were distilled from and *samogon*; a spirit similar to American moonshine and capable of leaving your head feeling just as fuzzy. A group of locals sat on the bar stools, enjoying the local flavors.

The atmosphere felt more spirited than usual. It reminded Ernie of a Slavic version of Fat Tuesday's pre-Lenten celebrations. He meandered along, enjoying the room's energy. Plush high backed booths packed with people lined the opposite side of the bar, pictures and artwork filling the walls. Knowing he was at best a third wheel, he let Owen and Tanya settle at a table toward the back, lingering on an old woodcut that caught his eye. He had not remembered seeing it before.

The image showed a man standing in a field and pointing an old flintlock rifle at the clearing's edge. The sun blazed high in the sky. The man's target, a wolf, lurked in the tree line. Just its head showed. The foliage concealed the animal's body. At that, Ernie frowned. The proportions appeared way off.

"Interesting wood carving, no?" One of the waitresses stopped alongside him. She balanced an empty tray on her hip, her blonde hair tied back. Many of the locals spoke English, something that surprised Ernie to no end considering the lack of linguistic diversity he had encountered in other small European villages over the years.

"It's one of Dibrovno's oldest surviving works of art, dating back to the fifteenth century," She said, tilting her head in admiration.

"It's an interesting piece," Ernie responded, noting the hint of pride in the woman's voice. "But, and forgive me, the scale is all wrong for such a composition. Regardless of the overly large sun the wolf's head is far too high off the ground."

"First, that's not the sun." She laughed, teeth flashing. "Second..." Her smile faded, "That's not a wolf."

Ernie flinched as if she had raised her hand to strike him, face drained of color as the waitress skittered off with a mischievous look on her face.

Owen was smiling at something Tanya had just told him when Ernie joined them.

"Don't mind her," Tanya said, watching the waitress approach another table. "She likes playing games with the tourists."

"What're you talking about?" Owen said.

"Werewolves."

Owen grinned, brushing her off. However, a brief shot of concern flashed across Tanya's face at the sight of Ernie's expression. She reached over to grasp Ernie's rigid forearm. "That carving depicts one of local lore's foremost werewolf hunters. A man named Ivan Mistrov – in this case pictured dispatching his foe sometime in the middle of the fifteenth century."

"You can't be—"

"Serious?" Tanya's eyes danced as she responded to Owen, "Of course not. But people *believed*. Some still do."

"And you?" Ernie said.

"I believe Ivan killed a lot of innocent wolves."

Tanya squeezed Ernie's hand, her grip warm and comforting. In spite of his turbulent emotions Ernie relaxed.

A young waitress set down three glasses of the village brewery's offerings. The deceptively strong server spilled not a single amber colored drop before taking their dinner order and disappearing as silently as she had come. In the ensuring hours and over steaming plates of smoked pheasant and trout, dumplings, potato pancakes, and thickly buttered rye bread washed down with sloshing glasses of ale - Owen and to a lesser extent, Ernie told their tale, from their friendship's origins to how they had ended up in Dibrovno.

Tanya had listened attentively, following her ale by nursing a glass of the cloyingly sweet local mead. The entire time her fingers teased along the handle of the glass as she leaned into the conversation, barely contained breasts swinging forward heavily in her thin blouse and dominating Owen's attention.

Ernie struggled to read her. *She carried herself like a male fantasy of what a Slavic woman should be, but Tanya's questions about the dig always flowed back to their interpretation as to how the German soldiers ended up in a mass grave. If she didn't get a sufficient answer then she waited, and asked the same question phrased differently. He couldn't help but key in on her back and forth with Owen regarding his findings as to the German unit's identity and date of disappearance. It evinced knowledge of historical matters that bordered on the professional.*

Owen had just finished stating his belief the men had died sometime in either July of 1941 or March of 1944 when Tanya interrupted once more...

"What makes you so sure?"

"You wouldn't be interested."

"Try me."

Owen blinked, his mouth suddenly hanging open.

"You're looking at me like I was your boss and just asked to jump on your computer," Tanya said with a grin. "Don't worry, just tell me."

Owen gulped, shocked that such a woman would be so interested in his work, but then he began answering her question...

The remains indicated the mass grave's contents came from an infantry battalion in the German army. However, the German army deployed roughly one thousand infantry battalions in three huge Army Groups during the June 1941 invasion of the Soviet Union, no less the myriad replacement units in the years that followed. That said, because of the mass grave's location German Army Group South seemed to be the most likely source of the battalion in question. Even so, this meant they still needed to figure out which of the army group's component armies, corps, divisions, regiments, and then battalions the lost soldiers has been assigned. Though significant fighting in the region surrounding Dibrovno only occurred during July of 1941, and then once more during the German Army's retreat through the region in March of 1944 - that didn't help nearly as much as one would have thought.

That is because one key element toward identifying the bodies revolved around reviewing individual *Kriegstagebuch* or unit war diaries created by the Operations Staff of the various German commands. They had started with the Army level war diaries, with another set of key documents coming from Army directives to its subordinate Corps level command staffs. Beyond that, they had also examined the *Morgenmeldung* and *Tagesmeldungen* - each day the Corps level headquarters passed these morning and evening reports up to the Army. As Owen explained to a surprisingly still observant Tanya they had spent the better part of three weeks reviewing these combined primary sources from Army Group South's Armies (as several armies form an army group); Corps (as several corps forms an army); and Divisions (as several divisions form a corps). The goal was to reach a point where it made sense to review records of individual battalions from divisions that reported losing an entire squad in the region near Dibrovno. This however, had led them to their next problem.

A German army battalion featured numerous sub-units; primarily *Kompanien*, or companies further broke down into several *Züge*, or platoons, and within each platoon the seven to eleven man *Gruppen*, or squads. Given the number of bodies found in the mass grave, they assumed the men came from a lost squad. Absent additional evidence however, they didn't know for sure. They had collated their findings and organized it into a structured database but this combined effort revolved around solving a final underlying issue. Whoever disposed of the bodies had removed much of the identifying information that would have survived seventy years in the ground. For weeks, they had been stumped. Then two days ago they got a break.

A grad student had found an intact *Erkennungsmarke*. This identifying tag that soldiers in the Second World War era German army wore told the researchers that the bodies had not been recovered and reburied. That was because the tag featured a perforated middle. Normally half would remain with the body. The other half would be turned over to the *Kompanie* headquarters, which possessed a list of each soldier's tags. This list was regularly updated to reflect men leaving the unit as casualties, or through transfers. From there these lists were tracked and recorded by the German Armed Forces Information Office for Casualties and War Prisoners. To help filter through these records, Owen had contacted a friend at the *Bundesarchiv – Militärarchiv*, or German Federal Records Military Archive.

"So…" Owen finished. "We await a response from my query. Then we can identify one of the bodies, and thus his unit. Though figuring out *how* these men died is something that remains a mystery."

"Your diligence is quite remarkable," Tanya said.

"No one's accused me of being hard working before," Owen said, laughing.

"That may be, but I approve of your efforts," Tanya said. "When I sink my teeth into something I don't let go either."

"And how often is that?" Ernie interrupted.

"Is what?"

"That you sink your teeth into something?"

"Not as often as you seem to think."

Ernie leaned back in his chair. *Tanya outwardly fit in, several of the townspeople recognized her when they walked in, but it's not like she got a warm response. And on top of that there was the way she spoke, as if she had spent significant time in the western world. Plus there was...Oh my—* Owen had once more dipped his eyes into Tanya's substantial cleavage. Ernie suspected that no matter how smart she was, this Tanya would go heels-to-Jesus for Owen in less time than it took them to wrap up the dig.

For that matter Ernie had his own reasons for being here, reasons brought to the forefront by his and Cindy's work. The stratigraphic method used for excavation had been chosen from the many possible procedures for disinterring a mass grave because it allowed them to maintain intact the dig's walls as they removed human remains and artifacts. In doing so, they had hoped to identify how the grave had been created. Nevertheless, nothing found indicated signs of tool usage. It was as if somebody had dropped the bodies into a pre-existing hole. In addition, the human remains featured a total absence of ballistic or projectile damage. Cindy found long scrape marks instead, including a large tooth fragment driven through the middle of—

Ernie suddenly noticed the late hour. He unfolded several bills, dropping them on top of a hand written check the waitress had left in a copper colored tray. Tanya and Owen took the hint. They all hustled outside and said their goodbyes before going their separate ways. Ernie had hardly taken a few steps when he stopped. He felt it again, the inescapable tingling feeling of being watched.

He spun about, seeing nothing at first. Then he looked up, gasping at the sight of a huge bat zigging and zagging across the moonlit sky. It sounded like an umbrella opening and closing as the creature winged through the air, appearing even bigger than the eagle sized fruit bats he came across in Fiji on vacation several years prior.

But fruit bats didn't live anywhere near this part of the world.

Heart beating faster Ernie looked to Owen, but he hadn't noticed. Ernie turned his attention to the sky once more. The big bat was gone.

Smaller cousins danced in the night, chasing the humid sky's rich bounty of bugs.

Ernie glanced up again, seeing nothing and shaking his head in confusion before wandering off. Owen stared after Tanya a moment longer then turned to catch up with Ernie, neither man aware of the figure observing from the shadows of a nearby alley. Oblivious to the fact that in one way or another *he* had been watching them the entire evening.

CHAPTER 14

August 2016 – Southeast Michigan

Martin sipped his coffee, standing in front of the kitchen door. A red line on the horizon announced the impending daybreak. Strips of bacon sizzled and popped in a greasy pan on the stove. He had been up for over an hour, the same as every other morning since he first saw that God-forsaken tooth. He still couldn't believe it. *For the Bureau to have flown in their gunner from the East Coast meant something serious was going down. To make matters worse, they hadn't been talking five minutes, and the guy nearly asked him about freaking werewolves. He was damned if he was going to have that conversation go into some file—* Something heavy and insistent pressed against his leg.

One of his big Rottweilers, Whitaker, stared up expectantly. Trammel, his other dog, padded into the room, the same look on his face. Martin glanced outside. They lived on ten acres of woodland backing up to the state park. Out here nighttime was not for pets, though he hadn't seen many coyotes of late. However, the moon had almost sunk from view. The sky more gray than black. A persistent whining distracted him. He sighed and slid the door open. The big animals bounded past. Martin turned back to fixing breakfast, bending and grabbing the eggs from the fridge's lower shelf—

The carton hit the floor with a splat as an explosion of growling, snarling, and barking sent his head straight into the swinging door. The cracking impact left him woozy, but adrenaline kicked in. He snatched up the Remington 870 twelve-gauge pump gun that he had taken from the safe several days ago. It was hot, four shells of buckshot in the mag and one in the chamber. He flicked off the safety as he stumbled outside onto the dew-laden grass, eyes searching.

The din of battle had moved into the woods. Orange hues spread like fingers through the sky. He squinted, *there*. A dark shape lay crumpled next to the small shed where he kept his riding mower. It was Trammel.

Martin slid to a knee next to his pet as a pitiful whine escaped the dog's muzzle. One foreleg hung limp and shattered. Tears blurred Martin's vision as he gasped at the huge parallel gashes running along Trammel's side, oozing blood through the dog's coat. It looked like someone had taken a sharpened rake to the poor animal. The dog struggled to raise his head.

"Easy boy," Martin said, patting his neck, which appeared unhurt. He might survive. That left—

From down the hill came a savage snarl cut short by a keening yelp. Martin charged into the forest, the morning sun breaking free of the earth's curvature, yellow light filtering through the trees in brilliant beams. Broken branches and a broad blood trail cut an ugly swath through the softly illuminated underbrush leading down to a small pond. He burst through the final layer of foliage, shotgun up, murder in his eyes.

Whitaker was lying on the pond's edge.

Something had ripped him in half. The dog's eyes stared sightlessly, blood flowing into the once peaceful pool of water. A twinge of fear tempered the veterinarian's bloodlust. He spun in a circle, heart pounding, but whatever killed Whitaker had vanished. It was more instinct, but somehow he knew.

He lowered the shotgun and stalked back up the hill to help his surviving pet. His tear filling eyes shimmered wetly, missing the welter of abnormally large footprints.

They were human.

November 2006 – New York City, New York

Brody gawked, trying not to let his mouth hang open as the secretary led him into the massive office. Everywhere he looked expensive Renaissance artwork worth more than he would make during his career hung on wood paneled walls. In front of him a huge picture window provided panoramic views of the Manhattan skyline. Just before the window was a hand-carved desk the size of his parent's kitchen table. Behind that desk paced Jimmy Donnelly, the CEO of the world's largest bank, issuing rapid-fire commands into a phone.

"Goddamn it, I don't care," Donnelly barked. "Just buy what I told you, and keep writing the CDS' on the CDO's from the pools…Huh? No, the other mortgage pools…Yes, those. I'm telling you investor demand is there," Donnelly said, waving with one hand for Brody to sit down. "Are you kidding me? Spreads are tighter than your wife's snatch when you married her virgin ass; of course they'll sell… What? Yes, that's right. The prop desk hedges the entire portfolio if it has to… What? Jesus Christ, Lew. When you get a chance to pull the trigger you take it. Don't fuck this up."

Donnelly flipped his cell phone shut as Brody tried to control his nerves.

"I want to start by stating that this bank is serious about meeting its compliance requirements," Donnelly said as he eased into his chair, observing. *A few months out of Quantico and Special Agent William Brody had already made his mark authoring a ground breaking report on the dangers of fraud in the real estate market. A report that had brought the agent first into a plum spot working the Wall Street beat, and now into his office for an interview. Impressive. Then again, few pleasures in life matched those attained by corrupting the true believers.*

"I appreciate that, sir," Brody said. "Given the froth in the housing market it's more important than ever—"

"Why don't we forget about that?" Donnelly grinned as he cut the younger man off. "I'm sponsoring a golf tournament at my club this weekend, a two-man scramble followed by a reception. All proceeds to charity, of course. Anyway, I would be delighted to have you join us."

"I'm sorry sir, but no," Brody said. "The Bureau's rules on such matters strictly preclude me from—"

"Nonsense, your boss will be there, and so will the attorney general." Donnelly's eyes twinkled as he took in the way the agent's shoulders filled out his jacket. *Guys like this only hit the gym hard for one of two reasons. Either they were fags or pussy hounds. And nothing about this guy's off the rack suit, Fantastic Sam's haircut, or beat up loafers even remotely implied weekends spent pillow biting.*

"Besides, one of our new hires is still seeking a partner. In fact, she just happens to be right down the hall," Donnelly said, waving off the suddenly pale looking special agent as he pressed the button on his intercom.

Within a minute there was a knock at the mahogany office door, followed by soft footsteps on the plush carpet as Donnelly's secretary escorted in a professional looking and attractive young woman.

"You won't believe your luck, Julie. I've found you a partner for this weekend's outing."

"And who might that be?" Julie said.

Donnelly choked back his laughter as the FBI Agent tripped over his chair attempting to stand. *But why wouldn't he?* Not only did Julie have an irresistible girl next door quality but six months prior she had graduated first in her class at Columbia Law School.

"It's a pleasure to meet you," The FBI agent said. "I'm special agent William Brody, but everyone calls me Brody."

"I'm Julie. Julie Hannover," She said, taking his hand, her grip firm as she held his eye contact an extra beat. "It's nice to meet you, Brody."

Fifteen minutes later Donnelly gleefully watched Julie's swaying ass escorting Brody to the elevators.

It was all too easy.

His smile faded as he returned to his office, and noticed that his eleven o'clock had already settled into the chair across from Donnelly's desk. As the man finished adjusting the cuff on his suit Donnelly fixed him with a withering glare.

The man bolted upright.

"Goddammit George," Donnelly hissed. "I told you months ago to shut this bitch up. So why the fuck am I still hearing about her?"

George Strieber, a managing director at the bank, wilted before his CEO, "Well sir, you see—"

"Results. That's what I want to fucking see," Donnelly said, slamming his fist down on his desk. "You need to understand something. This bank makes money hand over fist because of exactly what this cunt of a deal manager of yours is trying to shut down."

"I know sir." Strieber whispered, cowering in his chair.

"Do you? Because the mortgage market is as hot as it fucking gets. I *just* managed to convince Fannie and Freddy to let us in on the action. That compliance manager of yours could fuck all that up."

"Yes sir, I—"

"Look at me Strieber," Donnelly said.

A chill slithered through Strieber. Donnelly's eyes appeared huge and dark, blazing at him with a barely contained reptilian fury. "I don't give a rat's ass what's in the fucking mortgage securities. Nor is that my job. My job is to sell. It's the buyer's freaking job to know what he's buying, and if he doesn't then tough shit."

"Yes, sir." Sweat beading on his brow Strieber winced at Donnelly's anger over the woman that had become the bane of his existence, a compliance manager who had emailed virtually the entire management team about the originator's crappy loans.

"I don't care if these loans are complete shit." Donnelly's jaw somehow remained set as he raged, "It doesn't fucking matter. By the time we dice 'em, package 'em up, and sell them off to the dipshit investors it's not our problem. Now, you fix the reports so they look good. Got me?"

"Yes sir," Strieber said. He stood, unconsciously stepping away from Donnelly.

"Remember every loan is approved. No matter what," Donnelly said. "Keep that in mind, and we'll be very rich men."

August 2016 – New York City, New York

"It's brilliant!" Arnold Graham exclaimed, forgetting all about the newspaper he had grabbed moments before and its headlines screaming out the sordid details of the latest banker disappearance. None of that mattered given the audacity of the deal that had been outlined for him by his new business partners.

"Without Jimmy we wouldn't even be sitting here," Ronald Parker said, the business tycoon dipping his spoon back into a steaming bowl of lobster bisque. Next to Parker sat Jimmy Donnelly, a man who in any other context would have been the center of Graham's attention.

Graham, CEO of a multi-billion dollar real estate firm, couldn't shake his amazement. Though Donnelly's backing was crucial to getting the deal done it had been Parker's idea. Graham took another bite of his pear gorgonzola salad, contemplating the genius arrayed around him.

Parker had proposed a new development on the Upper West Side.

The idea was simple. Take advantage of a tweak in New York City's zoning codes meant to spur the development of more affordable housing in Manhattan's otherwise stratospheric real estate market. Their planned real estate coup revolved around an apartment high-rise featuring mostly multi-million dollar units for sale. To maximize their tax credits it would also include a section of two dozen modest rentals for middle class families. This way they could turn an even more obscene profit. However, one potential glitch loomed large. Who would deign to live in the same building as someone making less in a year than they would during this business lunch? Parker responded to Graham's worries by explaining how the section for those people would be sealed off from the rest of the building.

Graham waved the waitress over. He could care less that it wasn't even noon yet. *Time for a glass of his favorite port. What the hell. Maybe one of the pastry chef's delicious confections is in order as well.*

None of the men knew they were being watched.

August 2016 – Dibrovno, Western Ukraine

Owen sat down, it had been a long day and he was happy to rest. He flipped open his laptop, the lid cool to the touch. His homepage newsfeed jumped out at him: *"Wall Street Bonuses Soar, Median Income for Family of Four Lower than 1998."*

He closed the laptop with a thunk, staring outside. The evening's final rays of sunlight streamed in through the open window, a slight breeze wafting past the breakfast nook's faded curtains; distracting him from the depressing reality of life back home. His thoughts drifted to Tanya's long black hair, playful smile, glittering green eyes…

With a grin on his lips he reached across the kitchen table, grasping the richly bound book he had found on the pension steps earlier that morning, savoring its weight and the leather cover's smooth caress on the pads of his fingers. A note affixed to it stated "From a friend". An avid bibliophile, Owen delighted in the thoughtfulness of the gift.

"What's got you looking so lively," Ernie said as he shuffled into view, rubbing his lower back after yet another day of manual labor.

"A nineteenth century Ukrainian work about local folklore and history."

"Who's the author?" Ernie said, eyes fixed on his smart phone as he thumbed to his email.

"Markiian Shashkevych, Ivan Vahylevych, and Yakiv Holovats'kyi."

"The Ruthenian Trinity," Ernie said. "That must be *The Dniester Nymph*."

"How'd you know?"

Ernie didn't respond, sighing as he stared at his smart phone's screen, "The research desk at The National Scientific Library in Lviv will not leave me alone."

"Just tell them we're done," Owen said.

Ernie felt bad about putting fellow researchers off, but he just didn't see how they could have helped. What's more, Owen was right. The trucks would be arriving tomorrow morning, and in two days, maybe less, everything would be packed up. He looked up at the sound of the back door squeaking open.

"Hope I'm not too early," Cindy said with a smile as she stepped inside.

"You look like a proctologist who just saw Nikki Minaj walk into his office," Owen said.

"I see you were reading. That the Kim K selfie book, or maybe something a little less intellectually demanding?" Cindy shot back, welcoming the banter ever so momentarily brightening her sour mood. *She detested Dibrovno, its weird medieval castle, and the smell of boiling cabbage that seemed to be everywhere she went. The dark woods and isolated valley creeped her out even more. There was nothing even remotely romantic about it. If it weren't for the friendships she had forged with Ernie and Owen she would have already been on a flight home to California.* Yet, in spite of the fact they would soon be leaving, Dibrovno had just given her another reason to dislike it.

Ernie knew why she was there. He pulled a chair out from the white kitchen table.

Owen's smile faded as he took in Ernie's grim expression and the light draining from Cindy's brown eyes.

Cindy sat down. She exchanged glances with Ernie, who nodded in response.

"Have you noticed anything unusual about the remains we've uncovered?" Cindy said to Owen.

"Not really—" Owen started to say before falling silent as he took in once more his friend's concerned expressions. He stared out the window for several moments before turning his attention back to Cindy, "Look, I'm no forensics expert, and wouldn't pretend to be one. But I'm kinda surprised I haven't seen anything that looks even remotely like ballistic damage."

"We think there's a reason why," Cindy said, casting a furtive sideward glance at Ernie.

He nodded again, encouraging her to elaborate.

"We believe claws and teeth killed these soldiers," Cindy said.

"*Animals* killed a squad of armed men?" Owen's shock pulsed hot in his chest.

"We sent DNA out for analysis."

"DNA?" Owen said, "I damn well know—"

"You don't," Cindy said. "In 2005 a paleo biologist—"

"A paleo-freaking-biologist? What's next? You discovered a mosquito in amber, extracted the DNA and lookie here— these guys were killed by dinosaurs?"

"Let her finish," Ernie said, his voice loud in the small kitchen.

Owen shot a hard stare at his friend, but nodded his assent.

"In 2005 a paleo biologist from North Carolina State University was examining remains from a *Tyrannosaurus rex*. Even though DNA has a half-life of roughly five hundred years they found a chemical analogue that suggests they could potentially extract DNA remnants." Cindy said as Owen listened attentively. "We followed similar protocols, and profiled all the samples extracted, plus matched them to short tandem repeat loci. We still need to analyze mitochondrial markers, but the labs came back. They're a positive match for human DNA."

Owen's stomach knotted up. *Think it through. Weigh the claim against scientific methodology, and the need to establish a chain of factual causation.* His anger dissipated, curiosity taking over, "And?"

"The primary DNA results came from a piece of what must have been a six-inch fang embedded in a human arm," Ernie said.

"Must've been a dude with a hell of an overbite wandering around," Owen said. *Jesus, this is crazier than a pet possum.*

"C'mon." Ernie shrugged off Owen's need to joke about everything, "We'll show you what we've got."

Cindy scowled as they stood, chairs screeching on the kitchen floor. In spite of appreciating Owen's openness, she wondered when his immaturity would land Ernie in a situation they wouldn't be able to overcome.

Ernie stepped onto the back porch, fumbling with the lock.

A man stepped from the shadow cast by the neighboring house, hand up, wallet open, the setting sun gleaming off a— "FBI Special Agent Will Brody," The man said, displaying the Bureau's distinctive shield. "I have a few questions and could use your help."

"Absolutely, special agent..." Cindy offered without batting an eye.

"Please, call me Brody. Now, how about we talk over dinner?" He clapped his hands together, "I'm hungry as a wolf."

Ernie and Cindy exchanged pensive glances.

"By the way," Brody said. "Somebody ought to feed the dog. Those scratches on the kitchen door are something else."

Owen and Ernie turned to stare.

Five deep furrows had been carved into the door. The splintered wood freshly exposed against the otherwise dark timbers. It looked as if it had been laid open within the last night.

"C'mon you guys," Cindy yelled out, already bounding across the yard.

"Yea, okay," Ernie said, his legs trembling ever so slightly.

The FBI agent was right.

It must have been a large dog to leave such marks.

But that was just it.

Not only didn't the landlord have a dog, nobody else in Dibrovno seemed to either.

CHAPTER 15

August 2016 – Kiev, The Ukraine

Brandner sat near the front window, just inside the café. Body almost preternaturally still as he sipped his evening tea and waited for Roberts. Only his eyes moved, cataloging each person entering his field of vision, dismissing some, lingering on one in particular. The café took up the ground floor of a sturdy three story building not far from his unofficial office at the local CIA station. It was one of his favorite places in the Ukrainian capital, though at the moment he was frowning.

He had seen Roberts coming long before he sat down opposite him. A corpulent man who wore a perpetual scowl, he was impossible to miss. A second man, this one athletic looking, leaned against a wall on the opposite side of the street. He wore a windbreaker in spite of the stifling summer heat. A third and fourth man sat down at a table on the sidewalk just outside the café. Both heavily muscled, one watched the street. The other never took his eyes off those inside.

"Remember that FBI agent you helped smuggle out east the other day?" Roberts said, looking outside as he spoke.

"What about him?" Brandner said. He had worked with Roberts on several off-the-books-projects but hardly tolerated the man's presence. Nevertheless, thanks to Roberts prominent role in Kiev's recent changing of the guard rumor was that he had the inside track for a high-level job in the new administration.

"Our friends at the MVS say that not only didn't he check in yesterday, but he also shook loose his tail."

"Is that so?" Brandner remarked, one eyebrow rising ever so slightly. "I didn't figure him to be the wandering type."

"I need you to find him."

"And…"

"Just watch him, for now," Roberts said, head turning toward the intelligence officer so his cold blue eyes could fix Brandner in his stare. "But you report to me on this one, nobody else. Got it?"

"Since when did the State Department start tailing FBI agents?"

"That's not your concern."

"No, I guess it isn't," Brandner said. The concept *need-to-know* had been virtually pounded into him since his first days at Langley, but in this case he couldn't resist prodding. He had no confidence special agent William Brody would find Karlovic. However, Roberts almost comical concern at the Bureau's meddling around in what he regarded as State Department turf was too juicy to let go. Then again, and though killing had become second nature to Brandner during a professional career that reached back to the closing days of the Vietnam War, special agent Brody seemed like a nice enough fellow. He would hate to terminate him.

"Good," Roberts said, standing. His goons followed as he disappeared up the street as efficiently as he had come.

August 2016 – New York City, New York

Graham patted his stomach as he waited for his car. *Maybe the pastries had been a bit much.*

The sweating doorman, a tall black man resplendent in his uniform despite the heat outside, stepped inside the crisp climate controlled lobby signaling that Graham's car was ready.

Graham marched outside where the driver held open one of the spacious stretch limousine's back doors. Graham hardly noticed. He ducked inside and slid into the hand-stitched leather seats. His brow furrowed as the door swung shut. *Not only wasn't it his usual driver, but he wasn't even the same guy that had dropped him off two hours prior.*

The driver smiled as he settled into his seat and looked back toward Graham.

It was only then when Graham noticed that the driver was staring *past* him.

The hair stood on the back of Graham's tingling neck at the same time a feral musky odor oozed into his nostrils. *Something was behind him.* He spun around, eyes straining to adjust to the car's overly dark interior, then widening in shock.

The driver's glass partition hummed closed at the exact moment *it* ripped Graham's scream from his throat.

Rupert sniffed in disgust as he turned and walked toward the lobby door. *Mr. Graham had ignored him again. You can only walk all over people for so long before—*

A jolt shot through his body. He had served two tours in Iraq and recognized the feeling. Rupert whirled in time to see the limo rock heavily on its shocks, hearing what sounded like a high pitched scream from within cut short.

He took a step toward the car, but that was it.

The driver locked onto him, the man's eyes shining with a malevolent glint that froze Rupert in place. It was a look Rupert had seen once before, during his first tour of duty. His platoon had been waiting on standby security for a team from Delta Force. They were not needed. Later that night the Delta chopper landed and Rupert had wandered out to see six heavily armed Americans marching along the tarmac. Two slightly built Iraqi men stumbled along with them, black hoods over their heads, hands zip-stripped behind them. Rupert made eye contact with the Delta operator bringing up the rear. Though he had heard that combat vets had a "thousand yard stare" what he saw in that man's expression was not even remotely vacant. It was like staring into the eyes of a panther...

Rupert snapped back to the present, staring mouth agape at the limo driver whose eyes shimmered with a similar predatory intensity. Then the driver smiled, revealing unusually big teeth.

Rupert's sphincter involuntarily tightened.

The driver wagged a long and crooked finger, its nail strangely curving, extending well past the fingertip.

Rupert couldn't move away quick enough, legs weak he staggered against the building, grasping at the door handle. With safety at hand however, and against every instinct of self-preservation he turned back.

The driver's face appeared calm, teeth even and normal in size. He tipped his cap, and the tinted window whirred up. The limousine accelerated away from the curb, cut into traffic, and was gone. Rupert leaned against the door, panting. His uniform soaked through with sweat.

Maybe it was his imagination.

Then he saw a single drop of crimson blood gleaming on the concrete.

August 2016 – Dibrovno, Western Ukraine

Brody followed the professors through town, his mind spinning. It had taken him most of the day to shake the Ukrainian police and then make the wearying drive to Dibrovno. A drive that had been made more troublesome yet by a call his boss had opened with the dreaded, "There's something you should know."

"I take it the dead bankers piling up aren't going over well with the powers that be."

"Cut the crap, Brody. You're on thin ice as it is, if we had anyone else possessing anything close to your Wall Street experience you wouldn't even be in on this investigation. Besides, things are getting worse back here. Beat cops are still treating black people as target practice. Meanwhile, veterans are getting cashiered from the service with nothing to show for it but the chance to throw out the first pitch at a ball game or maybe shake a senator's greasy hand. Need I remind you that some of these guys are taking what they learned overseas and trying it out at home?"

Brody listened, letting Wilson vent.

"On top of that, left-wing groups are getting outside help from contractors too scared to whistle blow for fear of getting the Snowden or Manning treatment. That's got players on the left pushing a second amendment response for the first time since we broke that habit back in the 70s. The gun manufacturers are short stroking themselves silly as everybody but the local PTO arms themselves to the fucking teeth."

"Annnnddddd..."

"And smartass, between the resources we've diverting to the banker murders and the public's ambivalence—"

"The public's ambivalence? I can't imagine why these killings aren't generating greater sympathy."

"Find your fucking suspect."

Several hours later, and in spite of Dibrovno's failure to show up on his rental car's GPS unit Brody walked across the Main Square. The picturesque setting and friendly people made him wonder all the more about the weird looks he had received back in Kiev when he had asked about the town.

Upon reaching the tavern, Ernie selected a table out back. The river shimmered under the evening sun, the castle looming over them. Ernie ordered for everybody. Dinner came quick, allowing them to do little more than exchange pleasantries, which was fine with Brody as he surreptitiously assessed his companions. *Cindy was perhaps the most impressive as a Latino woman in a research field dominated by white men. Ernie would have been a leader anywhere. Then there was Owen. Though book smart the younger man seemed to have a bit of the man on the moon in him.*

Brody watched as Ernie teased Owen regarding his choice of after dinner beverage; hot chocolate done in the Eastern European style - meaning creamy melted cocoa in a cup. Cindy smiled as Ernie playfully suggested to the waitress that his grandson always enjoyed chocolate milk with his meals.

"A few days ago we found a body in Detroit," Brody said, quieting the table. "Genetic material from the crime scene led me here. It seems that you've uncovered DNA that matches that of our murder suspect."

"That can't be," Cindy said. "Our sample is seventy years old."

Brody shared as much as he could.

In turn, Cindy and Ernie explained their findings.

Yet, when it was all done Brody felt no closer to an answer than when he had sat down. He pushed back his chair, "I have a few calls to make. Why don't we get back together in a few hours, here is fine. I have some more things I want to run by you if I could, and in the meantime maybe you can see if there isn't something you've missed?"

They nodded their assent.

"Great," Brody said, decided to take one more shot at getting a feel for them. "Yesterday I was out by the Russian border. It's way worse than what the papers are reporting."

"What's happening in the East is hardly a surprise," Ernie said. "It doesn't help that some in Kiev are pointing fingers at the 'degenerate others' who need to be purged from Europe. On top of that, the IMF is doing its usual damage, pushing austerity and whatnot. If you think everything is going to work out for these people—"

"It just about never has," Owen said. "We're as nasty a species as it gets."

"I don't buy the idea that people are inherently bad," Brody said, standing. "I can think of plenty of times where I couldn't have won even a small measure of justice for crime victims without the assistance of regular folks who stepped forward and offered their help."

"Justice is a fine notion," Ernie said. "But in practice it's a malleable concept, is it not?"

"What are you talking about?" Brody said, tamping down a surge of irritation.

"Your belief in the system is admirable, though naïve," Ernie said. "Historically speaking, crime pays. Most of the Nazi's responsible for murdering millions got away with it. Given current events, they're hardly the only ones to do horrible things and walk away clean."

Brody turned in disgust and stalked off.

"Weren't you a little hard on him?" Cindy said to Ernie as she watched Brody go. She liked him. He had an earnestness that she found refreshing, plus he was handsome.

Ernie didn't respond.

August 2016 – New York City, New York

Jimmy Donnelly smiled. Regardless of what had been a satisfying if overindulgent lunch he had finally caught up with the hundreds of emails that had stacked up during his recent trip to Europe. Then, just as he was about to leave for the night, several members of his board of directors had burst into his office and whisked him away on a corporate helicopter. Within minutes, he had been deposited on a colleague's spectacular beachfront estate in the Hamptons, and his surprise sixtieth birthday party.

Everybody that mattered attended. CEOs, congressmen and

senators, the Governor of New York, three former treasury secretaries, the former attorney general, reporters from the *Wall Street Journal, New York Times, Washington Post*, celebrities, and more. All topped off with a special performance by the queen of the Big Apple herself - Beyoncé. Then came his impromptu speech. As a performer, he had been every bit her sweet brown assed equal, delivering a rousing birthday diatribe against regulation capped with a flourishing finish.

"Only the strongest survive the market." He had said, perhaps more than a little tipsy on $15,000 a bottle French wine flowing like a river, "For the best the rewards should be the greatest. Should they not? After all, this isn't the Soviet Union. This is the United States of America. And it's a Free Fucking Country!"

The crowd had roared their approval.

Life was good.

Fuck that, life was awesome.

No sooner had he stepped off the stage, shaking hands left and right, than he had snatched a thousand dollar cupcake off a server's tray and plopped into his seat at the head table. He bit into the cupcake and his mouth exploded with the combined flavors of champagne infused pastry cream, cultured butter from Normandy's finest farms, hand raked Rhône River delta sea salt, Tahitian vanilla beans, Tuscan Amedei chocolate, New Zealand honey, and 24-karat gold flakes sprinkled across icing topped off with a drizzled limited-edition Courvoisier. Donnelly's second bite into the delicious confection had nearly melted him into his chair when he frowned, spotting the loathsome Lew Sager heading for his table.

Lew, a senior vice-president at the bank, had been with him for longer than he cared to remember. Nevertheless, they only talked when there was bad news. He could tell by the dour little man's stick-up-his-ass-stride that this was going to be a doozy.

"We got a problem."

"Go figure," Donnelly said, sighing and reluctantly setting down the half-consumed cupcake.

"The associate attorney general is bragging about our settlement."

"Sixty million is nothing, you know that."

"That's not it. The associate AG is stating we admitted to filing fabricated documents in court, allowing us to foreclose on thousands of homeowners. To that point the settlement contained no admission of liability."

"Let him say whatever the fuck he wants, it's over."

"Look, boss," Lew said. "You just got back from London and know what's going on with our commodities guys. We need to let things simmer down."

"Simmer down? I'm not—"

"You hear anything else about the VP that took a roof dive while you were there?" Lew interrupted, "That was some nasty business. I can't believe I'm saying this, but thank God for all the Brexit stuff or we would have had even more of a public relations mess to clean up."

"Don't even get me started on the Brexit vote," Donnelly said, quickly changing the subject.

"A report came out today," Lew said. "From the American Journal of Preventive Medicine and it's getting traction in the media. Suicides are up big time. The authors attribute this to economic reasons."

"Like I care if some asshole let us take his house and couldn't handle being a sucker. Jesus Christ Lew, what's wrong with you? You ready to start subsidizing the loser's mortgages or something? What's happening to this country? The real crime isn't in taking what's there to be had; it's not seizing everything possible. It used to be you sink or swim on your own, and if someone couldn't hack it then too bad. "

"Sink or swim *on our own?* Without government handouts—"

"Watch it," Donnelly said. "I'm goddamn well aware of what we got. We deserved it. You know how much we pay in taxes. But now everyone's looking for a free ride just because those of us who earned a break got one."

"The optics are terrible," Lew responded. "Talking heads are linking the two stories. The DOJ might even reopen the investigation."

"Now hold on—"

"We're talking about hundreds of lives ended, and millions ruined," Lew said.

"Are you kidding me?" Donnelly said. "What's wrong with you? My employees are hard-working people. C'mon Lew. Maybe you can explain how far up your ass you reached to pull out that steaming shit pile of an idea that whatever's on TV might be a concern of ours."

"Please talk to the AG," Lew said, not wanting to tell Donnelly that he had misunderstood what he meant. That he was fully aware the majority of the people he worked with were dedicated to their jobs. Not wanting to tell Donnelly that he thought the rot was oozing down from the top.

"This fucking guy," Donnelly said, smirking and shaking his head. "Why don't you try stepping away from the fainting couch? Do you believe one of our esteemed senators stuffing their fat face at *my* party is going to hurt us? Or that one of the cable news guys pounding down shots at the bar is going to wake up tomorrow and decide jeez maybe I should do an investigative report telling the American people how all these settlements don't mean a thing? Wake up, man. Nothing is going to happen. Now go and get wasted, laid, or whatever. And stop messing up my birthday with shit I give zero fucks about."

Lew had known Donnelly a long time, perhaps too long. As a result he had often overlooked a certain aspect of the man's appearance. Not that it was something obvious. Donnelly hid *it* well. But that wasn't true when he lost his temper, like now. When that happened, Donnelly's mouth opened wide, revealing his strangely shaped teeth. Lew stumbled as he stood, backpedaling awkwardly, and then catching his balance as he rushed off in terrified silence.

Hearing a commotion Donnelly turned, his anger slipping away at the sight of one of his old fraternity brothers walking toward him with a glass topped wooden box in hand. Donnelly forgot all about foreclosures, suicide rates, or anything else as he rose. He looked into the box to see a rare Smith & Wesson Model 27 Snub-Nose .357 Magnum Revolver. It was accompanied by six commemorative bullets and a signed certificate bearing the Paramount Pictures stamp. Donnelly skimmed the certificate, his breath catching in his throat. He was a huge fan of Mafia movies and it appeared that he was being gifted the same weapon Luca Brasi had carried in the original *Godfather* film.

Yes indeed, life was phenomenal.

August 2016 – Dibrovno, Western Ukraine

After dinner Ernie and Owen returned to their pension to get some packing done before meeting back up with Brody. Meanwhile, Cindy and the other researchers planned how they would wrap up the remains for travel. After several hours and still nowhere near finished, Cindy called Ernie to inform him she would be late for the follow-up meeting with Brody.

The stars winked above them as Ernie and Owen set off to meet up with Brody, and Tanya, who had offered her assistance. The two good friends walked without speaking.

"What's got into you?" Owen finally said as he grasped Ernie's elbow to pull him aside.

Ernie didn't respond.

Owen held his tongue.

"It's nothing," Ernie said. "Besides we're late, and Brody's waiting."

"Don't give me that."

"I can't," Ernie said. "Not now."

"Okay, then when?"

"When the time is right," Ernie said. "You have my word."

Owen stared into Ernie's eyes and nodded his head okay.

They arrived at the nearly empty tavern to find Brody slumped over an empty glass, beer suds clinging to the vessel's sides. The waitresses seemed filled with nervous energy, zipping to and fro even though it appeared there wasn't much to do. When Ernie and Owen sat down, one of the servers deposited a round of ale and rushed off without the usual chitchat.

As they settled into their beer Brody caught them up with what he could reveal from two hours of fruitless conference calls with Vance and Wilson. Ernie told him what little more he could remember about the dig. It wasn't helpful. Brody was so despondent he didn't even comment on Cindy's absence.

They fell into silence, staring into their pint glasses.

After a long moment, Owen half smiled and leaned close to Brody, winking at Ernie who rolled his eyes, knowing Owen was up to some ridiculous stunt.

"Hey," Owen whispered.

"Yeah?" Brody said.

Owen glanced around and leaned in closer. He dropped his voice, and while doing his best impression of one of the backwoods rapists from *Deliverance,* drawled, "Y'all know what they call panties down south?"

Brody's eyebrows shot up.

Owen leaned in closer yet; his voice resonating lower, Southern drawl more pronounced, "Do ya?"

Brody shook his head 'no', a look of bewilderment plastered across his face.

"Squirrel covers."

Brody grinned.

Ernie shook his head, smiling nonetheless.

"You love it," Owen said, finishing his beer with a flourish. He waved the waitress over for another, the alcohol's warmth spreading through his stomach.

"I hope I didn't miss something," Tanya said as she arrived.

"Trust me," Brody said. "You DO NOT want to know."

After introducing Brody to Tanya, Owen turned back to their new acquaintance, "So why FBI? You don't seem like a spook? We haven't heard you mention terrorism once."

"Just so you know a spook is a term for a CIA agent. Furthermore, and at one time, the FBI did much more than counter-terrorism." The lines creased around Brody's eyes, his response sounding almost wistful. *In spite of recent setbacks he was still hopeful he could find Karlovic and leverage that success into another crack at the system.*

"Like there's a difference," Tanya responded, her face flushing red. "Isn't your FBI spying on everyone? What happened to you people?"

Brody leaned back in surprise at her sudden attack.

"Your laws once promised equality and justice. But now? Forget the *militsiya,* or as you call them the MVS, the KGB would be proud." She spat out the last line like a lover who had discovered her boyfriend had been cheating.

Ernie exchanged glances with Owen.

"Okay, let's just take it easy. To be fair, the last I checked your government wasn't so hot either," Brody spoke calmly even as the blood rose in his neck. *Tanya would be a formidable ally or a powerful enemy; he would have to be careful.*

"Your leaders can't understand the hate burning under their feet," Tanya snapped, "but they will."

Nervous glances shot toward them from the few others lingering in the emptying bar.

"I pledged an oath once," Brody said. "I'll be damned if I won't honor it by making as much right in this world as I can."

"Here you are, doing fine I might add, "Owen said. "Just keep rolling with it."

"Like your strip club scheme?" Ernie grinned at Owen, equally anxious to lighten the mood.

"Whatever are you talking about?" Owen replied in mock indignation.

"This clown came up with the bright idea of putting strippers on ice," Ernie said, jerking his finger at Owen. "He wanted to name the place *The Frosty Beaver*."

Brody smiled.

Tanya tried to hide the twinkle in her eye, but failed miserably.

"It's a great idea," Owen said.

"Yea, right," Brody said. "Haven't you ever been in an ice skating rink? Who'll want a lap dance when the room temperature is as cold as a meat locker?"

"I got that covered," Owen said. "A covering that guys could wear on—"

"Oh my," Brody said, chuckling as he shook his head in disbelief.

"Hear me out," Owen pleaded. "It's a good idea. The softcover solves everything. It's like getting two birds stoned at once."

"*What?*" Brody said.

"Stop, please," Tanya said, laughing.

Brody pounded down his beer. *Goddamn that's good.* The waitress served up another round, eager hands grabbing at the ice cold glasses. Brody took another pull from his mug and sat back with a smile on his face, surprised at how relaxed he felt around a bunch of strangers.

Owen was still grinning when he saw Ernie staring at the TV, "What's up?"

"Huh?" Ernie tore his gaze from the BBC world news, "Sorry. Wall Street is moaning once again about the sanctions our government slapped on Russia."

"Your glorious capitalist banker's paradise not quite turning out to be all it's cracked up to?" Tanya said.

"Nice. Don't you know screwing over people for money is a national sport in our country?" Brody said, ignoring the TV screen that had switched to a clip of a reporter interviewing Jimmy Donnelly.

"What's nice are all those financial stats trotted out by your Pravda-esque press trying to convince people that the economy's wonderful, and they should spend those pennies trickling down from the billionaires and their apparatchiks in the government."

"There's a big difference between what happens in my country and what happened over here."

"How true," Tanya said with a grin. "For instance, there's the electoral process of staffing and running our respective governments. I believe, in your country, the term for bribing politicians is lobbying. Or is it campaign donations?"

"Touché," Brody said. "At least my country is still a democracy."

"You really believe that?" Tanya said, leaning in. "I'm afraid that there's much you need to learn."

"I suppose you're the one to teach me?" Brody said, holding her attention, oblivious to Owen's mounting anxiety at his open flirting with Tanya.

The muffled sound of a smart phone came from under the table.

Tanya held Brody's eye contact a second longer. Then she fished the ringing phone from her purse, "Hello."

Something in Tanya's voice caused Ernie to take note as she walked off. He strained to listen as she defensively snapped at somebody on the other end of the line while she weaved through the empty tables toward the pub's front door.

Meanwhile, Owen was gawking at her ass like a lustful seventeen year old. When he returned his attention back to the table, Brody was snickering at him, both men missing the intense look of concentration on Ernie's face.

"How about you?" Owen said to Brody, nervous something was developing between the FBI agent and Tanya. "You got a special lady friend?"

"Maybe I should see what Tanya's doing tomorrow night."

"She's busy," Owen said before catching himself. "I mean we've got plans."

"That still leaves the night after," Brody smiled inwardly at Owen's jealousy, before deciding to back off. "Then again, I probably can't hang around that long."

"You ever wish you could be someone else?" Owen changed the subject.

"Naw, but I'd take a do-over."

"No you wouldn't."

"Why's that?"

"To alter your past would change you into someone else."

"In that case, it sounds like we want the same thing."

"I doubt that very much."

"Shut up, and buy me another beer," Brody said.

Owen smiled, waving at the waitress.

"When's the Bureau going to do something about the banks?" Ernie said, looking away from the TV interview of Donnelly.

"What do you mean?" Owen said. "From what I've heard they got slapped down hard by all those fines."

"Let's talk about those fines," Brody said. "What if I said that we should pass a law so *armed* bank robbers give back a small percent of their take in fines, but they get to keep the rest and avoid jail time or any personal liability."

"That's ridiculous."

Brody nodded his head in agreement and stifled a burp, glancing at his half empty mug. *It was a good lager, but it was getting a bit too smooth.* He set his beer glass down and looked at Owen, "Do you know what a CDO is?"

Owen stared back.

"It stands for collateralized debt obligation."

Owen shrugged.

"Do you have any loans out? Maybe a mortgage?"

"Sure," Owen said.

"Your lender earns a profit on the money you borrowed. That's the interest rate. It reflects your risk of default."

"Yea, I know," Owen said. "Just because I'm younger than you doesn't mean I'm an idiot."

"Yes, of course," Brody responded. He softened his tone, "Here's the thing about lenders. They always look for ways to reduce risk. In this case they took many loans and made it so that no one lender owned more than a part of each, while keeping the same interest rate. That's a basic type of CDO."

"What's wrong with that?" Owen said.

"Nothing," Brody said, his feet tingly from the alcohol. "But people got greedy. The banks knew their products were crap, but sold them to investors anyway while making side bets that the CDOs would blow up."

"That's fraud," Ernie said.

"Bingo," Brody said.

"Who cares?" Owen replied. "Most investors are pretty sophisticated."

"When I say *investor* I'm not just talking about other rich guys," Brody said. "I'm also talking about pension funds for people like teachers or nurses. They might as well have been putting their money into the preacher's basket for all the good it did 'em."

"Faith can be a powerful experience," Ernie said.

"So is telling fairy tales."

"Again, who cares? The banks got fined." Owen interjected as Ernie frowned at Brody.

"Technically speaking each bank got hit with a fine for *one* of the fraudulent CDOs it sold," Brody said. "But each bank sold *many* CDOs. For example when Jimmy Donnelly's bank settled with the SEC for half a billion they announced it was for one CDO. But in reality, it represented *all* the garbage CDOs they sold. And now the head of enforcement at the SEC is a partner at a Wall Street law firm, representing guess who?"

Ernie folded his arms across his chest. *Brody was barking up a tree he couldn't hope to climb. Only a complete naïf would have thought such venality was extraordinary in this day and age. For Brody this was personal, Donnelly wasn't just his white whale. There was history there, and that blood had run bad.*

"Remember our former Treasury secretary?" Brody continued, "Mister let's use foreclosed homes to '*foam the runway*' when the top dogs loot their banks so badly they crash? He's now the president of a private equity firm, even though he had zero experience when hired."

"What about Madoff?" Ernie said.

"He only got busted because he ripped off rich people," Brody said.

"Couldn't indictments cause a bank run?" Owen said. "Then the economy goes up in smoke."

"That's a con," Brody said. "If you start indicting individuals the bank won't fail. It's the people within it doing the stealing. That's the inside job that blew up the economy."

"C'mon, isn't all that mostly over?" Owen said. "You want to get worked up over something try the student loan mess and tuition scam."

"That's not illegal," Brody said.

"It's wrong just the same," Ernie said.

Brody took a swig of his beer. When he spoke again, his voice was quiet, "Back when I was a kid there was this teenager named Frank Castro that lived in my neighborhood. His dad gave him whatever he wanted. That wasn't enough. Frank liked to shake down the younger kids. My best friend and I had a chance to even the score, but Frank got back most of what we took away." Brody's face darkened, "That's just it. Guys like Castro or Donnelly, they never really lose. Every time I've tried to change it I've failed, and I'm sick of it."

"How sick of it?" Ernie said.

Cindy walked in. The meagre crowd had thinned down to a couple of stragglers hurriedly paying their bills. She slumped into a chair, her nearness distracting Brody.

"Sorry I'm so late, but I was on a last minute conference call. Your buddy Vance gave the Detroit medical examiner clearance to brief me on the investigation," Cindy said to Brody. She grabbed his beer and tipped it back; hoping nobody would notice the shiver that raced through her as the vision of a partially consumed body flashed through her head.

She needn't have worried.

Tanya had returned.

Cindy eyed the Ukrainian woman as she walked up to the table. She exuded a smoldering sexuality impossible to ignore. *She was glad her husband wasn't there, he would have been drooling. However, the way Tanya paraded around her big-play-with-me tits didn't jive at all with the intellect Ernie had described.* Nevertheless, Cindy found herself sneaking another glimpse at the stunning woman. Then she turned on Brody.

"You could have clued me in on the canine DNA taken from the victim in Detroit."

"Canine, but I thought—" Owen's eyes widened.

"Yea," Cindy shot a disapproving look at Brody, feeling almost as unsettled by his lack of candor as when date night with her husband ended with him thrusting something throbbing in her ass she hadn't been ready for nor wanted.

"If they found canine *and* human DNA then there can be no other explanation for what killed the victim?" Tanya said. "It had to be some sick individual and his pet, no?"

"Ain't you pickin' up what I'm layin' down?" Cindy said, "We don't have a clue."

"We were brought together for a reason," Ernie said.

"Don't mistake happenstance for destiny."

"You shouldn't mistake belief as stemming from a weak mind," Ernie responded to Brody.

A commotion erupted at the tavern's front door as a young man burst in. It was one of the grad students, eyes wide, breathing heavily, as if he had sprinted to the tavern. He ran over, "You need to come with me. NOW. *Something's* happened to Anna and Liam!"

CHAPTER 16

August 2016 – Dibrovno, Western Ukraine

Exhuming the mass grave wouldn't have been possible without the tireless work done by the team's graduate students, each night a pair of whom guarded the dig. They did this from the platform built high up in an old oak tree into which ladder like steps had been nailed. For most it was a thankless job. However, on this night, Anna Konarski of the University of Krakow and Oxford University's Liam Headley relished their turn. Guard duty being far from Anna and Liam's minds as they hauled themselves through the trap door, pulled up the rope ladder bridging the final feet, and spread out their sleeping bags.

Outside the stillness of the night was broken only by the occasional light breeze rustling through the leaves, and the deep serenade produced by thousands of frogs. Inside, the sounds of two summer lovers made their contribution to the night's rhythm, until it was upset once more.

"What's that?" Anna stopped moving.

Liam ignored her, sliding his hands up to her gently swaying breasts.

Anna moaned, her worries pushed back by his soft touch. She ground down once more in response, but a warning nagged inside her head.

"The frogs." She whispered, easing up. "They've stopped."

Liam lifted his head off the pillow.

A twig snapped outside.

Adrenaline flooded their systems as they fumbled for their clothes. The plan in such circumstances was simple. Stay put, stay safe and call it in. But then—

"Quiet," Liam hissed.

"What?"

He held his finger up to his lips, and pointed to the trap door.

Anna kneeled and cracked the door open, translating as she listened. "Hard to understand, a man, voice faint, an accident, he was hiking and fell, hurt his leg."

"I'll check it out," Liam said as he finished tying his shoes.

Ice coursed through Anna's veins.

Liam kissed her, and slid outside before she could stop him.

Anna stepped out onto the walkway surrounding the observation platform. The whimpering sounded clearer, but there was an underlying darkness to it. The back of her neck prickled in response. "Liam stop!"

He had just stepped off the ladder, his hand braced against the oak tree.

The man groaned louder, well inside the forest.

Anna peered over the railing, face shining white in the moonlight.

"I'll be okay," Liam said, ignoring her look of worry and plunging into the woods. He crept toward the insistent moaning, pausing every so often to catch his bearings. He had just reached out to move from his path a dimly seen branch when he paused. Something soft rubbed between his index finger and thumb.

What the...?

Liam's free hand fumbled for his smart phone.

The moaning sounded closer.

He swiped his thumb across the screen, nearly dropping the phone, his hands shaking as his fingers danced in a coordinated rhythm of swipe, press, and swipe. His flashlight app clicked on and the forest around him came alive with a harsh white light.

Liam strained to see, the sudden brilliance jarring as he directed the phone's aperture toward the branch. His throat dried up at what he saw, the blood pounding in his temples.

He blinked.

It was still there.

A tuft of fur nestled in his palm.

Like what one would find from a dog, or a *wolf*.

A breeze ruffled the silky hairs. Goosebumps broke out on Liam's arms as he realized the branch that snagged this fur was approximately six feet off the ground.

No wolf was that big.

Then again, another part of him knew better, the reptilian primitive part.

What if the hair came from something worse than a wolf?

Liam recoiled, physical movement done unconsciously, as was the second step back. The third was not. A rivulet of sweat ran down his neck as he backed away. The man's cries became louder, more insistent, and ever more off. The voice sounded throatier, deeper, menacing. Not human, but not fully that of an animal. Liam's teeth chattered uncontrollably. *Patience lad.* The fear reached deep into his brain, a whimper escaping his lips.

A barely constrained growl resonated through the trees.

Liam bolted.

A deep snarl rumbled forth in response, an angry sound that for eons had triggered a near universal response in any human unfortunate enough to hear it.

"RUN LIAM, *RUN!*" Anna screamed.

Branches stung Liam's face as he fled, hands groping wildly, his breath coming in ragged gasps. He stumbled but caught his footing. Ahead a thin beam of light slashed through the trees, guiding him. *Anna, thank god.* A volt of energy shot across his tingling scalp as he realized someone *or something* was loping along to his right. A dark shape dimly glimpsed from the corner of his eye, swift in spite of its terrifying size, drifting closer.

Liam's guttural cry of terror carried through the night. His pumping legs carried him past the final grasping trees, and into the moon swept clearing. His vision tunneled in on the steps nailed into the tree trunk, chest heaving, hands grasping, first foot up, finding purchase, second foot stepping, tears streaming down his face, scrambling higher...

The trap door banged open. *Anna!* Pupils white, she stared past him at something looming below.

"CLIMB, LIAM! *DON'T LOOK!* CLIMB! FASTER!"

"Help!" Liam bleated, his foot skidding off a rung "OH LORD JESUS!" The rope ladder bridging the final feet to safety twisted wildly in his sweaty grip. He grabbed for Anna's outstretched hands, clambering inside, his body thumping hard onto the floor, pulling his legs up behind him as fast as he could.

Anna yanked the rope ladder up in one great heave and slammed the door behind.

Liam shivered uncontrollably, struggling to stop his fear from turning into overwhelming panic, eyes searching Anna's face. *She saw it.* He cupped her cheeks in his hands.

"It was big. Fast," She said, pupils dilated. "Bigger than any wolf I've ever seen. But not a wolf, the way it moved. Oh Liam, it stood on two feet, and its *eyes*. Like a man…"

Another shudder racked her body, a horrific vision seared in her mind's eye from when she had scanned down *its* massive frame.

Anna's became glassy, as if transfixed or slipping into shock. Liam gripped her hands and squeezed, screaming her name. Anna heard Liam yelling, and pulled back from the abyss. She had seen what *it* wanted. She shivered again, the god awfully obscene image grotesquely stuck in her mind.

An eerie howling cleaved the silence outside. Loud, immediate, and angry, the noise penetrated the observation platform's thin wooden walls.

Anna's fingernails dug into Liam's shoulders.

When the next howl erupted it sounded quieter, the savage sound mercifully moving away.

"Where's your phone?"

"I dropped it."

Anna ripped her smart phone from the overnight bag, marching to the window. She flung the wooden shutters open. They thumped loud against the outside wall, cool night air streaming inside.

"*Anna!*" Liam exclaimed, huddling in the corner.

"*Shhh!*" In spite of her racing heart she leaned out, phone in hand, recording as the howling echoed off the hills.

A few seconds passed and the howling cut off.

After a much longer moment the frog's croaking cacophony enveloped Anna and Liam once more in welcoming safety.

The great beast lowered his muzzle, his last blast slipping into the wind.

It had been too long since he fed. The humans, their fear, his hunger…

Saliva dripped from his tongue and lower jaw.

It had nearly killed him not to run the man down and tear his pan-icked, juicy flesh to pieces. There was nothing like the taste of meat after a good chase. Teasing, tantalizing images danced through his mind; flayed open salty skin, the enticing strips of subcutaneous fat cradling the chunks of fibrous muscle clinging to bone.

It was too much, the moon, fresh meat, and her.

Blinded by his extraordinary appetites his momentum had car-ried him into the clearing. There *her* intoxicating scent had mesmer-ized him with an aching all-encompassing lust. In the woman's eyes he saw uncomprehending terror cascading over in all its mouthwatering sweetness. His blood had rushed through his body in response to her pulsing fright, bringing him painfully erect.

No...No...NO!

By sheer agonizing force of will, he had bounded into the woods. There in the dark, he had prowled back and forth until the yearning awakened by the female receded. At that his massive shoulders shook, knowing what he faced. There was bad news to report.

They would not be pleased.

Ernie rushed outside, leading the way, smart phone to his ear. A col-lective wave of relief spread through them when Anna picked up the call. Owen and Tanya rousted the local doctor while Brody, Cindy, and Ernie rounded up a rescue party.

In less than two hours they had shepherded Anna and Liam to Ernie and Owen's pension. The doctor was waiting and pronounced the stu-dents physically sound, but for symptoms of shock; treated with a mild sedative.

At daybreak, Owen led a group out to pack up the field lab and the remains for shipment to Krakow. Though everything went smooth, by mid-afternoon Owen's nerves had gotten the best of him. He drifted back to the pension where Cindy, Ernie, and Brody waited for Liam and Anna to awaken.

Cindy and Brody sat in the kitchen, making whispered small talk between Brody's incessant phone conferences with his boss. Each call leaving him looking more stressed than the last. Cindy glanced out the window, watching with helpless dread as the sun began its afternoon descent, the thought of the oncoming night almost too much to bear. "You know that professor from Michigan State University, Martin."

"How's he doing?"

"He stopped returning my phone calls, emails, you name it. It's like he vanished."

The sounds of Anna and Liam awakening filtered into the kitchen. After what seemed like an eternity, they crept down the pension's narrow creaking stairs, easing into seats at the small kitchen table. Ernie placed sandwiches and glasses of fresh juice in front of them, along with a bottle of vodka. Brody and Cindy settled in opposite the weary students. Owen and Ernie hovered in the background.

"Why don't you tell us what happened," Brody said.

"You aren't going to believe us," Anna responded.

"Try me."

"What do you want to hear?"

"The truth."

Anna gave a short, derisive laugh, but bit it back as she took in Brody's kind expression. After another moment she began to speak, slowly at first, then faster. At times, Liam chipped in. Anna finished their story with the howling, the dredged up memory of the night unsettling even in daylight.

She fell silent.

Brody let the quiet drag on.

"I saw it," Anna exclaimed, rewarding Brody's patience.

"You mean the wolf," Owen said.

Brody cursed under his breath.

"It wasn't a wolf," Anna said, trembling. Only with great effort did she still her shaking legs. For a long moment, she stared at the floor.

The clock ticked on the wall.

Brody struggled with his emotions; stricken by the thought his life was about to change forever. Anna lifted her head. Darkness danced across her face, twisting it into something ugly.

"It was a *werewolf*."

CHAPTER 17

August 2016 – Dibrovno, Western Ukraine

The word *werewolf* hung in the air, its very utterance throwing reality back centuries in time as Anna described a creature that more than any other personified one's deepest darkest fears. Brody listened; reeling with a freakish curiosity at the possibility Anna saw a monster.

A gust of wind rattled the kitchen window.

Six pairs of eyes jumped. Anna's and Liam's by far the most haunted. As Anna finished, Brody realized he had been holding his breath. A single tense voice broke the incredulous silence.

"We know," Cindy said.

"You knew," Anna said, "and you let us sit there anyway. Like bait!"

Brody winced.

"It's not like that," Ernie said. "We thought this was about a killing from years ago. You need to understand how unbelievable this can seem."

"I need to understand?"

"You have every right to your feelings," Brody said. "However, had Ernie come to you and stated 'you know we think a werewolf might be responsible for the deaths of these soldiers' what would you have thought?"

"Yea, that would've been something," Anna said, wiping away her tears with the back of her arm.

"Now what?" Liam raised his drooping head, eyes glassy.

"You did fine," Brody said. "Most people would've just folded up and quit in the face of what you two dealt with out there."

"But like he said, now what?"

"The dig's over," Brody put a reassuring hand on Anna's shoulder as his other handed her a tissue. "Just about the entire crew is scheduled to leave."

Everyone felt it. Ernie was no longer the leader.

"As for me," Brody's voice hardened, "I'm going hunting."

Ernie, Owen, and Cindy all offered to stay on and help a grateful Brody. He conferenced with Vance, who agreed they couldn't report anything as of yet without looking like fools. After his call Brody pulled Anna and Liam aside, insisting they remain silent. Liam just shrugged, but chilling Brody to the bone was *her* response.

"Don't you know?" Anna said.

"Know what?"

"*They've* always been here."

Ernie held open the kitchen door as Anna and Liam left an ashen faced Brody behind.

Cindy slumped at the table, eyes downcast.

Owen fidgeted nervously.

Brody fell into a chair, rubbing his temples.

"How many scratches did we see yesterday morning?" Ernie stared at the door.

"Five," Owen said.

Ernie counted ten.

"Why didn't you push Anna harder?" Owen said to Brody.

"She was positive."

"You're an *FBI Agent*," Owen said. "Yet you just sat there while Anna rambled on about seeing a *werewolf*."

"That's enough, Owen," Brody said. "There's a lot more going on."

"Like what?" Ernie said, turning from the door and motioning Owen to quiet down.

"I don't know." Brody thrummed his fingers on the table, his leg bouncing underneath. "I mean what Anna said," He trailed off, voice cracking.

"It's ok," Cindy said, encouraging him to speak.

Brody looked away, thinking of what had happened to those two college kids. It had reminded him of something he had hoped to keep locked up forever.

Cindy reached out, her hand warm as it slid over his, gently squeezing.

Brody stared at her hand, and then into her eyes.

Cindy smiled.

His reticence gave way, a feeling that he could trust his new friends granting him strength to tell them something that he had never told anyone else, "I was nineteen…"

He was at a house party in the next neighborhood over from his parent's place, getting tanked on Molson Canadian. He thought he had it all figured out. He drove a Camaro upgraded with an aftermarket turbo muffler and Alpine stereo. He lifted weights to look like his idol, of all people Arnold Schwarzenegger. He had a leggy girlfriend with stand-at-attention-tits, and an appetite for his cock that even he could scarcely believe. In retrospect, he was *almost* a first rate asshole, but not quite all the way there. That's because sometime after *House of Pain's* "Jump Around" had made its fourth turn on the CD changer and he decided to leave, he at least acknowledged that he was too drunk to drive.

He had dropped his jingling key chain into his pocket, smiling at the sight of the moon shining bright. In childhood he and Chris had explored every trail cutting through the quarter mile wide forest separating the neighborhood he was in from the one where he had grown up. However, he had never been on the trails at night.

Full of a sense of adventure and nostalgia he had marched off into *his* woods. Except that night, they weren't his woods at all. He was stumbling along, noticing how beautiful the silvery blue trees appeared in the cold moonlight when the hair had risen up on the back of his neck.

He had glanced to his right, but nothing stirred in the quiet trees.

To his left flowed a narrow creek creasing the bottom of a five foot embankment.

Then he had heard *it* again, a heavy footfall on the other side of the creek.

He had picked up his pace. Part of him felt he should look, yell, and confront his stalker. He couldn't. A voice told him not to, told him he would be better off if he didn't. Then he heard crunching dry leaves and twigs snapping underfoot on the other side of the creek. Saturday afternoon horror movies danced through his mind. Panic lanced his chest and he had broken into a flat out run. Though intoxicated, he was young, fit, and fast. Within moments he had burst from the woods and across a football field wide easement for the electric company, racing under the latticework of power lines before shooting through a narrow glade of trees surrounding the baseball diamond and park marking the western edge of his neighborhood. He sprinted past the first row of homes and crossed the street, his breath ragged. He hit his driveway, taking the concrete porch steps in one stride, fumbling for his keys, lock clicking open, squeezing past the door, slamming it tight, fighting back against his terror as he peeked through the living room curtains and out into the night…

As Brody trailed off Cindy stared at him in astonishment. The similarity to what had happened with Liam and Anna was entirely too real. Nevertheless, the rational part of her mind recognized that what happened to the graduate students was something different. That had been a message. In Brody's case…

"It wasn't a prank. None of my friends ever offered up even a hint that they had been out there," Brody said. "I was being tested. The way a predator would push a prey animal that could give it trouble."

"C'mon, Brody," Owen said. "How can you be sure it wasn't some kind of wierdo?"

"I've thought through this more than I care to admit," Brody said, shaking his head 'no', "Ever since it happened I've wanted to believe it was something more explainable. Call it a feeling, but to this day I remember how an instinctual part of me responded like it knew something much worse than a creep out there. So you wanted to know why I took it easy on Anna," Brody continued, "Well, what she described, along with my experiences, plus what every scientist is telling me about this case, that all led me to think." He wiped his forehead glistening under the harsh light swaying above the table. "What if it's true? What if *werewolves* are real?"

"We have to be sure," Cindy said. "If they exist then it's going to alter people's beliefs about this world and their place in it."

"Who's going to believe some students and their campfire story about a werewolf?" Brody said.

"You're thinking too far down the road," Ernie said. "We first need to get data and documentation to back their story. Then we can go public."

"Can someone at least acknowledge how crazy this sounds?" Owen said. *As far as he was concerned Anna and Liam saw a wolf, though he didn't know what to do with Brody's story. However, there was no way he was about to start believing an-honest-to-God werewolf was stalking the night.*

"No crazier than what most people accept," Brody said. "Organizing their lives around the magic man in the sky, and oh, by the way why don't you throw a little tithe in that there basket please."

"Watch it," Ernie said. "That soapbox you're on might topple over."

"Sorry if I'm not so generous about the fantasies some people need to make it through life," Brody said.

"That's rich," Owen snorted. "You suddenly believe in werewolves, but not God?"

"Lately, I'm seeing more proof one mythical creature exists over the other."

"We don't have time for this," Cindy said.

"She's right," Brody said. "Since we're thinking freely, there's something else. *If* all this is true, *if* werewolves are somehow real, then how much do you want to bet on our chances *if* they figure out we're onto them?"

Cindy's heart pounded in her chest. *She hadn't considered it like that.*

Brody gave them their marching orders. They would do their best to act normal. Owen had a date planned with Tanya. He would keep it. Maybe with more time to think things through he would be at least more open-minded. Meanwhile, Cindy and Ernie would visit the research desk at Lviv's National Scientific Library, taking them up on their offer to help. They would look for anything about the region's history that could be used to validate Anna's claims.

Brody called Wilson and Vance. He informed them that he had a lead on Karlovic and asked for surveillance equipment to help. Instead of congratulations he got Wilson yelling about how he had forty-eight hours to find Karlovic or they were pulling the plug on him. Brody mentioned that in the interest of saving time the Bureau should send the gear from Kiev to Lviv for pick up. Brody wanted to stay close to Ernie and Cindy, whose respective age and sex made them the likeliest targets.

In spite of everything Brody felt optimistic. He would be picking up a portable device that gathered cell-phone location information by sending out a signal tricking phones into connecting to it. He could adjust its settings to intercept not just location data but also conversations. A feature made even more useful by Vance's discovery that security systems at LaGuardia had recorded Karlovic's voice when he passed through customs. Thus, as Brody intercepted calls the information would be saved and entered into a special voice recognition program on his laptop. To cover the possibility Karlovic might not make or take calls the Bureau was also sending him a USB drive carrying software he could use for intercepting texts. They had been using similar devices in the U.S. for years and Brody felt confident he could monitor Karlovic's movements in real time while the Bureau put together a snatch-and-grab team. Nevertheless, with their minds preoccupied by the tasks at hand, no one noticed one significant detail.

Last night's moon would be even more swollen tonight.

CHAPTER 18

August 2016 – Dibrovno, Western Ukraine

It was late-afternoon when Ernie threw his overnight bag in the back of a battered 4x4 Lada Niva and then flopped into the passenger seat, the boxy vehicle protesting noisily.

"I see Cindy's running late," Owen said, strolling up. "Now's as good a time as any to talk."

Ernie furrowed his brow, recognizing what Owen wanted.

Owen squatted down so he could look into the open car window. "You got to trust me sometime."

Ernie sighed, "I've been thinking about my father."

"*And?*"

"You remember that my dad died during the war?"

"Sure."

"I left some stuff out," Ernie said. "Like the fact my dad fought with a frontline unit in the German army."

"That's not something I'd bring up at a cocktail party," Owen said. "But it's not the end of the world."

"That's not the half of it. What I'm about to say is between you and I. Nobody else."

Owen nodded his agreement.

"In Germany and before the War my family was middle class, our art gallery simple. Even so, when my mom brought me to the United States after the war, we settled into a posh neighborhood. Years later I did some digging. Only one other pre-war art gallery existed in our former home town. It was vandalized during *Kristallnacht*."

Ernie paused as a flicker of recognition passed across Owen's face.

"Add it up," Ernie said. "My mother didn't remarry until I was a teenager. My stepfather was a travelling salesman, and not a good one.

Yet we always had a new car in the driveway. I attended private school."

"None of this proves your parents stole from Jews," Owen said.

"One day I was flipping through an old photo album," Ernie said. "I found a picture of my parents at their gallery, taken just before the war began. Behind them you could clearly see a painting leaning against a wall. It was a Beckmann."

Owen stared.

"Max Beckmann was *Jewish*," Ernie said. "The Nazis confiscated his works as degenerate. The only way for my parents to possess one of his paintings so long after Hitler came to power is if they were given a special dispensation."

"Hold on, with your father's social standing he must've done something the Nazis didn't like to end up at the front," Owen said. "There must be more."

"Maybe, maybe not. Either way I—" Ernie cut himself off as he spotted Cindy come around the corner, bags in hand.

"You gonna be ok while we're gone?" Ernie said to Owen.

"Relax," Owen smiled. "It's not like I'm going hiking in the woods with a steak hanging around my neck."

"Yea, alright," Ernie said with a grin as Cindy jumped into the driver's seat.

Cindy looked over at Owen, winking and blowing him a kiss goodbye as she turned the key. The car sputtered to life with a loud cough.

Owen stepped back as she put it in gear. He stood on the hot cobblestones, staring after them. *A small part of him was thankful they were going. He hoped they would find something in Lviv to shed light on why Anna and Liam must have seen a simple wolf, and nothing more.*

Forty minutes later a shaved and showered Owen walked down the pension's narrow hallway, having forgotten all about wolves and ready for his first real date since his divorce. As he passed Ernie's bedroom he saw the door had been left open. Leaning inside to shut it he noticed a folder peeked out from a bag, its pages spilled out onto the flowery duvet. It was a report from their colleague at the *Bundesarchiv – Militärarchiv* in Freiburg, Germany. The cover letter was addressed to Dr. Owen Shaw. He sat down on the bed, frantically flipping through the mess of pages until he found the envelope he was seeking. It had been stamped Overnight Delivery, *but from two days ago. What was*

Ernie waiting for? And why had he stolen his freaking mail?

He turned to the report. One frontline German division had reported the disappearance of an entire squad, and that came in 1944. Several units from the German 168th *Infanterie-Division* had found themselves encircled during the Red Army's *Korsun–Shevchenkovsky Offensive.* It was a bloodbath capped by rampaging Soviet T-34 tanks grinding up German soldiers under their churning treads. Those Germans that survived the slaughter scatted throughout the western Ukraine; including the remnants of a battalion from the 168th that had crossed into the valley surrounding Dibrovno.

Owen's colleague from the *Bundesarchiv – Militärarchiv,* a man named Gruber, had included in his report the 168th's tables of organization and equipment (TO&E) – a byzantine mix of Roman and Arabic numerals used to designate it's three *Grenadier-Regiments*; one *Artillerie-Regiment,* an *Aufklarungs-Abteilung* (reconnaissance battalion), *Panzerjager-Abteilung* (tank hunter/destroyer battalion), *Pionere-Abteilung* (engineer battalion), and *Nachrichten-Abteilung* (signals detachment), and many other sub-units. Gruber had highlighted the composition of the battalion in question, the I./417 or 1st battalion of the 417th Grenadier Regiment. The positive identification came from a *KTB* found from March of 1944.

Nonetheless, that didn't help as much as one would think. That's because every ten days German army personnel officers sent to the highest headquarters (*Oberkommando des Heeres* or OKH) reports detailing casualties. In addition, medical units forwarded on their reports of killed, wounded, and missing. These figures were compared to the authorized strength returns, helping to allocate reinforcements. One of the problems a researcher faced in tracking down an individual soldier stemmed from the practice of wounded men staying on their parent formation's rolls for upwards of sixty days. This meant that just because they had found dog tags it did not mean the other soldier's exhumed from the dig came from the same squad. For example, a soldier could be convalescing with a hospital inside the combat zone and still be assigned to his unit, even if the unit received a replacement not yet on its books.

Regardless Gruber had been able to cut through some of those problems by reviewing all *KTB's* specific to the battalion and period in question. That enabled him to determine that on March 4, 1944, the I./417, or first battalion of the 417th Grenadier Regiment, and it's I./3./417 or the first platoon of the third company of the 417th had reported a missing nine man squad. Unfortunately, the squad members had only been identified by number. The squad leader represented the sole soldier listed by name: a *Stabsfeldwebel* or Master Sergeant by the last name of Dietrich.

Thus, though Gruber had come back with a rank and name to match the found dog tag they still had no actual record linking that man to the Master Sergeant. This would require Owen to review the divisional, corps, and army level reports that had been submitted to the old *Wehrmachtauskunftsstelle für Kriegsverluste und Kriegsgefangene* or Wehrmacht Information Office for War Casualties and Prisoners of War. Owen glanced at his smart phone and caught sight of the time. He was late, and at the thought of this date with Tanya he dropped the report on the bed.

Within moments he was hustling the short distance to the tavern; his anger at Ernie pushed aside by his thumping hormones. As he strode down the street he failed to notice the occasional villager rushing past, eyes furtively cast skyward. When he arrived at the pub, he missed, in his excitement, how empty it was compared to previous nights. How the few patrons never let their eyes stray far from the clock, how others hurried to settle their tab, leaving half-full pints warming on the polished wood.

Owen selected a table in the back just as Tanya strode inside, her smart phone against her ear. She weaved through the tables, finishing her conversation, "No, not yet…I promised I would do it…Yes, soon."

Owen stared, transfixed by her appearance. A touch of makeup highlighted her high cheekbones, and eyes framed by her shoulder length jet black hair. Her almost translucent black dress clung like a second skin to her swaying hips, plunging deeply between her semi-exposed breasts.

"Jesus Tanya…I mean, you look incredible," Owen said as she ended her call.

"Well, it's nice to know I'm normally not much too look at," Tanya said as she sat, her strained expression replaced by a smile.

"No, that's not what," he mumbled, before catching himself. "What I mean is you clean up pretty nice for a peasant girl."

Tanya chuckled, her irritation melting away.

"Is everything ok?" Owen finally asked, stealing another glance at Tanya's dress.

"Oh, it's nothing," Tanya said. "Just work."

"If you're too busy we can reschedule for another night," Owen responded, hoping to God she wouldn't take him up on the half-hearted offer.

"Don't be silly," Tanya said. Her eyes blazed with need as she crossed her legs, reflexively biting down on her lower lip when a tingling feeling shot through her midsection.

The waitress appeared, her gaze lingering on Tanya as she poured a full bodied blood red burgundy into their glasses.

They drank and talked. Owen found it easy to open up, briefly mentioning his divorce, and moving on. In turn, Tanya found herself enjoying his company more than she would have thought possible. In particular he exhibited an attentive and restrained manner that not once descended into the sophomoric humor that seemed to be his coping mechanism for a broken home life, instead exhibiting a caring intelligence made all the more endearing by his obvious affection for her. She reveled in the lack of awkward silences as they shared stories, laughing and feeling more relaxed in these few hours then she had in months. They ignored their food, including the blintzes the waitress had slipped onto the table with a wink for Tanya. An off menu treat, these fried golden brown flat cakes piled high with farmers cheese and lightly dusted in sugar and juicy raisins all but begged to be devoured. Instead, Tanya's hand grasped Owens, and they stood.

They walked out into the warm night. Moonlight shined through the pines towering over Dibrovno. Even the river had calmed its otherwise incessant gurgling. Not a soul could be found. Nearly every window shade had been drawn tightly closed on the home's lining the street. Owen felt a twinge of concern in spite of his recent reluctance to countenance what Anna had said. As Tanya leaned in however, her scent, a creamy musk of vanilla and wild jasmine, evaporated away his concerns.

They strolled onto a narrow moon swept path, Tanya's fingers stroking along his, sending his heart rate soaring. Not once did he even think to worry about the presence of anything other than Tanya and the fact he hadn't felt so happy to be with someone since long before his bank-rupt marriage had crumbled into divorce.

After a long climbing walk they halted before a country estate. Owen gawked at the structure's imposing gothic façade evident in the imposing stone tented roof and steep cross gables. They stepped onto the porch. To the right of an oak door a heraldic coat of arms had been carved into the stone, a black wolf on a yellow shield with a Latin engraving above.

"To serve and guard?" Owen queried, running his fingers over the inscription.

Tanya smiled and fingered the platinum bracelet on her right wrist. Owen glanced down. The coast of arms hanging from the brushed satin chain mirrored the one emblazoned on the wall. Tanya easily pushed the big door open. Owen followed, grunting with effort as he closed the door behind them. To his left a spiral staircase led up, intricately deco-rated with wrought iron bannisters and a wooden newel engraved with woodland animals. To his right were leaded glass French doors, fingers of light revealing shelves of books within the shadows.

Tanya glided ahead into a great room flanked by dark stained wooden beams rising to frame the high ceiling. An imposing stone fire-place bracketed by two picture windows dominated the living space. The open floor plan flowed into a large kitchen where a massive trestle dining table was attended by sturdy wooden chairs upholstered in lush fabrics.

Everywhere Owen looked he saw colorful tapestries, prints, and paintings adding warmth to what could have easily been a feeling of emptiness in the vast rooms. He lingered at one such wall-hanging, not sure what to think. Woven of gold, silk and wool it was a lavishly embroidered vision of two lusting satyr's carrying off a bare chested woman, bejeweled chalices overflowing with wine held aloft in their free hands. The creatures appeared as depicted in late era Greek art, humanized in appearance notwithstanding the animalistic lower bod-ies. He had come across such imagery before. Portrayals of the mythical beasts ranged from the savage to the childlike, to the erotic. There was nothing innocent about the image before him.

"You like?" Tanya sidled up, eyes glinting at Owen with hypnotic intensity.

"It's *different*," Owen swallowed, finding something to stare at on the floor, his heart racing.

"It was a gift," Tanya pressed close, "From someone who once knew me well. The satyrs were notable for their enduring love of both wine and women. Half beast and half man, they took particular delight in the pleasures of the flesh."

Owen's head swam with strange thoughts.

Tanya directed him to tend the fire.

He watched her stroll into the kitchen, and then crouched on the rug before the fireplace. Almost losing his balance, he reached down to steady himself. A brown bear's wide skull roared back. Owen's heart nearly leapt from his chest.

"He was quite a fighter."

Owen looked up at Tanya, who smiled as she twisted the cork off a bottle of wine. He turned his attention back to the fire, feeling increasingly languid. The wood popped and crackled, rapidly heating the room, the flames dancing hotter...

"Owen!"

He stumbled to stand in response, shaking the cobwebs off and accepting a glass of wine from a bemused Tanya, "Sorry, I just..."

"I know," Her tongue glided across full lips, voice deeper and in complete tonal control.

Owen watched her fingers teasing along the polished edge of her glass; the burgundy colored wine lightly lapping below, her gaze predatory.

Tanya could see how nervous Owen felt and stifled a smile, wondering if she were laying it on a little thick. However, she so badly wanted him to reward her attention. She spun around, her clinging dress caressing her legs as she bent deeply at the waist, elegant fingers setting her glass on a handsomely carved end table next to a deeply cushioned sofa where she took a seat.

Owen swayed, the blazing fire heating the room, and doing nothing to calm his swirling emotions. Just then he noticed a book perched on the table's edge. He craned his neck to see, making out a series of indecipherable woodcuts on the cover, barely readable was the author's name written in white on a black background...*Montague Summers*. Above it he spied letters printed in red but he couldn't quite read them in the dark. A strange feeling tickled the back of his mind as he glanced at the author's name again.

"Ahhh that, it's just a dry old tome," Tanya said, pushing the book into the shadows. She patted the couch next to her.

Owen stepped forward, and promptly tripped over the rug.

Tanya bit her lip to keep from smiling, catching him staring at her dress as he recovered. She responded. One leanly muscled leg came up and crossed over the other, wispy material sliding up her superbly toned thigh.

Owen sat down, drinking deeply from his glass, the brunette's leer evoking powerful but vulnerable sensations within. He blushed for the umpteenth time, "Nice place you've got here."

This time she laughed, "Is that what you want to do, talk about my house?"

The question hung in the air, unanswered.

Owen gulped, steeling himself to respond but Tanya stood in one swift motion, slipping the dress off her shoulders. Owen dove into her welcoming arms, his divorce, friends; everything was forgotten but this extraordinary woman before him. Tanya kissed him as Owen inelegantly shed his clothes. They slid to the floor, Owen holding their kiss the entire time, a moment of tender connection centering a need of something more. His searching eyes met hers - betraying the powerful depth of his feelings. She guided him to her, providing him with a contented closeness and hope that he hadn't felt in years. Afterward, they came down together, breaths of exertion lessening into softer pants of joy. Owen's throat tightened, a swirling vortex of emotions consuming him.

He didn't know how long they lay, silently staring into one another's eyes. There was a look of gentle sadness evident on her face. It was an expression he hadn't seen from her before. It triggered within him a brief twinge of anxiety quelled by the hope that maybe they had more in common than mere physical attraction.

The fire had mostly consumed itself when Tanya propped herself up. She liked being with him and her right hand trailed down his stomach, fingernails playing lightly back and forth, moving lower.

"You still haven't asked," Owen said with a sharp intake of breath; her searching fingers had found what they were seeking.

"About?"

"My divorce," Owen felt himself stir once more.

"At dinner I thought we—"

"We discussed nothing."

"It's not my place," Tanya said, her hand curling around his thickening response.

"I did something. Something I shouldn't have."

"Was it wicked?" Tanya said, her grasping hand rhythmically moving up and down.

"Very much so," Owen said with a moan.

"And…" Tanya tightened her grip.

"I enjoyed it."

"How exquisite," Tanya's full lips curled into a smile. "That's the *why* I want to know."

"Something inside told me to do it, so I did. Even after *she* caught me I couldn't help but feel that I would've done it again."

"Some people are drawn to the dark forest, or the bad part of town," Tanya's hand stroked faster. "Is that so wrong?"

"Yes," Owen gasped.

"It's only wrong if you let it be," Tanya's grin broadened, then froze. She snapped her head around, the clock confirming what her body knew, "You need to go. *Now.*"

Owen obeyed, not once questioning what she said. Within minutes they stood dressed at the open front door. A faint twinge of concern tugged at a dim corner of his mind. *Maybe she didn't really like him.* His worries vanished when she leaned in to kiss him.

"This won't be a one-time thing?" Owen's plaintive question when she pulled away all too nakedly revealed his raw vulnerability.

Tanya smiled and gave him a good-bye peck on the cheek, sending him on his way. She shut the door behind and leaned against it, eyes darkening as her happiness was replaced by a seething anger at what *they* wanted her to do.

She should have been full of joy, for the first time in she didn't know how long she had connected with someone. Instead, a single tear ran from her eye and down her cheek.

It came racing up from within.

She cried out, falling to the floor.

Owen was never going to make it back to town.

She didn't have a choice.

She was going to kill him.

CHAPTER 19

March 1944 – The Western Ukraine

Dawn loomed gray. The nights inky grip fading out as Dietrich dragged deep on his cigarette, hand rolled rice paper rough between shaking fingers. Gusts of frigid air pushed the previous day's precipitation into billowy white drifts blanketing the land. The fetid odor seeping from the pungent mess spread across the clearing overpowered even the tobacco's acrid bite, a sick lurching feeling roiling Dietrich's stomach.

The veteran *Stabsfeldwebel* scratched at the puckered scar slithering down his cheek, a gift courtesy of a Soviet rifleman's bayonet one year prior. Heavy lidded eyes surveyed his squad, arrayed in a loose semi-circle and squeezed into the icy meadow by the relentlessly dark forest. To a man, they looked away when their Sergeant searched their faces, puffs of breath hanging in the frosty air.

Dietrich savored the cigarette's woody flavor. Strong Turkish tobacco sent to him from a comrade in the *Luftwaffe*, far better than the *Juno* or *Eckstein* the men received from the quartermaster. He appreciated one last aromatic pull and flicked away the butt of burning embers.

He scanned the wall of spruces, gripped by a sense of something inexplicable.

After a long moment, he turned away. Shrugging off his lingering unease he squatted, the snow crunching under his fur lined boots. His cold blue unblinking left eye and watchful hazel right eye scanned across *Gefreiter* Erich Bekensteiner's remains, scattered about like so many discarded toys in a *kindergarten*.

As a child, his parents had chastised him when he stared too long at those made uncomfortable by his discomfiting focus. In the army, however, his eyes became an asset. His commanding officer once admitted that Dietrich reminded him of a predator; how he could fix someone in his stare without even turning his head. He pursed his lips, knowing a fellow predators work when he saw it. To his right, a *Marschstiefel* stuck inverted out of the snow. In it a ragged ankle bone stripped of flesh, providing a sharp contrast against the black leather of the slick jackboot. Pieces of hooded parka fluttered past, stained reddish-brown from the rank discharge of its former owner's bodily fluids. In the center of it all Erich's headless torso leaned against a log, scraps of meat stuck to the ribs like gristle on a picked-over holiday goose.

Dietrich gagged at the corpse's noxious odor but knew what he had to do. Wanting more than anything else to get it over with, he faced over his shoulder and inhaled a whooshing gulp of crisp, fresh air. Then he dropped to his knees. Fingers probed inside, flesh squishing like the fibrous pulp of a freshly opened squash. He held his breath, fighting off his rising nausea. The seconds dragged by, his vision dimming. He dug deep under the slippery collarbone, pulling aside clinging purplish tissue.

After another agonizing moment, he spun away, taking deep sucking breaths as the color flooded back into his face. Several more seconds had passed before he rose on unsteady feet, perturbed as much by what he hadn't found as what that might mean. As he caught his breath, he spied something a few feet away, projecting from the sea of reddened snow.

He stepped over, recognizing the flashing *Erkennungsmarke*. He bent down to pick up the soldier's identification tag, choking back bile and sipping at the crisp air. Brow furrowed he let his fingers roam over the disk's smooth zinc surface, wanting to lick his cracked lips but having survived too many Russian winters to make that mistake. The disk should have been woven into the laces of Erich's boot; with the issuing unit name, ID number, and blood type stamped on the tag. In the event of death, the perforated center was meant to be snapped in half. One part was supposed to go to graves registration. The other half stayed with the body. That is not what happened here.

He dragged a finger through the snow, staring off.

Nature's pitiless smile confronted him. Forested hills rolled away to the west, steadily rising up into the mountains overlooking the violence marring the morning's otherwise stunning beauty. He silently cursed the orders detailing his squad to this godforsaken valley. Candle straight pines towering one hundred feet above created a dank, gloomy canopy. Spruces and firs formed an intricately laced web of needled green underneath. Even on the sunniest day the wild existed in a semi-permanent state of twilight, settlements rare—

Goosebumps danced across his flesh. This time he could feel *it*, as sure as he felt his heart pounding under his tunic. A palpable presence hung in the air, stilling the wintry woodland. Even the crows were quiet. The men's eyes darted everywhere and nowhere at once. Teeth chattered to Dietrich's right. He fixed the soldier with an icy stare. *Gefreiter* Peter Bix had been with Erich in the listening post and had stumbled into camp not two hours prior, babbling nonsense. Dietrich turned his attention away from the young soldier.

Everything he needed to know was in the footprints.

Two tracks. One ran from the listening post, Erich's. They marched toward the second set. These were of *bare* human feet big as snowshoes, descending from the foothills as if on holiday at a Baltic beach. That is until the tracks met Erich's. What remained of the soldier's body looked like a pig on a spit after Oktoberfest. Hailing from the Black Forest, Dietrich knew the stories - *the legends.* The insistent warnings from his grandmother…*Stay on the path. Don't go into the forest.*

He shook his head in disgust. It had started with the farmer's house. They had been sweeping the area for partisans when they found it, fallow beet and potato fields surrounding the tidy homestead. They would have moved on had not Heinrich discovered an MP-38 hidden under a bale of hay. The wayward German machine pistol prompted a more thorough investigation. No sooner had they started when a loud explosion ripped the air. He remembered coming around the side of the house to see the cellar door wrenched off its hinges, shattered planks scattered across the yard. Erich stood on the stairs, staring. The pull cord from a stick grenade dangled from his shaking hand. Dietrich ducked inside to see a farmer, his wife, and what looked like a ten-year old boy painted across the cellar walls. That had been three days ago.

Dietrich balled his left hand into a fist, his face hot as he stared at the abnormally large footprints. They tracked back into the forest, accompanied by droplets of blood. The trail too obvious, Erich's killer wanted them to follow.

Dietrich raised his eerie heterochromatic stare. He had slain just about every kind of person that walked this continent. It was time to kill one more.

With a murderer's gleam in his eyes, he gathered his men.

They were going hunting.

August 2016 – Lviv, The Western Ukraine

Ernie fidgeted in his car seat, looking out the window. Eastern European woodlands normally hummed with activity during this time of year. Parked cars would be lined up along the roadside, marking locations where people had plunged into the forest in search of the wide variety of mushrooms favored in so many of the region's dishes. But not this afternoon, beech trees interspersed with firs, maples, and alder blanketed the land undisturbed. Only the rattling rental car marred the suffocating stillness as the narrow winding lane finally broke free of the sullen woodlands.

Small farming villages pressed tight to the road. Modern homes featuring red tiled roofs and brilliant yellow or burnt orange colored walls were interspersed with communist era designs, some touched up, others looking like drab concrete blockhouses. Traditional wooden houses also dotted the landscape. Blue stripes marked several, reminders of a time when families advertised their daughter's eligibility for marriage. Ernie gazed in wonder, thinking of more recent events that had scarred this land.

"What's so fascinating?"

He jumped at Cindy's voice. Her formidable intelligence aside he remembered that she was no historian. He explained to her how in the spring of 1944 one of history's great battles had unfolded amidst these peaceful villages.

As Ernie narrated men and machines jumped from the shadowed landscape. The black clad Germans in their massive steel beasts facing off against wave after wave of diesel powered Soviet tanks, chattering machine guns lacing the air with bullets. When Soviet T-34 shells found the mark they often ineffectually defected skyward in long arcing blue streaks cast from thick German armor turned white hot from the heat generated by the powerful blows. In turn, often the last sound and sight a T-34 tank crew knew was the crack of the German tank's high velocity cannon. Armor piercing shells would then hiss shoulder high over rippling stalks of grain to rip into the thirty ton Soviet main battle tanks, and send long gouts of orange flame bursting forth in deafening explosions that left burning oily wrecks behind. To a layperson like Cindy, Ernie knew it would seem that the Germans couldn't possibly lose such lopsided engagements. As he explained however, when forced to maneuver the mechanically complex German panzers all too often came clacking to a halt as transmissions or engines faltered.

Cindy listened. Though not having more than a passing interest in the Second World War she enjoyed the distraction. However, she couldn't escape feeling worried. Nor could she ignore the tingle of dread that raced through her when she looked out the window, the sky turning iron gray as the sun settled ever lower on the horizon.

They crested a rise, and Lviv loomed before them.

Within minutes they had driven into the centuries old informal capital of Galicia. Regardless of Poland's overwhelming centrality to Lviv's past, Hapsburg, Jewish and Russian influences also stood out in the city's eclectic mix of Central and Eastern European architecture assimilated into buildings bedecked with limestone carvings, delicately constructed brickwork, ornamented balconies, spires, turrets, domes, and more. After a few more moments they entered neighborhoods featuring rows of orange, aquamarine, peach and yellow colored Art Nouveau residences and shops crowding close to tree lined streets that finally gave way to the bustling medieval city center.

Ernie gaped at the diversity of architecture perhaps most evident in the city's churches; the distinctive triple dome of a Ukrainian Orthodox church; a spectacular bell towered Baroque-Rococo style Greek Orthodox church; Latin; Dominican; Jesuit, Armenian, and the only surviving active synagogue from the brief but brutal Nazi occupation. Cindy keyed in on the countless cafés; including one she eyed while sitting at a stop light. It was on the corner of a pink, white trimmed Renaissance building where under different circumstances she could have seen herself lost in a book and a cup of the local blend.

The light changed and she accelerated away, within minutes pulling up to their hotel near the old town center. The five-story neo-Renaissance building was surrounded by a dizzying array of restaurants, shops, and homes painted stunning shades of yellow, turquoise, and pink. Ernie ignored all of it, taking just enough time to check in, drop off their bags and get back to Cindy; who had been idling out front. After a short drive, the library's symmetrical cream and yellow façade came into view. Intricately designed iron street lamps stood at attention up and down the sidewalk where Cindy parked.

As she stepped from the car a tight feeling in the pit of Cindy's stomach pulled her eyes upward. The night had fallen like a black cloak on the unsuspecting city. She hustled Ernie across the library's dark courtyard and through an arcaded portico. As they entered the library, however, they missed the Mercedes sedan that cruised up behind their rental car. Had either of them glanced back they would have seen the car slow to a near standstill as a large figure slipped out from the back seat. Instead, Ernie and Cindy let the library's front door slam shut behind them as they spotted a librarian tending the quiet main greeting desk, youthful skin contrasted against eyes betraying a weariness of someone older. Her name tag read Kateryna.

Cindy couldn't shake her jumpiness. The building's gloomy interior hardly helped. She cast ever longer glances at the woman's teeth and shape of her jaw. After a moment, she caught herself, flushing red. *What were you looking for? A set of fangs?*

The librarian finally looked up.

Ernie greeted her in Ukrainian.

Kateryna smiled broadly, answering in English, "You are the American professors, yes?"

Ernie nodded.

"Unfortunately, the head of the research department has left for the day," Kateryna said, darting from behind the desk, "I would love to help you with your work. It has been big news here." She waved them through a Romanesque combination of arched walls and doorways as Ernie explained a summary of his research needs. The trio passed through a veritable cornucopia of learning, their footfalls echoing across the hardwood floors in room after room packed full of manuscripts, archives, periodicals, incunabula, paleotypes, cartographic publications, engravings, sculptures, drawings, watercolors, gouache paintings, photographs, music collections, and countless books. Kateryna directed her charges into yet another hallway, this one darker and narrower than those before.

A door slammed shut nearby.

Cindy's stomach cartwheeled.

Kateryna led them into the dimly lit archives located deep within the isolated east wing. There they stepped into a turreted room. Rows of closely packed bookshelves and russet colored desks crowded the floor. Slender, winding staircases led to open balconied levels above, each lined with bookshelves; the eye drawn ever up past the narrow clerestory to a soaring frescoed ceiling. Cindy and Ernie sat as Kateryna sought to fulfil Ernie's requests; hustling to and fro she stacked on a desk everything she could find about *Dubno*.

Ernie immediately recognized her mistake. Dubno had been a predominately Jewish town located on the Ikva River. During World War II Germany's *Einsatzgruppen* murdered thousands of its inhabitants in the forests outside the city. He coughed to get Kateryna's attention.

She turned.

"Sorry, but we want *Dibrovno's* history," Ernie said with a smile that promptly fell away as the librarian recoiled from him as if she had been slapped. Fingers of fear dug into Ernie's flesh even as he pleaded for her understanding.

She argued back in a sea of syllables. After several minutes of this Kateryna snapped her mouth shut, struggling with her thoughts. She stared at the ground for a long time before raising her head and angrily relenting.

She gestured for the two professors to follow.

They came to a sturdy wooden door hidden away behind several box-filled cabinets. Kateryna threw the bolt, exposing a narrow staircase leading underground into darkness. She stepped onto the groaning first step. Ernie and Cindy followed. The temperature dropped, and the humidity rose, imparting a glistening sheen on the winding steps as they reached the stairwell's bottom. Kateryna pulled from her pocket an old skeleton key. Her hand shook as she pushed the bronze shank into the lock, a click echoing through the enclosed space. She pushed open the creaking door and slid her arm around the corner. Her wrist jerked up.

A bank of grimy overhead lights flickered on, barely illuminating an old desk sitting a dozen feet into the room. Dusty rows of book lined shelves faded into the musty darkness, the air smelling of mildew, paper, and earth. Ernie and Cindy crept inside, wiping off the dirty chairs and quietly sitting. Kateryna scuttled off into the gloom.

Ernie willed himself to calm down, eager to see what was behind the stacks, especially curious to know whether other doors led into the room, fighting against a sick feeling enveloping him like a strange aura. Kateryna returned from her foraging, disappeared, and came back two more times. Each trip brought a stack of books, photo albums, and document boxes.

After the last of it had been unceremoniously dropped onto the desk in a cloud of fine dust Kateryna raised her index finger and glared at Ernie. She opened her mouth to say something, before changing her mind and stomping up the stairs.

The first book Ernie selected exuded a cloying vanilla scent of old pages. He glanced at the fraying cover and bindings then opened what turned out to be a communist era history of the region. He read aloud, translating the dense text for Cindy...

Dibrovno ranked among the oldest continuous settlements in the area, as befitted its location. The deep valley marked the entry to a series of passes through the Carpathians affording a traveler any number of options for reaching the relatively flat Hungarian plains to the southwest, into Romania's rugged wilderness to the south, or access to Czech and Slovakian lands to the west.

Ernie closed the book and Cindy sat back, deep in thought...*the town's setup astride a traditional trade route...*

He picked up another volume, much older; one that Kateryna had buried under a mound of surveys he had brushed past, knowing that time was at a premium. He swept the clinging grime off the soft dark leather binding. The cover featured a grooved design with red dyed letters etched into the leather. Ernie's fingers trailed across the distinctive texture. His meandering hand abruptly froze; eyes wide as he read the book's title...*Вовкулака vovkulaka.*

He exhaled in a disbelieving hiss, the blood roaring in his veins.

Cindy put a light but steadying hand on his shoulder. It felt like a knotted cable.

"This book, the title," Ernie said. "It's the Ukrainian term for *werewolf.*"

Cindy shot upright, terrified as to why Kateryna had left this book for them. She turned toward Ernie, but he was in another world, his eyes locked on the outside edge of the heavy volume, conspicuously lined with gold leaf.

He was so absorbed it didn't even occur to him to question Kateryna's motives. He turned the yellowish-brown pages. *They should have crinkled, but they felt soft, perhaps because of the resins used to bind the book?* Curious, he inhaled. The heavy sheets gave off an oily if not woody smell...

"Vellum," Ernie blurted in recognition.

Cindy stared in confusion.

"Sorry," Ernie caught Cindy's puzzled expression. "Vellum comes from the Latin '*vitulinum*' which roughly means 'made from calf.' Here, feel how smooth it is." Ernie directed her hand to the page, "Look closely; you can even see hair markings."

"But why?"

"Vellum was once used for the most important manuscripts. For instance, in 1455 a quarter of Gutenberg's first Bibles made with movable type were printed in vellum. But it's expensive." At that Ernie frowned, "Yet this book isn't that old. Based on the table of contents it seems to include events leading up into the late nineteenth century..."

He leaned in. The words jumped off the pages in an intricate calligraphic style of writing evident of the care and attention the author had given to each phrase, each description, each depiction, each fact, and to their attendant controversies. Several of the chapter captions were even gold-leafed.

Cindy ran her fingers over one such heading, recognizing it for what it was, and peering in wonder at Ernie.

He nodded affirmatively and closed his eyes, imagining the author hidden away in a dank candlelit room probably not unlike this one. His materials spread out on a heavy table, gold leaf, delicate brushes, wood-handled agate burnishers ready to polish the gold into a smooth lustrous finish. For the text there would have been bottles of ink, quills...

But why?

Then the answer hit him. He turned the book on its binding and stared at the gold leaf gilding the outside edge, the *fore-edge.*

He fanned the pages.

The savage face of a werewolf jumped out at them, lavishly rendered in blacks, whites, and reds.

Cindy stifled a cry.

"I haven't seen a fore-edged book in," Ernie trailed off, taking in the frightening image. Whoever had created this had been a real artist, those horrible eyes felt like they were reaching into his soul. "This style dates back to the tenth century, though the hidden or disappearing image like this didn't begin appearing until the middle of the seventeenth century." Ernie stopped fanning the pages. "By the nineteenth century it wasn't as common, but on high-end works it still showed up from time to time."

This didn't make sense.

Though the fore-edge painting was not dated, the use of vellum had been by the late nineteenth century. That would have made this a wildly expensive book to publish.

So why did the author go to such effort?

A worrying feeling worked its way through him as he cleared his throat, and with his finger pressed on the corner of the first chapter's first page began reading aloud...

No one knew for sure where the legends began. Some said in Germany, others in France. Others yet claimed to have traced the origins back to the age of antiquity, and the writings of a Gaius Petronius Arbiter - that is before he mysteriously took his life in 65 A.D. Regardless, one institution more than any other latched onto the idea of werewolves; the church.

By the Crusade's end the Papacy was desperately casting about for a new enemy to justify a renewed Holy War that could attract followers. The Inquisition became the vehicle for the Church's subsequent war of terror waged on Europe's population, bringing new life to the idea of werewolves. For the most part however, werewolves or *vlko-dlak* and the word's numerous linguistically derived variants across Eastern and Central Europe's Slavic populations, didn't appear in any real sense in European folklore until the absolute horror show that represented life in the fourteenth century, when the Plague's ravages decimated Europe's population. Shortly after the first sustained appearance of werewolves in the historical record, the Black Plague diminished. The legend of the werewolf did not. Ernie's breath caught in his throat, the fear close, and disquietingly *real*. Cases of werewolf attacks plentifully and richly described. Trials recorded in England, France, the German states, and more. He glanced over at Cindy. It was only then, when his eyes left the page, that he realized how deathly quiet it had become beyond their little circle of light.

His heart skipped a beat.

"Did you hear that?" Ernie said. A vein throbbed in his forehead.

Cindy's lips quivered. She thought she heard the ceiling creak, but wasn't sure.

After another moment, she shook her head no.

Head cocked Ernie waited, the page fluttering as his hand shook. Hearing nothing else, he shook off his initial instinct and plunged back into the book, half-listening for any other unusual sounds...

A woodcut by Lukas Mayer graphically illustrated the sixteenth century public execution of the "Werewolf of Bedburg." The accused had been arrested and put to the rack where he admitted to devouring approximately sixteen women and children. The bloody killing featured flesh torn by hot pincers from the accused murderer's body while he had been mounted on a wheel engraved with a wolf's form. The executioners ripped away his arms and legs, subsequently broken to prevent his return from death and use of said limbs. Then they decapitated him, burned his body, and mounted his head on a pole.

Another werewolf killed five young boys in Denmark. The Danish king's men hacked several ribs from the accused man's spine. From there they pulled his lungs through the holes and spread them across his back to beat like a bloody pair of wings until he fell into shock and died.

Ernie translated his way through a long discussion of how the *Völsungasaga*, a collection of tales and poems originating in late thirteenth century Iceland, spoke of men fighting as wolves. The *Mittelhochdeutsch*, or Middle High period of the German language, also described such things. Ernie and Cindy took in row after row of precisely arranged text strangely festooned with variously colored shapes and religious iconography burdening the thickly inked letters in a dissonant unsettling fashion. The dark tales and haunting text, however, could not outweigh Ernie's visceral reaction to the richly rendered drawings and engravings. Many showed the beasts exactly as Anna had described; on two legs, a well-muscled body lightly covered in fur, with a wolfish head. A slavering brutally lethal vision of death and strangely sexual overtones; the last thing a terrified villager would have seen striking from the darkness alongside the path. Ernie shivered, goosebumps breaking out on his skin.

Across Europe werewolves continued to strike, and in turn, be hunted down. The last few trials took place in eighteenth and nineteenth century France and Austria, accounts of werewolf killings markedly declined. Then they vanished nearly all together.

A cold icicle of terror knifed between Ernie's shoulder blades.

This time Cindy heard it too, a light footfall.

Then came another one, heavier, coming down the stairs...

CHAPTER 20

August 2016 – Lviv, The Ukraine

The footfalls stopped.

Kateryna burst into the room clutching a photo album. Something large moved in the shadows behind her.

Cindy's heart skipped a beat. Then she relaxed. It was Brody, frowning at Kateryna as he squeezed past.

"I take it all that melodrama about Dubno was a charade?" Cindy said.

"You of all people must know that werewolves are not a topic you casually bring up."

Cindy scowled at her.

"Please understand," Kateryna pleaded. "When I heard that you were working on a mass grave outside Dibrovno I just had to—"

"Do what?" Ernie said; the dark circles under his eyes cutting into his lined cheeks.

"You *still* don't know what's going on in Dibrovno?" Kateryna gasped.

"What do you mean?" Cindy said.

"Oh my god, it's—"

"Show and tell is over," Brody said, his voice gruff. "We have to go, now."

They gathered up what they could as Brody hustled the jumpy professors up the stairs, explaining meeting Kateryna at the library's front desk plus her strange insistence she could help. When Brody reached the top step he waved everyone into silence, peeking into the dark library. Moon light streamed in from the window, eerily illuminating the book stacks as deep shadows danced across desks, chairs, and office furniture. An image of Cameron's ravaged corpse skittered across his mind. He shook it off. The harder he stared the more the moon light seemed to penetrate less into the old building—something grabbed his arm.

Brody nearly leaped out of his skin, eyes wide as he pivoted.

Kateryna clung to him, eyebrows raised.

Trying to calm his jackhammering nerves Brody gave the all clear. Kateryna eased past. He let her. She would know the best way out. Cindy and Ernie followed, moving painfully slow. Ernie's eye sight wasn't what it had once been, nor was his hearing. Trailing behind his friends he abruptly startled, fumbling loudly with his armload of books.

Everyone froze. Multiple sets of ears and eyes strained to pierce the gloom.

A branch swaying in the wind scratched up against a window.

Brody's mouth felt uncomfortably tight and dry. After several more seconds he waved them on.

They came to a steel exit door.

Kateryna pushed it open and hurried outside, her shoes grinding into the asphalt as the warm night air enveloped them in its humid embrace. Tall buildings blocked most of the moonlight from filtering into the dark alley.

"Our car is parked—"

"No," Brody silenced Ernie, and motioned them to his rental car parked along the back wall of the library. They piled in and Brody threw the car into gear. As far as he could tell no one had spotted their escape. Nevertheless, he needed to be sure. He executed a tight turn, maneuvering up the alley. He let the car drift forward, nosing out into the main street running in front of the library. Evenly spaced lamp posts marched along the sidewalk, casting pale circles of light - except for the one that should have been above Ernie and Cindy's car. The only one not working.

Brody pointed down the avenue to make sure everyone noticed not only the broken light, but the way the parked car sagged to one side – as if something heavy was waiting inside. Brody shifted into neutral to let the car slide back. He abruptly stood on the brakes, the car rocking to a stop as he stared in disbelief.

Twin headlights had snapped on from further up the road, past Ernie and Cindy's car. Brody's eyes locked on the second car; a big sedan.

He wanted to flee, but waited as the car drove under a streetlight. He verified three passengers in a sickeningly familiar looking late model Mercedes. He let his vehicle roll behind the building. Upon reaching a side alley he turned the car around, unable to ignore the hot buzzing feeling in his ears. The one telling him he had screwed up.

"Wait a minute our hotel is where—"

"We're *not* going," Brody said to Ernie. "Once I picked up my gear I played a hunch and headed for your hotel. When you and Cindy checked in I wasn't the only one watching, you're being hunted."

Ashen faced, Ernie glanced over at an equally dismayed Cindy before responding, "Are you sure?"

"None of the suspects were wearing wolf print t-shirts from Walmart if that's what you mean, but the car that followed you from your hotel to the library kind of clued me in," Brody said as his they coasted down the alley, his eyes affixed to the rearview mirror. "I figured you were safe in a public place. So I slipped back to your hotel and let myself into your rooms."

"How did you?"

"They do teach us a thing or two at Quantico about these situations," Brody said, staring past Ernie in the rearview mirror. He dropped his foot. They accelerated ever so slightly, his heart pounding. *The alley seemed to go on forever.*

"I thought initially it was the MVS tailing you," Brody continued. "However, your rooms were bugged. High end stuff, manufactured in the west. That's when I knew we were dealing with someone other than the Ukrainian police."

Cindy put her head in her hands.

The tingling feeling in Brody's spine turned ice cold as a big car eclipsed the alley mouth behind them.

It was the Mercedes.

There was no question anymore. It was the same car that had followed Ernie and Cindy to the library. With one hand gripping the wheel Brody slid his other down to snap on his seat belt. Kateryna jumped at the distinct click and then fumbled to follow his lead. In the back seat Cindy and Ernie exchanged wide eyed glances, scrambling to yank their belts into place.

"We'll hit Kateryna's place and regroup there," Brody said.

"But she's a—"

"Librarian?" Kateryna shot back, her grip tight on the door.

"No, I meant someone not caught up in all this," Ernie pleaded.

"Wrong," Brody said. "The minute you stepped into that library she landed in it."

He stared at the rearview mirror, his breath catching in his throat as the set of headlights loomed larger.

Cindy and Ernie craned their necks to see, hearts pounding as reality sank in.

"The library's supposed to close in forty-five minutes," Brody said, the urge to floor it increasingly hard to repress. "When it doesn't *they* will figure out who skipped out of work. After that I guarantee you *they* will be stopping by Kateryna's place for the kind of introduction we don't want."

Brody slowed when they approached the end of the alley, a main street beyond.

The Mercedes braked as well.

That was enough for Brody, who hammered the accelerator, the car fishtailing before the tires caught and they shot forward. He wrenched the vehicle into a tightly controlled slide at the next intersection and onto a narrow side street. The screaming tires straightened out. He punched it. Buildings flashed past on either side.

"Where am I going?" Brody growled at Kateryna, fingers wrapped tight around the steering wheel, his eyes jumping from the rearview mirror to the road.

She pointed in response.

Behind them the Mercedes slewed around the corner, lights flashing wildly, all pretense of maintaining discrete surveillance gone. Brody streaked through another intersection but their vehicle couldn't match the German car's power. Steel and high beams loomed large in the rearview mirror.

The little Lada jumped every time Brody pushed his foot down on the soft pedal, trying to coax more speed out of the straining engine. They crested a slight rise, tires leaving the road's surface, hanging in mid-air, followed by a sharp shrieking sound as their car thumped down. Brody wrestled the wheel to regain control. Two tires caught the sidewalk's edge and held. He let the car go, racing along at a listing angle before he jerked the wheel, just missing a buttoned up news-stand. The acrid smell of burning rubber assaulted their nostrils.

Behind them breaking wood and glass rent the night as a corner of the news-stand shot into the sky. The Mercedes jagged violently, bouncing off a parked truck with a gnashing spray of sparks before pulling free. Brody zig-zagged across the road but he couldn't shake their pursuers. The other driver gunned it, gaining quickly.

Had they been stuck in any kind of extended straight away they would have been doomed. However, Kateryna represented their trump card. She directed Brody on a dizzying series of rights and lefts, avoiding the broad main avenues, bodies thumping into the door panel each time they spun around a corner. Brody expertly negotiated the streets in a frenetic whirl of acceleration, downshifting, and braking as he maneuvered the stodgy sedan in a way the manufacturer never would have believed. He power slid through one more such turn, fighting the wheel of the slewing car but feeling better about their chances as he opened up a slight lead on the Mercedes—

A Volvo pulled out in front of them.

Brody slammed on the brakes, their car swerving crazily as the back end broke free.

Cindy and Ernie screamed as they spun out, slewing to a stop in the middle of the street and facing back the way they had come. Wide eyed, they stared in horror at the looming Mercedes. A broad Slavic face, white with desperation cranked his steering wheel. They braced for impact.

It never happened.

The driver had pulled too hard, the big sedan moving too fast for such a maneuver. The passenger side tires lost their grip on the road and the car's front end tilted down. The hood blew out as its trunk shot toward the sky, the car airborne over the Lada and its complement of passengers howling bloody murder inside. The sedan's hood came down and caught on the sidewalk's edge not five feet to the Lada's left, the passenger cabin tilting crazily. Then the entire vehicle slammed down on its roof, sliding, spinning, and sparking along the cobblestoned streets for what seemed to be forever until the German car's torn and ragged fender caught an exposed drain vent. The car's undercarriage angled up into the air and the gas tank cracked into a street lamp.

The Mercedes exploded, a bright flash and whooshing WHUUUMP lit the night, sending a fireball hurtling down the street to match the red and yellow flame shooting into the sky. A secondary explosion ripped through the car at the same time the speeding inferno slid to a halt.

Brody, Cindy, Ernie, and Kateryna gawked in awe, rivulets of sweat streaking their faces, eyes squinting at the burning car's brightness. Brody snapped out of it first, cranking the ignition as a part of him wondered when it was death had ceased to be a surprise.

The Lada sputtered. Then the engine caught, and they sped off as the caterwauling sound of approaching sirens carried over the buildings. The blood pounding in his temples, Brody relaxed his white knuckled grip on the wheel and eased off on the accelerator. At this point speeding would only call attention to them.

"Do you think they're—?"

"What about Owen?" Ernie cut Cindy off.

"We can't call him yet," Brody said, not wanting to think about what Cindy had been about to ask. "His phone could be compromised. We'll drive back to Dibrovno. I have secure communications equipment but the range is limited. Besides, our showing up in town will be the last thing they expect. Once we contact Owen we can grab him and go."

Lights pulled out behind them.

Brody tensed, but the car turned off into a parking lot. He exhaled audibly, his nerves jumping as his eyes flicked back and forth from the road ahead, to the rearview mirror, to the side mirrors, and back again in a continual loop. Kateryna stared outside. Vague shapes moved in the darkness. She snapped her head back around, fingers digging into the seat.

Within five minutes they pulled up to a row of well-maintained buildings near the edge of town. Kateryna led them into a narrow two story residence and up the creaking wooden stairs. They walked down a poorly lit hallway, coming to a sturdy looking door. She stopped, throwing the bolt open on not one, not two, but three locks. Brody glanced back at Cindy and Ernie. They were huddled like a couple of scared kids, gaping down the narrow hallway at the dark stairwell. He sighed and cleared his throat, waving them into the apartment.

Overpowering light assaulted Brody's eyes. Every lamp in the apartment was on, tripped by bulky timers like the kind his grandma owned.

Bars girded the twin windows in the living room, unusual for a second floor flat in this part of the world. The apartment was spartanly furnished minus several packed bookshelves.

Kateryna locked the door behind, and then rummaged in the small kitchen off the main sitting area. She produced a loaf of dark bread and a tin of smoked fish. After throwing some plates and silverware on the kitchen table she grabbed a bottle of bison grass infused Zubrowka Vodka. She muddled apple, cucumber, and mint then added the mixture to everyone's glasses along with ice, and a generous amount of the yellowish tinted vodka. Finally, she grabbed another bottle of vodka, taking hers neat - pausing only to relish the hints of rye and vanilla. For those not drinking she boiled water, placing several delicately decorated white and blue porcelain tea cups on a serving tray. Then she slipped off to her bedroom.

Brody stood sentry at the window, riveted on the glade of trees across the street, eyes playing tricks on him in the silvery moonlight, not sure if he was seeing movement amongst the dark trunks and bushes.

Cindy and Ernie sat at the kitchen table, drinks in hand, chewing numbly on the soft and flavorful fresh bread, but tasting nothing. After a couple of minutes Ernie gently touched Cindy's hand, "I need you to know something."

Cindy's eyes widened.

"We've got to remember that Brody's got a job to do," Ernie whispered.

"I trust him," Cindy said. "In fact I'm not worried—"

"No, you're missing my point," Ernie said. "This isn't about Brody. It's about where this all goes. I just need you to know that I don't care what happens to his investigation or me, for that matter. We've got to get Owen. He's like a son to me. I couldn't live with myself if—"

Brody turned away from the window.

Ernie sat up in his chair, pretending as if he was reaching for another slice of bread. He needn't have worried.

Brody stared at the bottle of vodka, oblivious to anything else.

He turned away from the bottle and then looked back.

After several more seconds he gave in, stepping over and pouring himself a shot. He eyed the clear liquid dancing in the tumbler. It was then that he realized how badly his hand was trembling. He glanced up guiltily. Cindy and Ernie's attention was turned toward Kateryna as she strolled out of the bedroom, a small suitcase in one hand and a thickly stuffed photo album in the other. Brody blinked; it hadn't taken her more than a couple minutes to get ready. *She must have had a bag packed and ready to go.* He tilted his head back, the burning liquid washing away the metal taste of fear in his mouth. He drained the glass and glanced up, this time taking in Kateryna's well-proportioned frame.

She caught him looking, suppressing a smile as she plopped down at the kitchen table.

In spite of his exhaustion Brody realized that it was the first time in forever that he had exchanged some light flirting and hadn't thought of Julie. He slid into a chair opposite the librarian.

"What I'm about to say is unusual. Even so, its better I tell you about the town where you have been staying than you learn the truth in a more unpleasant manner." Kateryna said as she opened the cracked and faded album cover. The photo album was filled with newspaper clippings, documents, and sticky notes overflowing with a densely jotted scrawl. Kateryna's fingers carefully turned the page and stopped at a portrait of a handsome young man. He was named Aleksandr and had been her fiancé. She tapped the picture as she spoke, her eyes shimmering. It was the last picture she had taken of him before he disappeared outside of Dibrovno.

A freelance artist Aleksandr had taken a job photographing Ukrainian fauna for a local conservation group. He headed out on a Thursday, planning to spend a four day weekend getting the shots he needed. That Saturday afternoon Kateryna received a parcel addressed from Aleksandr. It was sent from the post office in Dibrovno. She found inside a World War Two era Soviet TT-33 semi-automatic pistol. Artifacts from the war turned up all the time, but this weapon's clean surface hardly matched its age.

Nevertheless, the mystery surrounding the pistol became an afterthought when Aleksandr did not return from his trip. An initial investigation went nowhere. Six months later the authorities declared him dead. Kateryna fell into a deep depression. She quit her job, cut herself off from family and friends. Months passed in a fog of pain and sorrow.

Finally, on a bright and sunny day too beautiful to ignore she roused herself from her suffocating bed and began rebuilding her life. She was cleaning out Aleksandr's stuff when she found the long-since forgotten pistol. Needing the money she decided to sell it.

The next day she went to one of the several local stores specializing in WWII and Soviet era militaria. The gloomy shop reeked of oil, leather, and cigarette smoke. Three old men played poker, ignoring her. She dumped the bulky weapon on the table, scattering chips and cards. One of the astonished men introduced himself as the proprietor, alternating between asking if she were a cop and where she had gotten the weapon. His eyes widened when she told him. He led her into the dank Cold War era fallout shelter that served as the basement. Row after row of bracket mounted sub-machine guns and assault rifles lined the cool gray concrete walls. Producing a beat up ledger the man scrolled down until his thumb stopped next to an entry for a TT-33 with the same serial number as hers. One of his smugglers had been travelling with a load of weapons stolen from an old Soviet-era arsenal. His runner had called in stating he was outside of Dibrovno and would be at the pick-up point within a couple of hours. No one heard from him again, or from two other smugglers later lost in the same area.

Meanwhile, alarm bells had been going off in Kateryna's head. She had been a reporter prior to her fiancé's death. Old instincts died hard. She took a job at the city library where she was horrified to find that a disproportionate number of missing person's reports originated from near Dibrovno. There was no master database. Instead, she compiled the evidence as she went. There would be a story in the newspaper.... *father of...or long time worker...not seen since...pronounced dead...* Kateryna flipped the album's pages, revealing countless yellowed newspaper clippings.

"Then I compared the dates the smuggler gave for his lost couriers to when my Aleksandr vanished, putting both against the dates for the other missing persons..."

Brody, Ernie, and Cindy's eyes drilled into Kateryna.

"*What? What did you find?*" Cindy finally bleated.

"They all disappeared during the night of the full moon."

CHAPTER 21

August 2016 – Lviv, The Ukraine

"That's just wonderful," Brody said.

No one responded.

Brody glanced at the clock. His chest tightened as he realized how much time had passed. He looked over at Cindy, who caught his stare. She turned to Ernie.

He didn't notice, resting an elbow on the table, one of his large hands rubbing his forehead as he stared at Kateryna. She appeared *too* composed. He wondered when the dual strains of personal loss and the immense research burden would prove too much for her to handle.

"I found a lead," Kateryna said, breaking the near suffocating silence.

"Can we discuss this in the car?" Brody said. "We've already been here for fifteen minutes—"

"That means we still have some time, no?" Kateryna said.

"Look, maybe you guys don't understand," Brody said. "If I don't get results, and fast, then none of this means anything."

"I get it," Cindy said. "Nevertheless, whatever's out there thrives in the shadows. The more we learn the likelier it is we'll be able to bring *its* existence into the open."

"Brody's right," Ernie said. "We're not learning fast enough. Every piece we uncover, every connection put together – it makes things worse for us. That is, unless we can put the whole story together."

"You're overreacting," Kateryna said.

"Are we?" Ernie shot back. "Do you honestly think Brody can protect us from these *things*? None of us can tell anyone what we're thinking. We're on our own." Ernie turned toward Brody. "Even you are. Try telling your boss you think Karlovic might be a werewolf, and see what happens."

"As I was saying, a few months back I found an article in the newspaper," Kateryna cut back in. "It was about a missing Roma man whose mother came from Dibrovno."

"Really?" Brody barked, his irritation coming through as what Ernie had said sank in. "Let me guess, you contacted this gypsy woman who might have knowledge of all sorts of legendary creatures. Leaving aside the borderline racism do you really expect us to buy—"

"As I was saying," Kateryna said. "This spring I visited the man's mother..."

The Roma community lived in a row of shabby houses near Dibrovno's cemetery. Plum, apple, and cherry trees burst with life outside the cemetery's wrought iron fence, moss-covered tombstones, and granite crypts. Kateryna parked her car on the sunken lane leading to the edge of town. As she stepped from her vehicle she spied a barefoot boy. He helpfully led her to the woman's house.

A small garden abutted the single story residence. Several of the roof's red shingles were fractured, the paint faded on the house's walls. The police report had indicated a woman aged forty-five. But the person who answered the door appeared closer to sixty. Poverty and loss had taken a toll on her wrinkled face and heavy body.

"Hello," the woman stated warily, her hand firmly grasping the door.

"I'm a reporter," Kateryna said, offering her friendliest smile to paper over the lie. "I would like to ask a few questions about your son, Boiko."

The woman tried slamming the door, but Kateryna snaked her foot in at the last minute, waving a picture of her fiancé, "Wait! My Aleksandr also disappeared outside Dibrovno. There are many more."

All pressure on the door ceased so abruptly Kateryna almost fell over the threshold.

"I'm Vadoma," The woman said as she glanced up and down the empty street. "Come."

She ushered Kateryna in, bolting the door shut behind.

The pungent smell of cabbage smacked Kateryna in the face. The home was dark. The late afternoon sun had started its descent from the sky, and there were few windows. A portrait of Boiko took up much of the space on the cracked plaster wall opposite the entrance.

"Sit," Vadoma said, waving her hand at the rickety kitchen table as she shuffled over to a cabinet and pulled out a liquor bottle. She set a small glass on the grimy countertop, filling it with strong *horincă*, or plum brandy.

Kateryna sipped at her drink.

"So, Miss…"

"Kateryna."

"Aren't there others you could speak with?"

"No," Kateryna stated. She noticed an old hunting rifle leaning against the wall just below a wreath of garlic. "Boiko is the only missing local. The others were outsiders."

"How many?" Vadoma said as she stepped over to a kettle on the wood fired stove, stirring a pot of boiling cabbage.

"At least three hundred."

Vadoma's shoulders stiffened visibly, "Yes. That would be about right." She wiped her hands on a towel and sat down, "What I'm about to tell you must not be repeated, ok?"

"I guess…" Kateryna mumbled.

"Don't sound so unsure. Yes or no?"

"Yes."

"Very well," Vadoma said. "For centuries my people have lived on the fringes of Europe. However, by being excluded we're able to see life as it is and not as it's made to seem."

Kateryna knew of the Roma's plight, and the ancient hatreds many mainstream Europeans had released upon these nomadic people.

"Your openness is most welcome." A smile crept up Vadoma's leathery cheek as she took in the sympathetic look on Kateryna's face. "Nevertheless, the wolves you should fear most are amongst you and not in the forest."

"Who are *they*? *Who* took my Aleksandr?"

"My poor girl," Vadoma said. "Your prejudices betray you. It's as if you walked into a theater after the movie started and that trustworthy looking person in the expensive suit explains to you how the story has unfolded. But he tells you only part of it. He leaves out the juiciest bits about how life works in this world, and what that means for people such as us."

"I don't…"

"Let's talk about why you're here."

"You know why," Kateryna said, gritting her teeth.

Vadoma shuffled over to a cabinet as Kateryna glanced out the one open window in the house, the shadows deepening on the wall. After what seemed to be forever Vadoma placed a tea pot on the stove. Smoothing her apron she sat down.

"What do you know of wolves?"

"Don't you mean—"

"I mean wolves," Vadoma said.

"They are vicious animals, responsible for killing thousands across Europe."

"According to whom?"

"The history books. There was the beast of Gévaudan in France. He killed over a hundred people." Kateryna said. "Another wolf killed twelve people in Sweden. There were others."

The tea pot shrieked, the eerie noise causing Kateryna to flinch.

"What happened when the villagers killed the wolves in question? Did the attacks stop?" Vadoma said, standing and preparing two cups.

"No, but—"

"Now that the wolves are repopulating Europe are we hiring hunters to protect ourselves?" Vadoma sat down and sipped her tea. "There's something else going on here, yes? Tell me, in all your research when did *all* of these people go missing?"

"You know?"

"Of course."

Kateryna's stomach churned.

Vadoma glanced sharply out the window, "It's late."

"Wait, how do I stop it?"

"You don't know enough," Vadoma said. "Even if you did I'm not sure you possess the fortitude to do what's necessary."

"How can you say this? *It* took your son?"

"I respect nature and the lessons it teaches us," Vadoma said, rising and trundling off to her bedroom.

A twinge of anxiety slipped across Kateryna's skin at the thought of what was happening down the hall. Then the bedroom door swung open. Out stepped Vadoma appearing human as ever, but clutching a folder. "Take it," She waved Kateryna to stand, pressing the folder into her arms. "You'll have more time to make use of this than shall I."

"Vadoma!" Kateryna exclaimed.

"There will be questions. I hope that is all," Vadoma said, hustling Kateryna outside. The sun was a deep orange ball peeking above the horizon.

"Are the methods for battling their kind, are they—"

"Forget it. All of it. Don't ever come back to this place," Vadoma said, slamming the door shut...

Finished with her story, Kateryna sat back, her eyes flickering from Brody, to Cindy, and Ernie.

Cindy sat back in thought. *Dibrovno's geography, the book from the library; it all made sense. As the entry point to one of the few passes through the Carpathians, Dibrovno would have seen a constant infusion of random strangers served up as perfect victims.*

Ernie stared out the window, a sickening understanding turning to nightmarish dread.

"What are you saying?" Brody said, staring at Kateryna. "That Dibrovno is a *town* of werewolves?"

Chapter 22

June 2016 – Dibrovno, Western Ukraine

Vadoma cursed her stupidity.

She had lingered in the forest for far too long.

It had been a gorgeous afternoon and she had plucked countless brown capped mushrooms littering the forest floor. Such was her luck she also had found a bevy of elusive yellow striped *maslyata* butter mushrooms. Her thoughts had turned to dinner and frying up a batch with some onions when she realized how far she had wandered, and how dark the forest had become.

She started for home. Time and again she nearly tripped over branches lying across the slender path and which had been so easily avoided during the light of day. Though she had long since known the forest's risks she had never felt immediate personal danger, even when Boiko was taken. Then that reporter had come.

Why had she blathered on like such an old fool?

The night of the woman's visit she had slept fitfully; startled awake every hour by some strange noise or another. She had checked her windows and doors a dozen times over, but each time found nothing. Over the following days however she couldn't help but feel she was being observed. During the past week however, that unsettling feeling finally and mercifully disappeared. She felt comfortable outside again. *Perhaps too relaxed.* She glanced up, shivering as she caught sight of the moon rising between two towering pines. She picked up her pace.

A twig snapped behind her, back in the woods.

She froze, her breath coming quick and shallow.

Head cocked, she listened.

Something rustled in the bushes nearest the path.

It came closer.

Vadoma spun away as fast as her old body could move. In spite of the chill seeping into her bones a sliver of sweat slipped from under the *babushka* tied around her head. Between her rattling lungs and the swishing sound of her feet churning through the leaves she made too much noise. But something inside told her it didn't matter.

The wind shook the trees.

A voice came with it, whispery, tinged with anger and need... *Vadooommmaaa...*

"Who's there?" She said, stopping in fear and confusion.

Nobody answered.

A cluster of spruce trees crowded close, their branches reaching out.

Bad thoughts whipped through her head.

Something snarled.

She dropped her basket, arms raised, hands protectively grasping the small cropping knife as she backed away. She risked a peek over her shoulder, catching sight of a light flickering in the distance. It came from the Bibik homestead just past the cemetery.

The bushes crackled, the heavy breathing of a large animal within. Vadoma turned to run.

It stepped onto the path.

Vadoma skidded to a halt, eyes widening in terror.

A smile traced up one side of the enormous beast's long muzzle, exposing impossibly large fangs. Black yearning eyes fixed on her as if she were a suckling pig.

The werewolf covered the distance between them in two bounding steps.

Vadoma jerked her arm up. The knife's short blade arced through the air as she swung. Once.

The moon loomed fat and full above pine trees old to the world's bloody ways transpiring beneath their weighty boughs.

The screaming began.

Vasily Malinovsky had been raking leaves in the cemetery when a high pitched shriek broke the evening calm.

The scream was followed by another.

And another.

He shivered as the final scream turned into a long pleading babbling cry of pain and terror before abruptly cutting off. Petrified, he gaped down the eerie sunken land running past the Bibik farmstead. The pile of leaves dancing around his feet long since forgotten—

Something howled, a vicious sound hitting Vasily in the face with the whapping impact of a club. He dropped the rake and grasped his chest, momentarily afraid he was having a heart attack. The pain subsided, but his quivering hand couldn't let go.

That's not possible.

As Vasily fled toward town the blood curdling cry drifted ahead of him, into the ghetto where the Roma huddled and chanted while rubbing garlic and silver, hoping to keep *it* from punishing them for the sins of one of their own.

That terrible howling rode the wind into the town center where Yuri and Leonid looked up from their chessboard in the square that suddenly felt far too empty. As they scrambled to their feet the howling carried into Katya Cisyk's home on the dark riverbanks. She had been setting the family table for dinner when the unearthly noise caused the last plate to slip from her hand, shattering into a thousand shards on the tile floor.

At the town hall the young mayor rose at the sound of the beast, staring outside, shaking his head in disgust. Then he forgot all about his anger as he fervently hoped that he wasn't the only person left in the office.

That night everybody in Dibrovno heard *it*.

Hours after the sun had burned off the morning fog, old man Bibik shrugged off his wife and stepped outside; rifle in hand, his shoes squishing in the wet grass. He and Nastya, his wife of forty years, had spent the night on their tiny couch, trembling and staring at their thin paneled front door. Gaunt faces flickering in the dim light provided by the same kitchen lamp Vadoma had so mistakenly thought offered her a beacon to safety. The kitchen light which Nastya had switched on shortly after sunset, the only light she would touch that night, dinner ice cold on forlorn plates. Bibik's SKS semi-automatic carbine had rested across his lap, its stripper clip loaded with ten rounds of steel jacketed ammunition. However, the old man had learned much in his eight decades. He held no illusions as to what this rifle could, or more likely could not do, against what stalked the forest.

When Bibik crept out into the morning he didn't need to go far, fighting the sour bile that came rushing up his throat in response to what he saw. Spread across the path and hanging from the tree branches was the gutted carcass of what had once been a human being.

August 2016 – Lviv, The Ukraine

"Not a town of werewolves," Kateryna stated emphatically, as a corner of her mind wondered why Vadoma had ignored the letters she had sent since her visit. "Such a profanity would have been discovered years ago. No, the truth is even *worse*."

She flipped to the photo album's last page, ignoring Brody's pointed looks at the clock. Attached to the album's back cover was a small folder, the same one Vadoma had given her a few months before. She slid out a document sealed in a plastic bag, laying it in front of Ernie and Cindy, handling it as carefully would a collector showing off rare jewels.

Ernie inhaled sharply.

Cindy glanced at him and then at the old document, the ink faded on the yellowed page.

"You know what this is, yes?" Kateryna eyed Ernie.

"It's a ledger," He replied as his eyes scanned down the page. "Names, place of death for victims in Dibrovno. On the right is the month and day of death. There must be sixty names here, but no year."

"There are seventy two names," Kateryna said. "I too was initially stumped as to the *when*. But one day an American from the University of Arizona walked into the library. He was on a research grant. As it turns out, he specialized in dating old works." She pointed. Four ragged cuts marked the bottom edge of the page, each no more than one by six millimeters.

"Radio-carbon dating," Cindy said.

Brody scratched his scalp.

"Radio-carbon dating can give us the century in question," Cindy explained. "The University of Arizona has an accelerator mass spectrometer that does just that, via finding a unique radio-isotope found naturally in low concentrations. During their life cycle plants and animals absorb Carbon-14. When that living creature dies the Carbon-14 dissipates at a quantifiable rate."

"I discovered this ledger originated sometime between the years 1350 and 1450," Kateryna said. "However, do you notice anything else about it?"

"Some dates are repeated," Brody said. "That means that the dates of death must be from multiple years."

"Exactly," Kateryna said. "Though, I was initially confused as to what years. Then I understood. The answer was right there in front of me."

Ernie and Cindy glanced at each other.

"Your NASA has a list of tables that provide phases of the moon going back centuries," Kateryna said. "I took the tables for the centuries dated 1301 to 1500, calculated Dibrovno's time zone in comparison to the Universal time zone used by NASA, and this is what I found." She pulled out another piece of paper.

"These tables are focused on select dates during the years 1404, 1408, 1415, 1416, 1423, and 1442," Kateryna said, pointing as she spoke. "Each year is broken down into months, and a specific date for each month. For example, look at the data for the year 1404 and compare it to the dates on the ledger."

Brody's eyes shuttled from the tables to the ledger and then widened, "They match."

"Guess what else these dates correspond with?" Katernya said.

"The full moon," Ernie said.

"This is a record from a time when the people of Dibrovno were preyed upon as viciously as anyone else." Kateryna jabbed her finger at the page as she spoke.

"But since?" Brody said, shooting another glance at the clock screaming that they needed to get moving.

"The werewolves needed a sanctuary," Kateryna said. "The people of Dibrovno went from being victims to partners. Today a resident of Dibrovno who does what they are told lives a comfortable life. But for the outsiders, or those that break their promises…"

Brody's lips tightened, his jaw set hard.

"Ordinary men and women as it may be," Ernie mused.

"Huh?" Brody grunted, desperately trying to ignore the clock's relentless ticking.

"It's a theory about how regular people enabled or participated in the Holocaust," Ernie said. "Everyone in Germany knew what the Nazi's were doing, and the overwhelming majority looked the other way. It's the only way Hitler could have pulled off industrialized mass murder. Compare that situation to Dibrovno's. If the locals wanted to make trouble then the werewolves couldn't kill them all. The escapees would return with help, and no werewolf that survived the eighteenth and nineteenth centuries would want to return to its dark ages."

Brody pulled his vibrating smart phone from his pocket. From the second he swiped the screen everyone could hear the tinny voice on the other end as it screamed without pause, interspersed with Brody grunting in response. Another several minutes he ended the call, a look of exhaustion on his face.

"Two investment bankers recently died under mysterious circumstances," Brody said. "My people want to know what the hell I'm doing with my final thirty-six hours out here and the best lead I have on Karlovic is..." Brody's eyes widened as he glanced at the clock again, "We have to go, now."

This time nobody argued with him.

Brody plunged into the dimly lit hallway. His friends followed close behind, clutching their books and documents. Brody moved carefully, hand wrapped around the reassuring bulk of his .45 as he followed the creaking claustrophobic stairs down to the apartment's entryway.

There they clustered, peeking through the white curtained windows. Brody studied the woods on the far side of the street, and then shifted his attention to the car. Moonlight dappled across the hood. Far more time had passed than he would have liked. Someone could be hiding in the darkness.

He watched and waited.

After several more moments staring he decided it was safe.

Taking a deep breath, he signaled go and exploded out the door, hitting the car in a rush. He slid across the front seat, Kateryna on his heels. Cindy pitched into the car's back seat.

Ernie came last. He had just about made it when he tripped, sprawling across the sidewalk. Three sets of eyes searched the shadows as one, hearts racing as Ernie scrambled to regain his footing, shoes sliding on the slick pavers. Then his right foot caught the edge of an upraised cobblestone, propelling him forward, a horrible ticklish feeling skittering up the back of his neck as if something was reaching for him...He lunged for Cindy, falling into the car, pulling his feet in, the swinging door slammed shut behind.

Kateryna floored it, tires screeching. She executed a series of quick turns, doubling back several times before Brody was sure that they were not being followed, the full moon illuminating the winding road out of town.

They entered the forest. A dark tension pervaded the car. Several hours later they approached Dibrovno. The blacktop narrowed and then crumbled in the dim headlights, devolving into a single rutted lane. The forest throbbed and swayed with the threat of *something* awful within.

Something that might already have Owen.

Something that would be coming for them.

CHAPTER 23

August 2016 – Dibrovno, Western Ukraine

Owen couldn't believe how good he felt. Until tonight he hadn't realized how much he needed to be close to someone, how much he needed a woman in his life. *And what a woman. Tanya was smart, caring*—he skidded to a halt.

The silence was deafening.

The thousands of frogs that otherwise serenaded the night had been quieted as if struck down *en masse*.

Owen turned in a circle, flickers of fear tugging at the edges of his mind. In spite of his reluctance to believe Anna's story he would have been lying if he didn't admit that the tale creeped him out. On the other hand, the rational side of him couldn't help but remember that he and Tanya had made the same walk just hours before without once being threatened by anything, no less a wolf. Nevertheless, he looked around once more, carefully taking in the swaying waist high grasses shining white under the silvery moonlight. He saw nothing, but again a primordial concern welled up from within, his heart beating harder. Without looking he reached into his pocket for his smart phone, cursing as it slipped from his grasp and thumped onto the path's soft dirt—

He heard something, every hair on the back of his neck rising and tingling in unison as he held his breath, eyes wide.

After another long listening pause he bent for his phone, and altered his life forever.

From the corner of his eye he dimly perceived something huge, moving impossibly fast. Before he could react *it* slammed into him with the force of a blitzing linebacker. Owen's breath left his chest in a great whoosh as he was launched into the air, feeling a sharp tearing sting in his shoulder, his blood spurting into the sky. He had the briefest moment to take it all in; the surprise, searing pain, and sheer disbelief. Then he fell, skull bouncing off a hard and unyielding object. He groaned once, stars blinkering his vision as a massive shape loomed over him at the same moment he passed out.

She crouched on her haunches, off the path and behind a downed tree, a coiled ball of tensely packed muscle, teeth and claws. A light breeze blowing down the trail carried into her elevated muzzle. She inhaled Owen's scent long before he plodded into view. She tested the air once more then lowered her skull, body still behind the tree trunk, watching as he stumbled into the clearing as blind to the dangers of the night as a newborn fawn.

Tanya tensed when he approached the edge of her predetermined kill zone, her muscles rippling under her pelt, analyzing each way-point in this ancient process of killing she had long since mastered. Nevertheless, she procrastinated, filled with sorrow.

Owen was her first real lover in years. She should have been allowed to savor the pleasures he brought into her life. Yet, *he* had commanded otherwise. Tanya had fought against her orders, but *he* was at his wits end. *He* had thought such a command would have been unnecessary when Karlovic put the fear of god into them. Instead, the humans had become emboldened. *He* could not have that, not at this crucially important moment. When Owen's friends left Dibrovno Tanya had received her final orders. She braced herself to leap.

The wind shifted.

Tanya's ears snapped up, fur bristling. *Karlovic!*

Jumbled thoughts flooded her brain. She saw something big on the far side of the clearing at the same time Owen dropped his phone. She whined, a high pitched note of concern she hoped would carry to him.

Karlovic *moved*.

She whimpered louder, and then barked.

Run, oh God please run.

Her calls were useless. She watched in horror as the big werewolf narrowed the distance between him and Owen in a blur, then exploded through his final leap, jaws gaping open. Tanya's reeling mind calculated

Karlovic's trajectory. He would hit Owen in the neck; ripping through it in one brutal slashing attack carrying the destructive impact of a chainsaw. Her lover would be dead before his body hit the ground. Tanya whined again, her great clawed hands digging into the nearest tree trunk, shredding its bark. Owen bent to retrieve his phone.

Karlovic belatedly attempted to adjust in mid-flight but the sudden movement proved too much to overcome, even for his super attenuated athleticism. The werewolf's gaping jaws slashed across Owen's back and shoulder as the creature's heavy lower body slammed the smaller man to the ground. The steep angle of impact sent Karlovic spinning, thudding into the grass beyond the man's crumpled form. In one fluid movement however, the enraged beast sprang to his feet, straddling Owen's inert body as he lifted his grizzled muzzle to howl in victory

Tanya's triangular ears flattened as her emotions, already volcanic, turned to pure rage. She categorically inventoried his strengths and weaknesses in a cold military fashion. She knew death intimately. Though Karlovic outweighed her by over one hundred pounds, was older, more experienced, and in his prime, none of it mattered. Within a half-second Tanya knew what she needed to do, whom she would have to betray, and how. She had one chance. If her initial rush failed she couldn't hope to defeat him. She flexed her calves, leaping from her hiding spot. A deadly streak of black rippled over the clearing's grasses and flowers.

Far too late a chill shot down Karlovic's spine, his howl dying in his throat, the tight feeling of terror paralyzing him as her teeth punched under his jaw, thrusting his head up and back, ripping into the loose, exposed flesh. Then she danced away, crouched low, her face a mask of snarling spitting anger.

Blood sprayed from Karlovic's throat. He stepped back, stiff-legged and confused. His eyes rolled white and with a tortured yelp he pitched forward, an accusation unsaid floating through the air between the two beasts. He hit the ground with a booming thump.

Tanya kicked once at Karlovic's motionless body. Then she turned to Owen's broken form, blood dripping from her muzzle...

CHAPTER 24

August 2016 – Dibrovno, Western Ukraine

O wen twitched and turned, sweat pouring off his body.
He ran, being chased.

No, he was the pursuer.

Screams of terror, his mouth opening—

He slammed awake with a start, breathing in ragged gasps, wincing at the sharp sunlight streaming in through the open window and a cacophony of noise jackhammering at his sensitive ears; birds, frogs, crickets, buzzing bees all crowded into his skull. In an effort to shake off the disorienting blizzard he focused on a wooden door opposite him.

It appeared to be throbbing.

He fought off a sudden rush of nausea and tried again, this time attempting to figure out his location.

After several straining seconds a moment of clarity burst through. He was on the second floor of a home—

He lost the thought as the scent of carrot, beet, radish, dill, cumin, mint, raspberries, currant and more filled his mouth with saliva. He couldn't remember being so *aware* of the sheer volume of information brought in by his formerly nondescript nostrils. He pressed his hands to his ears, battling to settle his flitting, fluttering mind.

Concentrate.

He took stock of his surroundings. He was in a bed, every creak in the house audible...no...the floorboards, the porch. *Please stop.* Even the trees groaned, popped, and squeaked in unison. *Stop.* His senses pulsed in a way he hadn't experienced since the time he had dropped acid at a hippie music festival. He smacked his head, struggling to regain the present, beating back the insipid melodies of *Rusted Root* and their happy fuzzy ilk.

The forest and house doubled down, yelling with greater ferocity. Owen wobbled on the edge, his mind reeling from the stomach-churning attack on his sanity. This time Owen's bloodshot eyes honed in on the bedding, settling in on a sea of white.

That's it, think it through, stay with the sheets, what are they made of, how do they feel?

He bore down, having never known such sharp acuity, analyzing the sparkling ivory linens, the sheets and pillows of a decidedly decadent Egyptian cotton, creamy smooth, the luxurious covers caressing exposed skin. His flesh came alive with goose bumps as if the softest hand roamed across his body. He stirred between his legs—

Goddamn it, stop!

Owen centered his attention on the room. He willed himself to catalogue its contents, and layout. A high arched ceiling provided dimension to the otherwise box shaped space. To his left an espresso colored dresser and night table rounded out the sparse furnishings.

Perspiring heavily, he finally felt the room slow around him, every additional second bringing under control the world of sights, sounds, and smells otherwise driving him mad. To his right a painting hung on the wall, a rendering of a valley at sunrise done in thin brush strokes. Light airy yellows and oranges cascaded down the gorge's brightly illuminated green walls. He stared, something about it drawing him in. After another moment he recognized it as the valley surrounding Dibrovno. A partially closed door led to a bathroom. He craned his aching neck, taking in the polished clawed foot of a porcelain tub, the edge of a white pedestal sink, the camphor like smell of lavender.

Pleased with the minor triumph over his senses Owen belatedly noticed the duvet had slid from his naked body. He pulled it up, squealing in pain. Surprised, he looked down to see a huge white bandage wrapped around and over his entire shoulder. The sight of it jagged loose fragmented memories painfully flickering through his mind's eye—

The bedroom door swung open.

Tanya bounced in, radiant in snug fitting blue jeans and a straining white t-shirt. Owen stared at the overloaded tray of food in her hands, his stomach growling.

"Rise and shine," Tanya beamed. "That's how you say good morning in America, yes?"

She placed the tray astride his lap and sat on the edge of the bed, the cinnamon musk of her body crème trumped by his raging hunger. He sat up, wincing then diving into an American style breakfast replete with fluffy scrambled eggs, strips of salted bacon, juicy sausage links, moist ham, and rye bread lathered with black currant jam. He used his good arm to feed, at first feebly then with increasing vigor.

Tanya watched, biting her lip. It pained her to see him hurt, but *it* was a process.

When he finished eating Tanya leaned in, peeling the tape from his skin and pulling back the dressing. A long puckered scar zigzagged up his chest, over his collarbone, and across his upper back. It looked light-years better than it had just a few hours before, when it appeared as if someone had dragged a freshly sharpened garden rake through his flesh.

Owen contemplated the painting on the wall as she tended to him.

"Do you like art?" Tanya asked, having noticed the direction of his gaze.

"It depends on what you mean," Owen said.

"Do you appreciate such beautiful images, or don't you?"

"Since you put it that way, I always had a certain fondness for the centerfolds in my dad's Playboys."

"So vulgar," Tanya laughed, feeling a bit more relaxed, "and so very American."

"Yea, I've heard it all before. When are you gonna grow up. Yada, yada, yada."

"I wasn't judging you. Sometimes vulgarity can be fun."

"But not Americans?" Owens said, watching her carefully.

"I didn't say that."

"You didn't have to," Owen responded. "Anyway, nice painting you got there."

"It's too impressionistic for the décor, but I couldn't pass it up," Tanya said. "It's by Fedir Krychevs'ky. I met him not long before he died in 1947."

"Jesus, Tanya," Owen said. On the other hand, he somehow knew that she understood the sensations and feelings battering his sanity. Not once did a patronizing look cross her face as she tended to him. Not once did she seem bored, or even worse horrified by his dependence on her. Instead, she seemed elated. She caught him looking and grasped his hand, fingers interlacing.

Owen's struggled to regulate the welter of conflicting emotions buffeting him "I…" He stopped, grimacing, once more pressing his hands to his head. "This is too much. I can't. The sights, sounds, all of this. I can't process it all."

"You'll learn how," Tanya said.

"I need to know what's happening."

"You know."

"Say it. I need to hear you say it."

"You're a werewolf. Just like me."

Scenes from horror movies raced through Owen's brain… *"In the made-up stories, the guy who's the werewolf only changes when the moon is full, but maybe he's like this almost all the time, only as the moon gets fuller… You can't tame what's meant to be wild, doc. It just ain't natural."*

Owen shook his head to clear it. Then settled his attention on Tanya, eyes narrowing, one thought overriding all others.

"Leave."

"What?" Tanya said, surprised at his sudden shift in demeanor.

"I trusted you," Owen said, his voice rising. "Get out!" Tears ran down his cheeks, his old life sliding away. *Good or bad there would be no going back.*

He stared at the door long after she was gone.

August 2016 – Dibrovno, Western Ukraine

Nobody slept. On top of the usual reasons Brody's boss had called in yet again, the conversation inescapable in the tightly packed car. A Citigroup managing director had been found dead in his New York City apartment, an apparent suicide. Brody's face had said it all as Wilson's voice screamed over the speakers, warning him once more that if he didn't want to find himself working security at Target he had twenty-four hours to come up with something. Mercifully the call dropped when the forest thickened near Dibrovno. The glowing dashboard clock read four in the morning when they halted in front of Ernie's pension, four doors squeaking noisily open, eight feet clattering across the street and to comparative safety inside. Owen wasn't home.

The wind kicked up, moaning eerily in the old home's eaves.

Multiple sets of eyes looked up, confusion and fear writ large on their faces as they stole glances out the front window and behind them into the dark house, each room potentially housing *something* unpleasant. Brody checked it out while the rest of them crowded into the kitchen. Ernie threw on a pot of coffee.

Brody reappeared within minutes, the house evidently clear of any threats.

"You think we're ok?" Cindy said as Brody squeezed in at the table with everyone else.

"No. But this is the last place they would expect us to come," Brody said, trying to appear confident but feeling shaken beyond belief by not only the fact Owen wasn't there but by how every move he made seemed to not be working out. "That should buy us just enough time if we act fast. Anyway, my place is around the corner. I just need to get—"

"You're not going out there," Ernie snapped.

"Take it easy," Brody said. "Remember I have one of these." He pointed at his holster.

"What about us?" Cindy said, her voice tinged with a note of anger and barely contained desperation.

"No worries," Kateryna smiled, hand emerging from her purse clutching a semi-automatic World War II era *Pistolet Wz. 35 Vis* pistol. "It was my grandfather's, though I've since adapted it for our needs."

Kateryna pulled back the slide, ejecting the round in the chamber while popping out the box magazine from the pistol's grip and expelling each bullet in turn. Within seconds eight silver bullets lay side by side, shining bright under the stark light hanging above.

Ernie whistled.

Cindy picked up one of the deadly beautiful blunt nosed rounds, "Where did you—"

"Kutná Hora."

"Of course," Ernie said.

Brody and Cindy gawked at him quizzically.

"Between the thirteenth and sixteenth century Kutná Hora rivaled even Prague's influence in Central Europe," Ernie said. "The city was blessed with bountiful silver mines, a particularly pure strain then in the greatest demand across Europe."

"But the plague's repeat appearances, numerous wars, along with a spectacular flood all conspired to ruin the silver mines," Kateryna said. "Then, late in the eighteenth century a last gasp attempt to revive silver production collapsed around the same time that—"

"The werewolves disappeared from Europe's historical record," Ernie said, remembering what he had read in the library. "In cities such as London or Paris well-armed elites would have made life very hard for the werewolves. That left the poor preyed upon in the villages, and farmsteads dotting the countryside. That's why the legends persisted amongst the peasantry. That is, before the werewolf population fell so low they became little more than a mythical creature."

In the distance a lonesome howl rose from just outside of town. Brody glanced at Cindy, who studiously avoided eye contact. *It was probably just a wolf.* He snuck a peek out the window and then turned his attention back to the table, "It's starting to make sense."

"What is?" Ernie responded.

"The way Cameron was killed," Brody said. "It didn't add up. The Bureau has recorded nearly a dozen dead bankers in the past couple of weeks with nearly all of them made to look like suicides or as part of some sort of kidnapping, all except Cameron."

"And that makes sense how?" Cindy said.

"Compare those deaths to Cameron being ripped apart," Brody said. "I mean, step back and really look at how Cameron died."

"It's not even remotely the same M.O." Cindy said, her eyes widening in comprehension. "Jesus, I can't believe I overlooked it."

"Hey, so did I," Brody said. "The point being, whoever did Cameron killed him that way on purpose. They wanted us to come here. There's no other way to explain how creatures so good at hiding as to be virtually invisible for the better part of two hundred years would allow us to get this close."

"I'm not following," Ernie said.

"Remember at the pub when we talked about how the best way to rob a bank is to run one," Brody said.

"Yea," Ernie said.

"Cameron's death is the same thing. It's an inside job," Brody said.

"One of the werewolves isn't happy with what's going on. Maybe they want to force their kind back into hiding before it all spirals out of control and they're hunted like they were two hundred years ago. Or maybe it's a turf war, who knows."

"What about Karlovic?" Cindy said. "Based on everything we've seen he's behind Cameron's murder as well as God knows how many other killings?"

"We got that wrong too," Brody said. "Karlovic didn't mastermind anything. He's a weapon that follows orders."

"Whose orders?" Kateryna said.

"Figuring that out will be the trick, won't it?" Brody said. "Because if there's one thing I know about operations gone bad it's that you don't want to be caught in the middle, and that's where we are right now."

Kateryna stood, returning a moment later with an old leather pouch. She motioned to Ernie. He released the pouch's brass clasp and a locked wooden box slipped from inside.

Kateryna handed him the key. Ernie opened the box, the mildewed aroma of ancient paper wafting from inside as a small stack of yellowed handwritten documents spilled out on the table; seals of all shapes and sizes marking the official stamp of Kings, Queens, and Princes from across Europe, handwritten texts marching across each page in a variety of languages - French, Polish, German, and more.

"Invoices, Bills of Lading, Receipts, Purchase Orders," Ernie said, flipping through the documents. "Are these from the library's collection?"

"Yes," Kateryna responded. "I found them hidden in a corner of the vault."

"Silver musket balls, daggers, swords, lances, pikes, arrows, crossbow bolts, even a silver battle axe and maul for one German prince. It goes on and on, with tons of gold paying for it." Ernie said, pausing in thought. "My God, the first waves of fifteenth century explorers weren't just looking for a shorter trading route to the east. They were paying for the silver used to fight the werewolves."

More howling filtered through the thin window panes and into the cramped kitchen.

"Hey that's wonderful," Brody said, glancing outside. "I like history too. When this is over we can have a hoot of a time going over it all. But for now, how about we focus on what's going to keep us alive."

"We can't forget about Owen," Ernie said.

"I'm not," Brody said. He was pretty sure it was a gathering pack of wolves outside, but he eyed the bullets anyway, "If those papers that Kateryna just dumped on the table mean what we think they do then those silver bullets take on a whole new meaning. Or they don't. For all we know silver might be as effective at killing werewolves as if I waved a magic eight ball around and shoved a lit candle in my ass while chanting some sort of crazy spell."

"That's a heck of an image you painted there," Ernie said, shaking his head. "As much as I'll try to forget it, in your own way you've made a point."

"True," Cindy said. "However, it's not like we can test them out."

"After visiting Vadoma I found a gunsmith who knew the old ways." Kateryna reloaded the magazine, holding each round up in the light before pushing it home with her thumb. "Did you know that silver is less malleable than lead? This makes the bullet unstable because it's harder to impart spin. That means you have to get so very close to be sure of hitting your target." She slapped the full clip into the pistol's handle.

Ernie watched, the sick feeling inside him worsening. *Whether she knew it or not Kateryna was ready to explode. Regardless, backing out on saving Owen wasn't an option. He had seen too much bad in this world. About the only thing out there that was worth a damn was love.*

Outside, the wolf pack howled again.

This time something howled back, its voice deeper.

It sounded angry.

Very angry.

CHAPTER 25

March 1944 – The Western Ukraine

Dietrich took point, the spruce's claustrophobic nearness enveloping the killer's winding path through the primeval maze of twisted branches. Dietrich's eyes tracked back and forth, white with tension as he rounded a corner. He stopped.

A headless raccoon lay across the path, blood staining the snow pink.

Dietrich read the implicit message broadcast by the animal's pointless death. The forest had frozen into a painted landscape. His senses strained to pierce the dense green needles, the hairs lining the back of his broad neck standing on edge…

What was that?

He snapped his rifle to his shoulder, his free hand up in a fist.

DANGER.

The silent command flowed down the line. Every other one of the eight soldiers faced the opposite side of the trail, weapons ready.

Dietrich held his breath.

Seconds passed.

He swiveled his head to the right, branches rustling as a large object rippled past.

Or did it?

A freezing whisper of wind shook snow off the leaden branches.

Dietrich held his position.

Nothing.

Dietrich's finger eased off the rifle's trigger, hand opened, fingers extended.

CLEAR.

As one the men rose, crunching deeper into the wilderness.

The trees parted. They spilled into a clearing ringed by towering pines nearly blotting out the sky. In the middle of the glade squatted an enormous tree stump. On it sat the half devoured remains of Erich's head. The man's bristly scalp had been peeled back and a scoop carved from the brain cavity. The remaining pulpy purplish gray matter formed a glutinous frozen mass.

Dietrich swallowed hard and glanced around, his eyes widening as he counted to himself. *One, two, three, four...*

"Where's Peter?" He said.

Karl reacted first. He swept Erich's head off the stump and unlimbered the long barreled MG-42, its belt of ammunition jingling in his hands. Capable of ripping off over one thousand metal jacketed rounds per minute, each slug could knock a grown man from his feet. A three second burst from "Hitler's bone saw" would cut a person in half. In the right environment no weapon could match it. However, the dense trees diminished the machine gunner's otherwise murderous field of fire. The men recognized the weakness in their position, but with no instructions to the otherwise they fanned out to Karl's right and left.

With a nod Dietrich sent Heinrich and Franz doubling back to find their comrade. They spread out into a sweep search pattern. The five remaining men squatted down in a rough firing line, tendrils of fog snaking around their snow covered boots as they laid out grenades and spare magazines for their weapons. Dietrich knew something was off but logic, reason, and experience overpowered his instincts. He shouldered his rifle, his finger slipping inside the trigger guard just as he felt something moving fast and close.

Behind them—

A low rumble filled the air, its deep resonance conveying a homicidal intent as old as the forest itself. Dietrich struggled against ancient terrors welling up inside. He heard his grandmother's voice scolding him. *Silly boy, you stepped off the path did you now? What did you expect?*

The crack of a rifle report reverberated through the woods.

Dietrich whipped his head around.

Two more shots rang out, the rifle fire coming from Franz's Mauser.

It was followed by a staccato burst from Heinrich's machine pistol, then silence.

Dietrich's breath caught in his throat.

Time stopped.

The tree branches bent and swayed.

It howled. A savage expression of triumph, the blood curdling sound rose up through the forest canopy. The men wilted. Even the trees shrank before the expression of bestial violence.

Karl sobbed. Dietrich elbowed the rattled soldier into silence and grimaced savagely, his breath rattling. The sound was like a wolf, but *ersatz*. If not for the volume and depth it could have been considered human. The soldiers closed ranks. Two men turned to face behind them. Whatever was out there would not be shooting back. Dietrich's chattering teeth rattled in his head, one last flash of white hot rage steeling him for impending battle.

A single crow took flight, snow shedding off a branch.

Something stepped from between two trees.

Murder hung in the air, pregnant with anticipation.

Dietrich couldn't believe his eyes. It was the most terrifying thing he had ever seen. *It was huge, it looked like, no, it couldn't be—*

Karl *moved*.

Time accelerated to a blur.

Karl squeezed the trigger even before the heavy barrel fully came around, the weapon's discharge deafening in the enclosed space. Bark sprayed from exploding tree trunks, branches stripped away by the high velocity rounds. The machine gun swung toward its target, the ripping noise of hundreds of bullets shattering the morning air as the big weapon annihilated everything within its field of fire.

The barrel suddenly swung up. Every fifth round a tracer it arced a red diagonal line across the forest canopy. Karl's scream choked off before it began, his throat ripped open, blood spraying skyward as if from a high pressure hose as his perforated body was propelled through the air by an enormous force.

Dietrich squeezed off a single round at the fleeting shadow that disappeared back into the trees. Automatic weapons fire echoed through the clearing accompanied by frantic yelling and inhuman snarling. A fragmentation grenade exploded, throwing up powdered snow and clumps of dirt to mingle with the haze of gun smoke. Dark shapes flitted about as bullets zipped through the air.

A burst of gunfire to Dietrich's right was cut short as something heavy slammed into his side. He staggered on unsteady feet as Hans fell away, arm ripped from its shoulder socket, his throbbing heart glistening and exposed, the man's life sickeningly spurting from him with each weakening beat.

Dietrich stood helpless. Screams echoed through his head, the sharp smell of cordite assaulting his nostrils, Rolf's machine pistol chattered away and then stopped, the soldier pitching forward into the snow. The side of his head had been caved in, pieces of his steel helmet driven into his brain. Dietrich felt blood dripping down his face and into his right eye, vision hazy through the red filter of his men's death. The coppery fluid and acrid gunpowder created a sickening smoky flavor in his mouth. He broke, fleeing from a fight for the first time in his life.

The darkest recesses of Dietrich's mind propelled his panicked legs away from the murderous presence putting to shame any vision Grimm or Aesop could have conjured, his only thought to put distance between himself and whatever hell had been unleashed behind him. He burst free of the forest and past a large oak tree, the sun peeking orange over the horizon, its warm embrace reaching out, eyes registering a strangely familiar looking farm house.

He could hear screaming. It was his voice. One of his arms lifted up and reached forward, but his legs wouldn't move. He thudded into the ground as something heavy blasted the air from his lungs. Hot breath washed over the back of his neck, his vision dominated by the wrecked remnants of a cellar door. Sharp pain radiated through his skull as if the back of his head and neck were crumpled in a vise. *Oh god no, not like this!* The crushing pressure gripped tighter, sharp knives slicing into his readily yielding flesh, bones popping, cracking, and splitting. Dietrich's life bled into the snow as his consciousness faded to black.

CHAPTER 26

August 2016 – Lviv, The Ukraine

"It doesn't make sense," Brandner said into his smart phone. A burned out Mercedes smoldered in the street behind him. Three recently filled body bags had been lined up by the wreck. Blue lights from multiple police cars flashed under the mid-day sun.

"C'mon, man," Roberts sighed in response. "Surveillance cameras pick up our favorite special agent passing through the lobby of a hotel *and* library, each not far from the scene of the wreck. The MVS has identified the driver's body as a local hired gun and you still somehow think Brody has nothing to do with this?"

"NSA intercepted Brody's calls. They were scrambled, but we know that they were made to and from his supervisor at Quantico as well as an agent in Detroit and done so at multiple times each day," Brander responded. "For what you're implying to be true would mean that the Bureau is involved in some sort of clandestine operation without noticing up anyone else, and I ain't buying it. That's not how they work. So, like I said, it doesn't make sense."

"Not unless Brody's free-lancing," Roberts pointed out, well-aware of the Bureau's full-court-press to figure out who was behind the *banker murders* as they were being called in the reports he was reviewing daily.

Brandner paused before responding, "I pulled Brody's file. There's no way. He's old-school, a throw-back-purist who believes in justice and the law to his core. Shit, the only time he got in trouble was for attempting to do something that should have been done a long time ago."

"Sounds like you admire him," Roberts warned.

"Maybe a part of me does," Brandner said. "But I've put down plenty of men like Brody."

"Good," Roberts replied. "Now, find him, and find out what he's doing. I need to know for sure."

"How sure?"

"Easy boy," Roberts said, ignoring the fact that Brandner was at least a decade older than him. "We'll take care of it once you locate your target."

Brandner hung up, wondering if Brody had any idea as to what kind of trouble he was heading toward.

August 2016 – Dibrovno, Western Ukraine

Owen rolled over, sensing Tanya's presence before she tiptoed into the room.

"I don't do apologies well," She said, sitting down next to him. "You have every right—"

"I'm sorry," Owen cut her off as he sat up, this time hardly noticing the slight ache lingering from his wound. "You don't need to help me, Tanya. I can figure things out on my own."

"I'm not helping because I pity you, or out of some sense of moral obligation."

"Sure. A beautiful woman like you has nothing else to do but play nursemaid to a guy like me."

"I care about you."

Owen swallowed hard, hugging her tight.

After a long moment he broke their embrace, a questioning look on his face.

Tanya headed him off, "Your concerns are important, and I will answer as many of them as possible. But first, just know that you can die."

"You mean like with silver bullets blessed with holy water and—"

"No, I mean yes. I mean, it's possible to survive silver, though just touching it hurts worse than getting kicked in the tits by a mule. The point is that though you have new powers, you also have new boundaries." *She had witnessed her fair share of tragedies. Including one young pup who recently had wandered east and been fatefully challenged by a Siberian Tiger.*

"This power you have, I liken it to a gift," Tanya said, taking both his hands in hers. "Your first change will be so overwhelming you'll feel like a god. When you return to human form, life, no matter what form you are in, will seem richer and…" her hand dipped under the sheets and into his lap, "We will have much fun in the meantime."

Owen's next question died in his throat, replaced with an appreciative moan.

The theme from *Magnum P.I.* blasted from the nightstand.

"It's Ernie!" Owen said, pointing at his smart phone.

Tanya bit her lip, motioning for him to answer it.

He snatched it up and pressed it to his ear, "Hey, how's Lviv? *What? You're back?* No, that wouldn't be a problem…Yes, I'm at Tanya's…I'm fine. It's easy to find…Yes, that trail…See you soon."

"We'll meet them on the path," Tanya stood.

Owen threw back the sheet, his erection waving in the air.

A wave of dizzying lust swept through Tanya. She glanced at the table-side clock, then at Owen, "Lay back, this shouldn't take more than a minute."

Tanya overestimated her talents. It ended up taking five minutes.

"Everybody get ready," Ernie shouted.

Brody looked up from the specialized equipment that had confirmed the location of Owen's phone while in turn masking their location. He stood and pulled Ernie aside, "There's something you should know."

Ernie raised an eyebrow.

"The investigative work the three of you have done is incredible, but it's not good enough."

Ernie's emotions summersaulted between feelings of elation that Owen was unharmed balanced against the danger they still faced.

"Even if the Bureau takes Anna's testimony, and looks at everything else we've gathered, and does so with all facts and inferences weighed in favor of the existence of werewolves there's simply not enough here to make a case, no less prove it."

"Don't forget Anna's recording. Anyone who listens can tell that howl is different than a normal wolf."

"Yes it is," Brody said. "However, the available data suggests to a reasonable person that werewolves *don't* exist. That's what the Bureau's analysts would defer to in lieu of relying upon the circumstantial clues we've gathered that they *do* exist."

"Meaning what? We need to get a picture or something?" Ernie asked uneasily.

"Maybe in a different era," Brody said, shaking his head no. "That's not how things work today. Even if we took a picture of a werewolf and delivered it straight to the TV networks every black-helicopter-nut-job out there would be screaming it was a fake. No, we need to catch a live one."

"Forget it," Ernie said, turning and striding down the hallway, shaking his head as he went.

Afternoon sunlight streamed through the parlor's front window. Cindy sat on the couch alongside Kateryna, flipping through one of the books they had spirited from the library. Both women looked up when Ernie entered, Cindy's hand absentmindedly flipping the page one last time...

"Okay you two, let's—" Ernie stopped in mid-sentence, staring at the book. "It's *her!*" He exclaimed, pointing at the book in Cindy's lap.

The page lay open to a black and white shot of Dibrovno's main square. The caption stated it was taken at the 1941 Soviet May Day parade, just before the German invasion. The photograph captured a crowd watching as a Red Army rifle platoon marched past in formation.

"Who?" Kateryna said, scanning the image. "Who is it?"

"Oh Jesus," Cindy cried, her right hand coming up to cover her mouth. She extended a shaking finger toward the picture's edge. There, an attractive teenage girl held the hand of a young boy. It was Tanya.

"That's it," Brody said, striding into the room, the glee in his voice unmistakable.

Ernie and Cindy spun around.

"Hey, hold on," Brody said, backpedaling at the anger evident on their faces. "I'm not overlooking Owen, but this is the break we need."

"Wait a second, who's—"

"Patience," Ernie snapped at Kateryna. "As for you," he said to Brody. "I expected much more."

"Don't you understand?" Brody said. "Tanya's the key. We grab

Owen, we get her. We get her, we got Karlovic. We take him, and I blow this case wide open."

"Using my best friend as bait, is that it?"

"Relax, we'll get him if for no other reason than this," Brody patted his holster. "Plus, what Annie Oakley over there is packing," He pointed at Kateryna, who was chewing on her fingernails. "Then the rest of you are on a flight home and I use Tanya to get my suspect."

"You still can't see ten feet in front of your face," Ernie said, looking like a teacher who had caught his prize pupil cheating on the final exam. "For all the talk about fighting what's wrong in this world you're so excited to drag your prize back to the people enabling the crimes you obsess about. For what? Stop and think about why this is happening."

"Don't give me that crap," Brody said. "I could give a shit about what my boss thinks. If I show up at the Bureau with Karlovic in a cage I don't just win my career back, I write my own ticket."

"Then what?" Ernie said. "You'll turn down the partnership at the Wall Street law firm that will be dangled in front of your nose. You're too honest of a man for that. Even so, do you really think you can transform a *culture* of corruption? Let's say you get a task force investigating Wall Street. What then? Sure, you'll take a few token scalps, maybe some lower level bankers, but then they'll cut your budget. You'll be pushed off into a back office, doing nothing."

"What are you? A fucking fortune cookie?" Brody said. "Don't tell me how to do my job."

"Your job is to bring *justice* to this world," Ernie said. "Whether you want to admit it to me or not that banker Donnelly was a big part of whatever's going on with you. Let it go. Or deal with it, because this is bigger than all of us. Until you figure out what justice means, nothing will change."

"Don't push your baggage on me. You might be here for more reasons than you like to let on, but I'm just a lawman working a file. Nothing more, nothing less, and I sure as hell ain't the man you seem to think I am," Brody said.

"You have to be," Ernie said. "You don't have a choice. People like Donnelly play for keeps. They want it all. They always have. They always will. They're the apex predators of our society, and there's only one way to stop them."

"You're wrong," Brody stated. "I had my chance and blew it. So as much as you may think I can or will do something, I can't. I respect the hell out of you Ernie, but what life means for me is my business. Not yours, nor is it anybody else's."

Ernie stared hard into Brody's eyes before turning away.

"You sure you're ready," Brody said to Kateryna, his heart racing at the thought this might require more of him than he ever considered possible.

"I can handle it," She said, staring at the book. "Now, who is this Tanya?"

"She," Ernie rasped, still corralling his anger. "Is our purported comrade, my best friend's lover, and someone who contrary to what you see in that picture will, when you meet her, appear no older than possibly forty years of age."

Almost two hours later Brody stopped walking and wiped the back of his hand across his brow. He was trying hard not to think of what Ernie had said, and failing miserably. He unclipped his water bottle from his waist and drank deep. The path through the woods had once more turned into a dusty trail clinging to the side of a cliff. The overhang projected above the forested valley floor several hundred feet below. In the distance, the river glinted next to Dibrovno's rooftops and the castle towers. Above him the path finally reentered the tree line, leading to the flat plateau marking the location of Tanya's house. Higher yet, the jagged ridgeline rose in the distance.

Though in the pension he had glibly spoken of "bagging" Tanya as easily you would a shoplifter, just prying Owen away from her would be hard enough. A crucial part of convincing Tanya to give up peacefully depended upon Kateryna. He hoped she was ready. The plan was for him to scout ahead, make sure there were no surprises. After Owen and Tanya passed by on their way to the meeting point he would create a diversion so that Ernie and Cindy could separate Owen from Tanya. From there he and Kateryna could intimidate Tanya into surrendering.

As he took another pull of water he thought about the plan and grimaced.

It was a crappy plan.

But it's all he had.

They clambered along the trail, moving slow under the pitiless sun. Ernie stopped and held up his hand, a pained expression on his face "Is it okay if we take five?"

Kateryna walked off and plopped down onto a felled tree trunk. Ernie bent over, hands on his knees to catch his breath.

"Should I speak with her?" Cindy said, squinting at Kateryna.

"Let's see if she works through it on her own," Ernie said. He figured Kateryna's fiancé must have died somewhere nearby, and he wanted to give her space.

"Good, because I don't care anymore," Cindy said, surprising Ernie with the vehement tone in her voice. "I don't care about Brody's case, curiosity, science, or Dibrovno. What are we doing out here, Ernie? We aren't trained for this."

"It's different for me. You know that," Ernie said, looking past Cindy at the deepening purple hue on the mountains, the crimson splashes of sunlight illuminating forested slopes enveloped by deep shadows. The late afternoon had always been one of his favorite times of day. He wondered when it would be again.

"We're betting everything on Brody," Cindy frowned, noting that Ernie had that same glazed look in his eye as he had on the drive into Lviv. "One way or another *they* will know we're a part of it, and if *they're* real what makes you think the government or whoever else can protect us?"

Before Ernie could respond a crunching noise came from up the rocky trail.

Footsteps!

To their left was the drop off. To their right a thin layer of bushes and trees clung to a vertical sloping rock and dirt wall. Forty feet further along the trail bent into the trees. Tanya and Owen stepped around the corner.

"Hi," Tanya said, smiling in a way that didn't quite reach her eyes.

Owen charged forward.

"Thank god you're all right!" Ernie embraced him, relieved.

Owen pulled away smiling broadly. He turned toward Cindy, his smile falling from his face.

She was eying Tanya like one would a crocodile drifting close to their canoe.

"Don't move, *bitch*!"

Owen twirled around, gasping in surprise. Not ten feet before Tanya stood another woman. She was brandishing a semi-automatic pistol, the big gun awkward in her tiny hands.

"I know what you did," Kateryna said.

Tanya smirked.

"*Put the gun down!*" Cindy commanded.

"Why? I would be doing everyone a favor," Kateryna said, her voice cracking.

Tanya shot a glance at Owen.

Ernie's heart skipped a beat as he caught the look exchanged between them.

My God, he knows.

"Owen," Ernie pleaded. "Please, come here. We can help you."

"What makes you think I want to be helped?"

"You need to forget whatever she's told you," Ernie said. "Tanya didn't just ruin that woman's life, she killed my father."

CHAPTER 27

March 1944 – The Western Ukraine

"Run," Her father commanded.

In one way or another Tanya had been running her entire life. Years prior her family had hid from the commissars by passing themselves off as poor woods folk and not farmers to be worked to death on the *kolkhozy*. Most of her extended family hadn't survived the purges, nor did seven million other Ukrainians. Then the Germans came.

Tanya drifted into town one morning shortly after the Germans arrived. Not a soul could be found on the street. Posters on buildings warned Jews and dogs to stay off the sidewalks or depicted hideously large nosed and beady eyed Jews holding bags of money taken from Slavic homeowners. The sound of large engines pierced the silence.

Tanya backed away from the road, watching as a fleet of German staff cars and bulky army trucks roared into the town square. The men that spilled out bristled with machine pistols and rifles. Nevertheless, their uniforms were different from the regular German army gray. They were festooned with a variety of SS tunics & insignia, police uniforms, piping, collar tabs, green shoulder boards, and caps in lieu of helmets. Most of the men had lined faces, some had gray hair. All had hard eyes.

Tanya slipped away. Later that afternoon her father came home. He took her mother by the arm and directed her into the bedroom, asking Tanya to watch her little brother. She snuck down the hallway instead, pressing her ear to the door. She heard snippets of her father's voice, "*Einsatzgruppen* and the police…they rounded up entire families…"

Tanya couldn't bear it. She ran from the house and past the old oak tree at the edge of the clearing. She didn't know how long she ran, but it was only when her breath began hitching that she finally slowed to a shambling walk, and then stopped altogether. Mosquitos hovered in the thickening air as dark thunderheads gathered in the distance. She looked around to find herself standing on an offshoot of the main road into town.

Gunshots rang out.

Tanya dove for the ground, hugging tight to the soft earth until she realized the shots were not directed at her. Brushing off leaves and dirt she sat up, listening. *The gunfire came from over the next rise.* Curiosity trumping fright, she climbed up the hill's forested slope. Just before reaching the crest she crawled under the low hanging branches of a sheltering spruce tree. Hidden amongst the heavy boughs she peered down the far side. What she witnessed would remain seared in her mind for as long as she lived.

In a narrow hollow a group of about thirty men, women, and children were lined up, all Jewish and all naked or in various stages of undress. Shirts, pants, belt buckles, wooden toys, blankets, hats, and more scattered about. Tanya's stomach clenched up at the sight of the wide-eyed children clinging to their parents, crying infants pressed tight to their mother's bosom.

A long ugly gash rent the ground. Bodies lay within; arms akimbo, faces staring blankly. Stacked shovels leaned against a German army truck parked astride a dirt track. German soldiers and Ukrainian auxiliaries wearing white arm bands stood about smoking and talking. Some took pictures. The Germans were the same one's she had seen pull into town, the one's her father had been talking about. These *Einsatzgruppen* stood near the pit's edge, executioner's eerie eyes conveying a religious zeal. Motion from left of the pit distracted Tanya.

A Jew she didn't recognize was shaking his head "no" as a tall German soldier leaned on a shovel, pointing at the Jew's gold teeth. Receiving yet another "no" the German shrugged. In one smooth movement he swung the shovel up into the air and slammed it down into the Jew's head. The man groaned and crumpled to the ground.

The German swung the shovel again, and again, and again.

With the fourth blow the moaning stopped.

At the fifth blow the man's skull came apart.

The German leaned down, peeling open the dead man's mouth and punching his dagger inside. He pried each gold tooth from the jaw, wiping the blood off on his pant leg, and then holding his treasure up so the sun would glint off the shiny metal, smiling approvingly as he dropped it into his pocket.

As Tanya fought back the urge to vomit she caught sight of an old Jewish man gesturing angrily at a teenage Ukrainian auxiliary. She recognized the man, a lump swelling in her throat. It was the town doctor, standing in nothing but his underwear, berating the boy by name. A sneering German officer looked on. He was dressed in black but for his immaculately shining SS runes. Without saying a word the German raised his arm, a small pistol in hand. He pulled the trigger. The doctor fell in a spray of pink blood.

A young woman clutching a baby boy screamed and ran to the dead doctor. Another shot rang out. Her lifeless body tumbled to the ground. A burly looking soldier grabbed the wailing infant and threw him in the air. Multiple gunshots echoed off the surrounding trees, the high velocity bullets ripping the baby apart. Tanya stared in horror, transfixed by the sight of a bloody stump of an arm hanging in a low hanging branch. One of the Ukrainian auxiliaries strode over and reached up with a shovel to knock the baby's arm into the pit.

A Jewish teenager screamed in anger and rushed the nearest Germans. A bullet dropped the boy before he got within ten feet of the nearest soldier. The other Jews ran for their lives. Gunfire exploded from at least a dozen weapons. No one escaped. The gunfire stopped.

An eerie silence fell over the killing field.

Ukrainians and Germans dragged the corpses to the pit and grabbed their shovels. They pitched great clumps of black soil onto the horribly torn bodies, some still moving as they were buried alive. Tanya's mouth was so dry she had to work her throat several times to produce saliva. In spite of every instinct screaming at her to run for her life she slid back down the hill an inch at a time, the sounds of genocide reduced to that of a banal work crew.

A low grumble of thunder was followed by the first patter of heavy rain drops. The sky opened at the same time Tanya hit the bottom of the reverse slope. With the rain masking her movements she ran, great wrenching sobs stealing her breath. By the time Tanya stumbled through her front door dusk had fallen. Her mother rushed to her, face pale with worry. Her father hugged her between them, somehow knowing better than to admonish her for leaving. That night Tanya couldn't sleep. She fantasized about having superpowers that would protect her family and friends.

The next morning she awakened as powerless as ever.

In the weeks that followed the Germans finished murdering the Jews they could find and robbed everyone else. The town's population, who had endured such horrible deprivations at Stalin's hand, starved again. Many resorted to digging up dead horses and cattle. Others remembered that pine needles boiled in water could provide the Vitamin C needed to stave off scurvy. Occasionally, she would see Jewish survivors drift into their homestead. Her father, who had carved out a garden hidden deep in the woods, fed the wraithlike ghosts and allowed them to hide in the barn for a few days at a time. Tanya also learned to hide, but for different reasons.

She had blossomed into a physical beauty, her swelling breasts and curving hips impossible to hide under even her loose work clothes. No matter how much dirt she smeared on her face, how raggedly her hair hung down from under a cap, her attractiveness was a dangerous beacon to the gangs of soldiers and militia roaming the town.

Her father built a shelter near the secret garden. Well stocked with clothing, basic medical supplies, food, water, and an old pistol, it could hold them all quite comfortably for short periods at a time. Nevertheless, it only ever held her. Tanya spent hours on end there, alone in what became *her* woods. Within a matter of weeks her overnight appearances in the forest hardly caused a ripple in the behavior of the animals.

In turn she felt secure in their presence, even when one night two glowing eyes stepped from the inky blackness and into her fire lit clearing. The wolf had stood in the light for over a minute, ears alert, his tongue lolling like he was smiling. For some reason she had smiled back. Then the great beast disappeared into the night as quietly as he had come.

It was late in the war's third winter, with the Red Army finally driving west, that the German soldiers called on her family once more. Though her father had ordered her to run to the shelter, shortly after entering the forest she had slowed to a walk. Something felt different; a feeling that danced its persistent beat around the edges of her mind. She had stopped. The anticipation of spring hung in the air, but winter was not ready to let go. She turned back, moving quickly, her heightened anxiety pushing her on.

As she approached the forest's edge she heard the godawful sound that changed her life forever - a sharp explosion. Shaking like a leaf, she had dropped into a crouch and crept forward to the forest's edge. There she peered around a tree. Her heart crumpled at the sight that greeted her.

The twin doors of her home's cellar had been wrenched open, mangled by the blast. A lone finger of smoke twirled into the sky and a German soldier stood at the cellar entrance, his machine pistol dangling loosely in one hand as he stared inside.

Tanya's lower lip trembled.

Oh please no. Poppa, Momma, Brother - please no.

"These things happen," A soldier with a cruel scarred face said as he emerged from the wreckage.

"Are they?"

"What do you expect?" The older man said, shaking his head. "A fragmentation grenade in that tiny space…"

The soldier stared in shock.

"Don't look so concerned. Wait until the SS ropes us into one of their *actions*. After this nonsense slaughtering a bunch of Jews will be a piece of cake." The older man said, and then raised his voice. "Move out."

His command was greeted by a rustle of activity as other soldiers appeared, marching off into the forest on the far side of the house. Tears filled Tanya's eyes as they disappeared down the path toward town. She squeezed her hands to her mouth, but a whimper escaped.

The young soldier from the cellar steps was still in the clearing. He spun about.

Tanya tried to hide but his searching eyes found her, pupils dilated.

Tanya's tear filled eyes bored back into his. She couldn't breathe, as if a giant fist squeezed her chest.

Neither moved.

Something passed between them.

He nodded and turned to follow his comrades.

This time she did the one thing she had always been taught.

She ran.

CHAPTER 28

March 1944 – The Western Ukraine

Tanya crumpled to the ground and wept. She was exhausted. Only after what felt like hours did she rise on shaking legs, her sobs fading into a final flurry of tears. Wiping an arm across her swollen eyes she breathed deep, an aching hollow emptiness at the center of her being. As she pulled herself together her pain was superseded by an all-consuming rage. She was done running.

Upon reaching her hideaway she grabbed the pistol and pocketed it. She turned to go, and froze in her tracks.

The wolf was back.

He glanced over his shoulder at the same time a man stepped from the tree line.

Tanya blinked.

The man was still there.

He strode forward to stand between woman and beast.

Tanya stared at him. He had a symmetrical face, prominent cheekbones, and a strong clean shaven jawline. He was dressed simply, as a peasant, but wearing spotless clothes. Even his large hands appeared freshly scrubbed, as if he had just stepped off a streetcar. In spite of his relaxed stride and pleasant expression he had an athletic look about him; as if he could spring into action at a moment's notice. A warning tremor raced through Tanya's body. She had noticed such physical qualities in men before. *In soldiers.* She tensed, pushing her hand into her pocket, her fingers curling around the pistol.

"Wait," The man said, holding up his hands, palms open.

His pupils were unnaturally bright, dancing with life. For some reason the tension eased in Tanya's body, her hand loosened its hold on the weapon's sweaty grip.

"I know what happened," He said. "I also know what you're think-ing. Please, don't go down that path."

Strangely, Tanya couldn't shake feeling comforted.

"I understand. Believe me, I do." He stood tall, the cadence and tenor of his speech precise as he lowered his hands, "But is your death what your mother or father would want?"

"Just go, and take your pet," she said, feeling dizzy. "You understand nothing."

He pointed at the wolf, "I know that he's yours as much as he is mine."

Tanya's head spun.

"He's been watching over you. You respect him, his world. We have all noticed," The man said.

Tanya whimpered. She tried to rip her eyes away, but couldn't. Her lips parted, mind fighting against the pleasant sensation warming her body.

"I'm speaking of your future, Tanya."

How did he know her name?

"This is a cruel world. To be alone is the last thing you want, no?"

She warily mouthed her assent.

He smiled, drawing her into his orbit.

Eyelids heavy, she tried to protest but couldn't. She swayed in place on increasingly rubbery legs...

"I have an offering for you, call it a gift."

She felt clumsy, as if her equilibrium was shot. Then a moment of clarity shot through the fog. *She knew what most men wanted for their alleged gifts,* "Oh, I bet you do. You can forget it, mister."

"Not like that," He said. "Look at me, *please.*"

He appeared to be twice her age, but he was attractive. She licked her lips, casting her gaze down to take in the bulge running down the man's pant leg. *He appears to be packing a gift all right.* At that she giggled out loud, and then clapped her hands over her mouth.

Where did that wickedness come from?

His eyes searched hers as if he had the biggest secret he wanted to tell her.

For some reason she trusted him.

Perhaps it was his demeanor. Perhaps it was the wolf. Yes, the wolf was the key.

"Okaaaay," she slurred. The sound of her voice was eerie. She felt tired, hot, and needful as her finger waved lazily in the air, "But no funny stuff, or else." *Or else I will jump on you and ride that fat cock until I squeeze every drop from it.*

His eyes sparkled, "It's *time.*"

They appeared, her eyes slamming open as the sight of the wolves. One…two…three…a dozen animals crowded into the clearing. A soft pressure pushed against her leg. She looked down at a large female, her big head turned up…

My God, she's reassuring me.

She stroked the creature's fur. In spite of the animal's bolstering presence Tanya swooned, her world collapsing around the comforting wolves and the serene voice of this strange man.

"Take off your shirt."

Tanya bit her lower lip, complying without protest. Intense waves of pleasure and need emanated from her midsection, overriding any vestige of modesty. She gulped, a tremor sweeping up between her legs.

"Sit on that tree stump."

Tanya obeyed. She vaguely noticed him gliding to her left, her mind registered a brief shock as his shirt came off, revealing a trim well-muscled torso. She wanted to turn her head and follow his movement, but it took too much effort. The hairs on the back of her neck suddenly tingled; he was standing directly behind her. She squirmed on the tree stump, an exquisitely delightful pulse coming from within. Her mind stared down from above as if floating, leering at a raven haired woman wearing nothing but pants and a bra. Tanya sat erect, her body tingling. *Give it me, please.* Tremendous warmth emanated through the man's hand as he placed it on her shoulder, his body pressed close. The female wolf snuggled across her feet, kicking the temperature higher. She squeezed her thighs together, willing her hands to not descend further into her lap. She had never felt this way, tickling fingers of fright and desire twisting and twirling from her head to her toes. She opened her eyes, *she had to see…*

"Don't turn around," The man said, his voice sounding different, thick. To her muffled ears the last word sounded impossibly slurred. *Like a growl?*

Tanya gasped. One of his fingernails had creased her upper chest, feeling like a knife slicing into her skin. Her eyelids fluttered, she hovered on the edge of consciousness. Then an exquisitely plush fur blanketed her upper back. A tingling feeling radiated down from her neck down to... *Oh yes, down there.*

Her bra snapped. She gasped as her breasts sprung free, nipples hardening under their swaying weight, needle sharp pain at the base of her neck, the sensations coursing through her body dulling the edge. She felt like she was being held in a hot vice. A coppery smell hit her nostrils as something wet ran from the throbbing heat at the base of her neck.

With colossal effort she opened her right eye. She swore that one of the wolves had moved over her shoulder. *A muzzle? It had to be one of the wolves, but his head was so big.* The last thing she saw was wat looked like an enormous wolf standing on two legs.

August 2016 – Dibrovno, Western Ukraine

Ernie's accusation echoed in the air.

"Are you out of your fucking mind?" Owen yelled, feeling like he had been punched in the gut.

Tanya pursed her lips.

"Say something," Owen pleaded.

"It's a horrible thing to leave a child without their parents." Tanya said to Ernie. "You should know, your father butchered my family."

"It was an accident!" Tears streamed down Ernie's face as his hands plunged into his pack. He fumbled about, producing sheaves of paper yellowed with age, "These are his last letters, written to my mother. Look!"

"Let me see," Owen said.

Kateryna's eyes flitted back and forth as Owen flipped through the papers.

"It's true," Cindy said as she turned to Owen.

"I don't want to hear it from little-miss-super-scientist," Tanya sneered, turning toward Ernie. "You tell me. What's written on your precious Nazi papers?"

"Enough talk!" Kateryna screamed.

Tanya snapped around to glare at the smaller woman.

Immense strain wracked Kateryna's face, her lips trembling as she fought to keep the pistol pointed at Tanya.

A hawk's whistling cry sounded in the distance.

Kateryna blanched at the sudden noise, nearly discharging the weapon.

"It can be spooky out here, yes?" Tanya said.

Kateryna whimpered.

"What's that you say?" Tanya taunted. "C'mon, spit it out sweetness." Her face twitched, something rippling under her cheek.

The pistol wavered.

Tanya staggered and fell to the ground. She threw her head back and let out a soul crushing scream that echoed off the surrounding cliffs as her body exploded in a rictus of spasms.

"Shoot her!" Ernie shrieked, his emotions boiling over.

The gun shook like a windblown leaf in Kateryna's tightly clasped hands.

Tanya grotesquely skidded around on the ground, head thrashing, lips peeled back from her teeth.

"Oh God, no," Cindy cried.

Revulsion and an unbreakable curiosity washed over Owen as Tanya's writhing spasticity picked up in intensity. It looked like a documentary he remembered from his high school biology class. A dramatically speeded up shot of an Arctic flower's life cycle, the clouds flowing impossibly swift, petals opening with a flourish. Tanya's clothes stretched and tore like she were Dr. David Banner, legs kicking and lengthening with each explosive thrust, shoulders massively expanding, blood dripping from her finger tips, grotesque popping sounds, fibrous claws springing forth through her skin, bones jumping and crunching all along her torso, her jaw pushing forward into a long muzzle.

It was over.

Fully formed muscles rippled under a jet black coat of fur as the monster stood and howled.

Kateryna blinked, taking in the enormity of the terror before her. A thin high-pitched scream burst forth from her lungs, the pistol clattering to the side of the trail as she tore down the path, her mind collapsing.

Ernie swept up the pistol before anyone could react.

Tanya turned toward him, but too late. She looked at Owen, eyes glistening with a look of surrender.

Owen launched himself into the air, slamming into Ernie just as his finger curled around the trigger. The impact folded Ernie's body up like a chair and propelled both men off the cliff. As Owen plunged toward the tree lined slope below his feet extended down, ancient instincts protecting their new host. He whipped through several stinging tree branches, the first brushing his thigh, but a second painfully cracking him in the ribs. He ricocheted off it and slammed down onto the ground, cartwheeling unevenly down the hillside, dimly registering another body tumbling next to him. He bounced off a tree trunk and came to a stop, rolling to his knees, surprisingly unharmed but for a thin line of blood running from his hair line. He touched his hand to his forehead a second time, but the jagged cut was already closing. Then he noticed it. Partway up the slope. A body splayed out like a rag doll. Head bent back at a sickening angle.

Ernie.

Owen rushed over and slid down in a cloud of dust. He turned Ernie over but his head flopped like a broken puppet, sightless eyes staring into nothingness. Owen's throat seized up, the rawest pain he had ever felt surging up from inside. He cradled Ernie in his rocking lap, tears spilling down his face, a hollow black emptiness spreading outward from his convulsing mid-section. Owen screamed out his anguish, wanting nothing more than to kill himself.

A golf ball sized rock tumbled down the hillside.

Owen looked up as it rolled to a stop, lost in his grief, not quite processing what the rock's movement meant. He turned his attention back to his friend and raised a trembling hand to smooth Ernie's ruffled hair, but stopped.

Owen glanced at the rock again at the same time a hot feeling brought new life to his muscles, something clawing from within, anxious to escape—

The clack-clack of a shell being chambered in a shotgun rang in his ear.

CHAPTER 29

August 2016 – The Western Ukraine

Owen pressed his forehead against a garage door sized window, sunlight baking the tears caked tight on his cheeks. The finality and totality of Ernie's death hung over him like a guillotine. He pounded his head against the glass, each blow producing a dull echo. Splintered images flashed through his mind's eye; slamming into Ernie, gun flying, soldiers, a bug shaped helicopter, landing pad, canvas hooded figures being herded toward— Owen picked his head up, staring outside.

Where the fuck was he?

He was at least ten stories off the ground, standing in the biggest of three curvilinear towers laid out like the outstretched middle fingers of one's hand, with his tower furthest forward. His window appeared to be one of hundreds set into a concrete and steel modernist façade redolent of a software company's headquarters. Outbuildings surrounded the towers, creating a campus like atmosphere. Trimmed shrubbery lined gravel pathways winding through a sprawling garden filled with people. Some ate and talked. A few kicked around a soccer ball. Others played with their smart phones. Owen's eyes burned with hatred.

He wanted to make them feel his pain. Bury his snout under each perfect little chin and rip—

The door slid open. A tall man in a black Tom Ford three piece suit strode in, a brown folder held in his well-manicured left hand. His lustrous shoes clicked across the marble floor and his face shined with a light belying his nondescript age, big teeth lining his mouth.

"Good afternoon, Owen," The man said as he drifted near, right hand extended. "I'm Sergei Mikhailovich Vukovich."

Owen recoiled. Vukovich looked even more imposing up close.

The proffered hand hung firm in mid-air. It looked like it could palm a basketball.

"What have you done with my friends?" Owen said.

Vukovich let his rejected hand fall to his side. He stood ramrod straight, his bearing courtly.

Owen caught his expression. It was the condescending look of a server in a fine restaurant who regularly employed *sir* as a substitute for *asshole*.

"This belonged to someone you cared about," Vukovich said as he deposited the folder onto the coffee table. "Call it a gift."

"Get out," Owen said, flinching as if he had been slapped in the face. His hands balled into fists, fingernails slicing into his palms.

"The fact that you are alive and in your present condition vexes me," Vukovich said, a smile creasing his face and revealing two long fangs at the same time. "But such surprises are what make life interesting, no?"

A strand of hair shook loose from Vukovich's forehead. He absent-mindedly combed it back with one immense hand, his wolfish eyes staring down his prisoner. Owen couldn't shake the sick feeling of being trapped in a small room with a large predator.

Vukovich departed, the door gliding shut behind him.

Owen staggered into the nearest chair. He glanced down to see palms stained with blood, but smoothly closing up.

August 2016 – The Western Ukraine

Some agent you are.

Brody had been perched above the trail, hiding in the foliage. One minute he was alone and the next Owen and Tanya loped past, leaving him sitting in stunned silence. He had waited then scampered to his feet, coming to an abrupt halt when a wolf's howl split the late morning air. His testicles had just completed their rapid ascent into his belly when his head had exploded, the world spun once, and slipped away.

Brody rubbed his sore neck, wincing at the memory of getting clubbed as he glanced around the ten-by-ten room in which he had been confined. He sat on a twin bed made up with a single sheet and flat pillow. In a ceiling corner a flat-screen TV was tuned to CNN, the sound muted but the news crawler flashing by: *"Criminal Prosecution Taken off the Table for CEO Jimmy Donnelly Following This Week's Hearing."*

At least some things never change, Donnelly robbing the country blind then skating free like he was Charlie White or Meryl Davis. Stifling an urge to smash the TV Brody eyed the rest of the windowless room. Walls painted battleship gray. A steel door with what looked like a mail slot but thicker marring its seamless expanse. A large mirror had been mounted on the wall to his left. He presumed it was a two-way. The TV clicked off. Brody sighed and fell back on the bed, hands over his eyes.

The door slid open.

Cindy stumbled into the room, the door shutting behind. She sagged into his outstretched hands, her cheeks flushed and pupils dilated. As he caught her she moaned, "Oh my, it's just awful. Ernie's gone."

Brody tensed. He wanted to ask her about it, but held back. *She needed him more than he needed answers.* He tightened his arm around her until she looked strong enough to sit up on her own, though still snuggled into him for support.

The flap in the door opened. A tray balanced precariously on the small lip projecting into the room. Brody reached out with one hand and grabbed it just before it tipped forward. Together, they examined the tray's contents; sliced apples, a collection of Boursin, Chevre, and Gouda cheeses, a baguette, two splits of German Riesling, and a pair of clear plastic cups.

"I guess *they* aren't total savages, but if this is meant to hold us—"

"Knock it off," Cindy said.

"You don't think this is the least bit odd?" Brody said, trying to play down the inappropriately electric jolt that her nearness had triggered within him.

She ignored him, pouring them each a drink.

Within minutes the ravenous duo had polished off the tray's contents.

Brody bent to set it on the floor, the quick movement making him dizzy.

"That was fucking outstanding," Cindy blurted out, hand flying to her mouth. She swallowed nervously, trying to understand why she felt so incredibly free.

"A little wine and miss forensic biologist turns into a longshoreman, huh?" Brody said, feeling a giddy warmth spreading through him.

"No, I mean," Cindy gulped hard, but was unable to stop herself from leaning in close to brush against him. "Is it hot in here or—"

"Is it just me?" Brody's grin widened at the stale joke that strangely sounded like the funniest thing he had heard in years. *He felt good, too good.* A warning flashed in the back of his mind. Then it disappeared as Cindy's devouring stare ate him alive.

Cindy's body tingled in a way that had her face flush, her mind fuzzy and swirling. *She had wondered once or twice, okay more than once or twice.* She shook her head as if trying to clear the cobwebs that accumulate after a deep sleep. A tingling sensation rippled across Cindy's skin, her hands roaming across her thighs.

The decrepit TV sputtered to life, volume first and surprisingly loud, a woman moaning coupled with the sound of deep grunting. Then the TV screen popped on in garish high definition. Cindy gasped at the most horrifically lewd sight she had ever seen. A pale skinned naked woman was on her hands and knees, braced against the pounding hips of a man kneeling behind her. Cindy stared harder at the man. *Was that some sort of Halloween mask, why was he getting darker?*

The woman's face turned sideways toward the unseen camera, dilated pupils black and devoid of emotion.

"My God," Cindy cried out, "It's Kateryna." Her hand slammed down and locked Brody's thigh in a death grip. "I can't believe it!"

Brody fought to analyze what he was seeing. *He couldn't believe it either. Something was very wrong.* His eyes widened as he recognized what Cindy was missing. *Kateryna had been drugged, and that monster was raping her.* Brody's fist clenched at the same moment a shockingly unexpected wave of pleasure jolted through his body. He glanced down to see Cindy's hand squeezing his thigh harder.

Cindy blushed at the depraved sight of the librarian's jiggling body. A part of her brain told her the images and sounds were utterly repellent, but she didn't care, rhythmically squeezing and stroking ever higher on Brody's thigh.

Brody's eyes fixated on Cindy's hand, his senses heightened, transfixed by a dizzy kaleidoscope of feelings, a hungering fascination fighting against the urges telling him to stop this before—

Cindy leaned in and kissed him hard on the mouth, beyond caring about her husband or anything else.

Brody responded. His attraction for Cindy was undeniable. However, a voice in the back of his mind became increasingly strident, overriding his physical need. He pulled back.

Cindy chased after him, flashing hotter at the incredible sensations floating through her, dimly aware her drink must have been drugged even as she attempted to get into Brody's pants.

Brody's head spun in a daze but he gripped Cindy's hand, his eyes boring into hers.

No.

Cindy's reacted in surprise, disappointment, then in shame. She wept. Brody let her bury her head in his chest, hugging her tight, burning with anger as he thought of what *they* were doing to him and his friends.

Owen's jugular vein throbbed as he stalked into the sparkling clean bathroom. He stared into his reflection in the extravagantly gilded mirror before bending his head to the marble basin, washing away the caked tears that had reddened his puffy eyes. He toweled dry and strode into the main room.

Grabbing up Ernie's papers he fell into a chair, perusing page after page of yellowed letters and notes dating back to the Second World War. Some were typed; others creased and wrinkled, bearing the furtive scribbling of a frantic mind. Old envelopes marked the letter's providence, faded blue stamps depicting a transport plane, the most common stamping from the *Feldpost*. The handwriting further placed the letters in the wartime era. It was the *Sütterlin* style, commonly taught in German schools from the First World War into the early 1940s - when the Nazi party banned it for being "Jewish". The script rolled in precisely clipped but closely placed strokes, so straight it was as if the paper were lined. Owen smiled wanly, finding the upper case "G's" as illegible as usual. Ascenders and descenders in one line crossed over to another. Nevertheless, he picked up the elaborate handwriting's cadence at the same time one letter separated itself from the pile. Dated March of 1944, it was written to Ernie's mother from his father - Erich Bekensteiner.

My Dearest Luisa,

Something dreadful has happened.

I have not slept a wink in two days. I do not wish to frighten, but there were stories we were told as children. Stories we at one time even believed. Then we grew up, and they were pushed aside. Now I am not sure that was wise. It seems that I have awakened an unthinkable evil. It wants retribution for what I did. Tonight is that time.

I long to see you and little Ernst, and I hope with all of my heart that he is well. Nevertheless, what I am about to tell you is disturbing. Heed my words, for your sake as well as his. The thought of my family suffering what is in store for me is too unbearable to consider.

If I do not return home then you must protect him from what I have discovered. That might mean travelling great distances. I know it will be unpleasant, but do not hesitate. There is more than enough hidden in our special place to help you start over, including our best silver. I implore you to take it, have it forged anew. Do this. I can't say any more, other than I pray that you won't need it.

By now I have hopefully opened your eyes to the nature of the unspeakable truth hunting me down. I will do everything in my power to rejoin you. But if I cannot, then you must know that my memories of you and Ernst will warm my heart forever more. Even though you are hundreds of miles away as far as I am concerned you are here, comforting me. Until we meet again my darling, I kiss you affectionately.

Yours in endless love,

Erich

Owen let the letter float to the floor.

There it is. Or was it? Could Tanya have murdered Ernie's father? What if Ernie's father had killed Tanya's family? Context, as it was whenever one examined actions of those caught up by history, was everything. How does one who has never been tested judge one that has?

Owen stood and paced, rubbing his hands as if lathering them up with soap. The door hissed open. Owen whirled about, nearly leaping from his skin, nerves burning. A well-muscled man wearing black jeans and a matching skin tight t-shirt entered the room. He wordlessly hung a suit on a closet door and disappeared, replaced in the doorway by Vukovich.

"Feeling tense?" The older man said, cruising into the room and sitting down by the window.

Owen contemplated testing the window's strength with the man's body. Then he thought better of it, easing down opposite Vukovich.

"Unrestrained impulses can destroy even the strongest of us, no?" Vukovich said, fixing Owen with a cold, knowing stare.

"Why am I here?"

"The question should not be *why*, but *how* it is you came to be here," Vukovich said.

Owen rolled his eyes, gripping the chair's puffy arm, feeling dizzy, "Where are my friends?"

"Why don't you see for yourself?" Vukovich said, snatching the remote off the coffee table.

The TV mounted to the far wall switched from the endless droning of talking heads to a split screen image. On the screen's left side Cindy and Brody were locked in a passionate kiss, their hands roaming across each other's bodies. On the screen's right Owen saw the Kateryna woman that had pulled a gun on Tanya was being mounted from behind by a man morphing into...Owen shifted uncomfortably in his chair, trying not to be obvious about his discomfort, or for that matter his swelling and inopportune response. He spun toward Vukovich.

"Don't look at me," Vukovich said. "Your friends are acting of their own free will."

"Free will my ass—"

"They had a choice," Vukovich said, jumping up. "Everyone gets a choice."

Vukovich thumbed his finger at the suit hanging on the closet, his voice firm in the manner of a man accustomed to having his orders followed. "Clean up. You want to see your friend's, fine. You can ask them all about that," Vukovich waved his hand at the TV, "this evening at dinner. Otherwise we have more meaningful topics to discuss."

He stalked from the room.

Moans and groans accompanied by the sounds of hotly slapping flesh echoed from the TV.

A tremor swept through Owen's crotch. He fumbled for the remote, pressing the 'off' button as *it* stirred more insistently within him.

CHAPTER 30

August 2016 – The Western Ukraine

Owen walked down the spotless hall, his suit's silky cashmere wool blend failing to distract him from the raw sensations coursing through his body. He couldn't focus on anything other than his escort's plump ass pumping along in a lascivious form fitting dress. The raging hungers churning within him fueled an overwhelming urge to stick his face, among other things, between her incredible cheeks.

As if on cue the woman glanced back over her shoulder, licking her full lips and nearly sending him over the edge. Her long hair swayed down her back as she put an extra wiggle in her hips before coming to a stop in front of a steel door in yet another barren corridor. There she pressed close to Owen, the scent of orchid, vanilla, and sandalwood bringing him achingly erect. "Enjoy your dinner. If there's *anything* else you need, please don't hesitate to ask." With that she slapped him on the butt, her eyes sparkling with mischief.

Owen entered and the door hissed shut behind him. Windows lined a westward facing wall, the orange-yellow light of a brilliant late afternoon sun streaming inside. A slate gray industrial style dining table dominated the room, the place settings marking service for seven.

"Please, sit," Vukovich said from the head of the table.

Owen complied, glancing at a bank of wall mounted monitors. Each flashed green, red, and yellow dots within white country borders. The majority of the brightly blinking dots marked London and the U.S. East Coast.

An ample breasted redhead emerged from the shadows to fill his glass with a blood red cabernet, her freckled cleavage swinging heavily before him. A predatory look crossed the woman's face. She glanced hungrily at Owen's crotch before stepping away, Owen's eyes trailing after.

Vukovich observed. *Owen's response to the females was as it had been to Tanya; laughably Pavlovian. Nevertheless, the man's mind appeared to be transforming along with his body. Perhaps he could be an asset yet.*

"This is the headquarters of my company, Security Services International," Vukovich commented as he swirled a robust semi-dry red around his wine glass. "One of the most exclusive private security firms in the world."

Owen half-listened, distracted by of all things his napkin. *It was embossed with the same coat of arms he saw at Tanya's.* Only after a stunned pause did he turn his attention back to Vukovich, "SS huh, I suppose the corporate logo is a swastika?"

"In our clientele's price point there is an enduring affinity for, how should I say, *certain* worldviews."

The door slid open.

Tanya glided into the room wearing a plunging black dress. Owen jumped up, hugging her tight. She let him go after a perfunctory squeeze and sat down to Vukovich's right. Owen barely had time to register his displeasure before the door hissed open again.

Brody and Cindy entered. Each dressed resplendently; they smiled at the sight of Owen. He nodded politely in turn. Behind them came Kateryna. Owen couldn't help but notice her breasts practically spilling out of a tight leather dress barely covering the bottom of her ass. She stumbled along, dazedly clinging to the arm of a handsome but rough looking man. The man's shirt collar shifted, revealing a puckish pink scar running the width of his throat…

"Karlovic!" Owen exclaimed, whirling on Tanya. "You said you killed him!"

"Not exactly," Tanya responded.

"Who are you? Bill-fucking-Clinton?" Owen snapped. "Silly me. I didn't make you specify what you meant when you said you nearly separated his head from his body."

"Owen's got the right idea," Brody said to Tanya. "It's a shame you didn't finish the job."

"Is that so?" Karlovic said.

"My father always taught me to put wounded animal's down."

"Taking a life isn't as easy as it looks," Karlovic said. "That is until you get used to it."

"There's a first time for everything," Brody said.

"It's more complicated than that, isn't it Tanya," Owen said, licking his teeth and noticing how sharp his canines had become.

"Why don't you lay off?" Brody said to Owen, reluctantly turning his attention away from Karlovic.

"That's rich, coming from you and your new girlfriend," Owen said. "By the way, I saw the two of you on TV, making out like teenagers barely hours after Ernie died. You should be ashamed—"

"We were drugged," Cindy said as she settled into her seat, noticing a painting of Adam and Eve on the opposite wall. *I cheated on my husband.* A red apple lay on the ground, two conspicuous bites hollowed out of its lustrous red exterior. A smiling serpent slithered across the sand.

"Enough," Vukovich said, rising to his full imposing height and leaning forward, knuckles grinding into the table top.

The server's rushed around, eyes shining like children's on Christmas Eve, a strange tension running like an undercurrent through the room. The wait staff unfurled napkins and placed them on laps jumping when eager fingers rubbed below the smooth linens.

"You have much to learn," Vukovich said to Owen.

Owen ignored him, downing his wine in one gulp and reaching for a nearby decanter of cabernet.

"I can't believe you fell for this guy," Karlovic said to Tanya.

"He killed his best friend to save me," She replied. "That's more than you ever would have done."

More servers swarmed into the room, laying out a lavish spread of caviar; pan seared sturgeon; roasted prime rib encrusted with salt, cracked peppercorns, and dried herbs; pork loin smothered in sautéed apples; a dazzling array of hand folded pierogi's along with heaps of sour cream and butter; hearty rye and black breads; fresh fruits and chilled decanters of vodka coupled with a wine selection ranging from dry and crisp whites to heartier reds. Vukovich surveyed the feast with pride.

"What's this all about?" Brody said. "With the exception of him," Brody gestured at Owen, "Kateryna, Cindy, and I are—"

"More valuable than you think. I wanted to wait until after dinner," Vukovich said with a sigh. "However, if you must know, there's a war being waged and your side is losing. Badly, I might add."

Owen glanced outside at the sun dropping lower, his right leg frenetically bouncing under the table.

"You know something is wrong," Vukovich said. "Yet for one reason or another you believe there are real choices offered by your 'Democracy.'"

Brody felt someone looking at him. He glanced over at Kateryna. Her eyes seemed to brighten in response. A weak smile twitched at the corner of her lips as she turned toward Karlovic and blurted out, "Oh, how I love the *Maidan Nezalezhnosti* during this time of the year. I can't wait to see it."

Everybody turned to stare at her.

She looked down and away. Brody's stomach clenched as Kateryna looked up again. Whatever brief glimpse of what had been her was gone once more, replaced by someone else. Brody stared at Kateryna a moment longer and then shot a murderous stare at Karlovic. The beast didn't notice, busy cramming a buttered hunk of rye bread into his mouth.

"You see your governments and leaders as failures. Yet, they are doing what their masters request." Vukovich said, having shrugged off Kateryna's interruption. "If you are one of the privileged few and make a bad bet in the Wall Street casino, then you are reimbursed. Blow up the economy? The system of socialized losses and privatized gains is granted to you as a birthright."

"Wonderful speech," Brody said, his anger boiling over. "I can't wait to hear what you've got to pair with dessert, perhaps a soliloquy on the pointlessness of human existence?"

"This wasn't always the reality of your existence," Vukovich said, shrugging off Brody's sarcasm. "By the middle of the last century the wealthy had been clobbered by their self-indulgent greed. For the first time ever they paid a fair share into the system that had enriched them. In turn, millions enjoyed the good life. Nevertheless, economic crisis gave the plutocrats the chance to unwind the wartime social compact. Leading the charge is a financial sector turning the screws on what had been the middle class. The rampant inequality, disintegration of the nation-state, and breakdown of social norms you see at home are all natural outgrowths of this war centralizing power into fewer hands."

Owen grimaced at a tremor wracking his heaving stomach. He hadn't eaten a bite even though he couldn't remember being so hungry in his life. He gripped his chair, his fingers whitening as Karlovic's fleshy lips smacked every time he licked his greasy fingers.

"Am I missing something here?" Brody said. "You're a werewolf, so excuse me if I don't get where the morality trip comes from?"

"An old one at that," Vukovich said. "That's why I know there's a road better traveled. One that can restore balance prior to the chaos otherwise set to come."

Owen dabbed his glistening forehead with his handkerchief.

Cindy grimaced at Owen sickly appearance, but couldn't resist answering Vukovich, "This smacks quite a bit of envy."

"Do you know how long it takes for wealth once acquired to disappear?" Vukovich responded. "I've read your work on the link between poverty and crime. Can't you see that society's winners are also predetermined?"

Cindy cursed under her breath. He was blowing up her academic findings and working them into an integrated worldview.

"The wealthy are different," Vukovich added. "I know, for I too was born into privilege."

"Just like Osama Bin Ladin," Brody said.

Vukovich shot a laser like stare of irritation across the table as Owen smiled and winked at Brody.

"I know quite a few wealthy people and they, this is ridiculous," Cindy said. "Stereotyping an entire group? You can't demonize people for being successful."

"I'm not talking about success," Vukovich said. "Look at the CEO of your biggest bank; he's little more than an organized crime boss granted state sanction to loot."

"So what gives?" Owen said. "In past centuries when it got this bad out came the pitchforks, public executions, and all that fun stuff you seem to admire."

"The people have been numbed up by decades of propaganda promoting the mythic free market," Vukovich responded. "Trust me, the average working person will look for help. In turmoil extremists speak to the people, offering them enemies to hate."

"I'm not saying I buy it," Cindy said. "But what does this have to do with *werewolves*?"

"Or more to the point where did we, the werewolf, come from?" Vukovich smiled. "For to know that is to answer your question."

CHAPTER 31

August 2016 – The Western Ukraine

"For centuries we were a whisper on the wind," Vukovich said. "Then the Black Death came."

"You're the result of a virus?" Cindy said.

"A bacteria would be the more accurate term. Your scientists have identified three of the four types of plague." Vukovich said. "Each has unique blood based symptoms, but one in particular stands out."

"Let me guess, the werewolf plague."

"We refer to it as the Lupine Plague," Vukovich said in response to Brody. "Similar to the Bubonic Plague, transmission comes from being bitten by an infected animal. However, the subject, assuming they survive contact with the carrier, experiences an evolutionary response. The plague reacts with underlying genetic material already predisposed by existing mutation to accept the coding brought by the bacterium. If symbiosis exists then the new host is equipped with the tools needed to survive."

"But we're discussing a disease," Brody said.

"What's a disease?" Vukovich responded.

"You know, getting sick," Brody said, recognizing he was out of his element.

"It's any *transformation* or stoppage of normal functioning or structure of any of the body's systems or organs." Vukovich replied.

"Why the Black Death? Why not in tandem with the Justinian Plague?"

"It lacked long term viability," Vukovich answered Owen. "With the Black Death the evolutionary advantage shifted to the bacterium."

"The sword versus the shield," Owen said, his bloodshot eyes flashing bright.

Karlovic and Tanya exchanged worried glances.

"An organism evolves and its competitor responds. It's nature's way, is it not?" Vukovich said.

"But a *werewolf*? Evolved from a human?" Cindy said.

"Scientists recently found in Spain a fossilized human femur one hundred thousand years older than previously thought possible. It came from a Denisovan. Up until then the only other place Denisovan DNA had been found was in Siberia. So how did that DNA get four thousand miles west of any other known location Denisovans have been found? The point is—"

"There may be extinct forms of humans we don't even know about." Cindy replied.

"Of the one's we do know there is much still tripping us up," Vukovich said. "Scientists now believe that Homo Sapiens cross-breeding with Neanderthals may have provided today's humans with the genetic material needed to handle the climate found outside of Africa. Some of these genes controlled obvious physical differences in people. This means—"

"That the genes responsible for creating the strength and power of a werewolf may not have come from today's humans," Cindy interjected. "It may have derived from the parts of the genetic code modern man inherited from species such as a Neanderthal."

"Or DNA inherited from a homo sapien that cross bred with a Denisovan, or a Neanderthal that cross-bred with a Denisovan, and passed it on to us." Vukovich said. "There are gaps in the human genome where Neanderthal genes must have existed, or Denisovan DNA for that matter, but which scientists now believe our bodies simply removed. What's most stunning is how quickly we shed the genetic coding that arose from those matchups."

"Thus the converse must be true," Cindy responded, thinking aloud. "If humans can *drop* much of the genetic code passed on by others, then we can *add* genetic code to jump up the evolutionary chain."

"Why is this so hard to understand?" Tanya sighed, glancing out the window at the darkening sky. "An Amur Tiger is genetically ninety-five percent the same as a house cat. However, tigers are rapidly evolving, exhibiting massive changes in metabolism, musculature, and even enhanced senses. All of which is by definition what happens when I change, just on a more rapid pace."

"With the Bubonic Plague systems that took years to develop break down within a single day." Karlovic added, his needs boiling, "If an infected animal as small as a flea produces such incredible results why can't the strain of plague passed on from the bite of a disproportionately larger creature produce more dramatic outcomes?"

"The point is that these microorganisms are unpredictable," Tanya said. "They react dissimilarly in diverse hosts in conflicting conditions. Here we have a type of natural selection whereby genes that when triggered kill in one context, but a mutated gene in another instance transform its host in a positive fashion."

"Assuming becoming a monster and eating people is positive," Brody said.

"But again, why did this happen in conjunction with the Bubonic Plague?" Owen asked.

"Those absorbing the lupine plague experienced an interaction in their genetic code triggered in response to a potential species termination event," Vukovich said. "The Plague didn't just happen. It needed underlying conditions such as inequality and instability to wreak havoc on humans consuming at rates beyond the capacity of their surrounding environment."

"This makes no sense," Brody said. "How does any of that relate to bacteria?"

"During the end of the thirteenth century in Europe a milder climactic period wound down." Owen said, his mind racing ahead as what Vukovich said began clicking into place. "The human population had exploded as agriculture flourished. Then the temperature fell. This brought down agricultural productivity. By the early part of the fourteenth century Europe's population exceeded its food base. This produced malnutrition."

"Malnutrition leads to sickness and compromised immune systems," Cindy said.

"Peasants piled into Europe's great cities, living in slums. Then in 1314 it began to rain and it just about never stopped." Owen grimaced as another tremor rumbled through him, "The worst famine in over a century followed."

"In the meantime the Black Death spread along ancient trade routes." Vukovich said. "When the plague arrived in Europe's malnourished and overpopulated cities—"

"Social order broke down," Owen finished Vukovich's sentence. "In a matter of years the plague killed nearly two thirds of Europe's population."

"Some people had been infected by a different strain," Vukovich added. "We don't know who patient zero was, and the assumption is that he or she was bit by an infected wolf, but regardless they had transformed forever. An interesting by-product of this Lupine strain derived from what it did not just to metabolism and appearance, but also to appetites."

"Appetites indeed," Brody said.

"We have since learned to moderate our needs, but we there's a reason why our kind must prey on yours." Vukovich replied.

"That is?" Brody felt disgusted and intrigued at the same time.

"Nature's imperative is to create balance," Vukovich said. "Remove one element and the system collapses. Look at the Chesapeake Bay. You killed the sharks. But the sharks ate rays. Rays eat oysters. No sharks meant too many rays and there went the oysters. An ecosystem that existed for millions of years was decimated all because one link in the food chain was destroyed. Similarly, in fourteenth century Europe humans created an imbalance. In that case nature created its answer but it spread unchecked. To control that answer nature responded yet again, by creating an organism that could stop those infected from sickening others."

"By removing the Plague's food source," Cindy said.

"However, healthy humans proved far from thrilled with nature's solution," Vukovich responded, noticing Owen's anguished glances out the window in response to the sun's diminishing rays.

"As a result this new balancing agent needed to imitate something that if seen in passing might be mistaken for an animal that would compel the observer to turn and flee, thereby limiting their ability to identify what they saw," Cindy said, thinking aloud. "In Europe at that time only one animal could strike that kind of terror in a person. This new organism took the sensory capabilities and cunning of a wolf, mated these abilities to the physical strength of the strongest primate, and finished it all off with the cutting and slashing power of the carnivore's fangs and claws. That's nature's chosen weapon for dealing with armed men who stood in the way of restoring equilibrium."

"Yes, and unfortunately many of our kind took liberties," Vukovich said. "These excesses produced the legends."

"Excesses, liberties," Brody said. "You sound like the head of the CIA inventing weasel words for torture."

"I will not deny our past," Vukovich responded. "But we've been there to right the ship every time you've nearly destroyed yourselves."

"Destroyed ourselves?" Brody said. "Hold on there. That was a bug, virus, bacteria, or whatever that almost took us out."

"Haven't you been listening?" Tanya flushed red, hormones jumping, *feeling* the moon rising.

"Calm your tits down," Cindy snapped back, sick of Tanya's overbearing self-righteousness.

Tanya threw a hostile stare at Cindy, before turning on Brody. "Overpopulation, destruction of resources, inequality, political instability, and climate change are what allowed the Plague to spread. These things are happening again as we speak. So though he," She pointed at Vukovich, "is focusing on inequality leading to fascism and World War Three, my concerns go deeper. What if nature comes up with a different genetic mutation in response?"

"The truth comes out," Brody said. "Worried about your own future are you?"

"Your fates and ours are intertwined," Vukovich said. "The evidence is in the historical record. The Bubonic Plague returned in 1603 to London, to Italy in 1629, to Seville in 1647, London again in 1665, Vienna in 1679, Marseilles in 1720 and to Eastern Europe in 1738 and 1770. Each time *we* checked its progress. If you don't believe me look at the spread of our legend."

"He's right." Cindy said. "Ernie and I found a history of werewolves in Lviv. The folklore spread with the Plague's worst hit areas, from the Anglo-Saxons to the Germans before reaching the French. Then the mythology journeyed east, and as the conditions that produced the plague receded the legends—"

"Faded away," Vukovich said. "So did our numbers. The first generation that survived the human backlash left behind a smaller, more circumspect second generation so selective in its methods we became invisible. That is until Emily Garard's writings regarding Transylvanian folklore stirred renewed interest in our kind. Luckily Bram Stoker deflected that attention in other directions."

"We evolved to prey on the weak. Like any other predator," Karlovic said, letting out a deep breath as he battled against *it* welling up within him. "For most of your history there have been few people who didn't fit that category."

"You had no problem ripping Cameron to pieces," Brody said. "The man had a family and you killed him for what? To make a political point?"

Karlovic glanced at Tanya then responded to Brody, "You are meat. Like any other beast."

"Open your eyes, Brody," Vukovich said. "To maintain balance we will do whatever it takes, including by forcibly dialing back the predations of your human 'one percent' if I may use the parlance of our current times."

"Via killing people? That's great, how good of you," Brody said. "By the way dinner was wonderful. Though I wasn't such a fan of the lecture, maybe Wagner should have been piped in to complete the mood."

"Don't be so naïve," Tanya said, "How else are we going to stop this madness? Fund a grass roots political organization with the goal of instituting a global wealth tax?"

"That's not a bad idea," Cindy interjected.

"Capital is mobile," Vukovich said, shaking his head no. "Given the political power this provides it also means it can't be stopped by conventional methods."

"Why are you speaking of this?" Cindy asked pleadingly. "That is unless you're going to kill us?"

"If I wanted to kill you I would have dispensed with the explanation, this isn't a James Bond movie. By sparing your lives I have shown you a path. The idea of being devoured is not pleasant but it's time to know your place. After all, every other animal on this planet is part of the food chain."

"No, you're the exception there," Brody said.

"That's not entirely true," Tanya shot a concerned glance at Vukovich.

"Nature is resilient," Vukovich said, pointedly ignoring her. "I have no doubt that if we abuse our position she will find an answer. In the meantime, the three of you are more powerful than you think, each with unique skill sets, access to critical information, and serving in networks crucial to protecting your nation's ruling class. Together we could—"

"This is madness," Cindy said. "You're discussing a revolution launched by *werewolves*."

"As if we're so odd?" Tanya snarled. "Get the fuck over it. Do you want to just sit back and watch the world burn, or do something about it?"

"I can bring purpose to your lives," Vukovich said. "Cast off the artificial construct within which you waste your talents. See man's world for what it is and not what it's made to appear." He rose, motioning toward Owen and Brody, "Nevertheless, time is not a luxury. I will first need the two of you to come with me."

"You said a test," Tanya gasped, leaping from her chair. "Not *that* kind of test."

"What choice do I have?" Vukovich's eyes softened. "You of all people must understand."

Tanya rushed to Owen who had also stood, albeit on shaky legs. She took his face in her hands. Owen's heart danced in his chest as he kissed her. After a long moment he pulled away, choking back tears, whispering so only Tanya could hear, "I miss him Tanya. I miss him so much. He is, was my—"

"Shhhh, I know," Taya said. "I too have lost, long ago. Even today there are no words that can describe the pain that I have felt. This pain, the pain that I have endured, the pain that can never be forgotten is, however, the pain that has made me into who I am. You too must be strong. Embrace your pain. Learn from it, and promise me that you'll come back."

Owen quelled his trembling lips, nodding 'yes' and flashing the broad toothy smile she had come to love.

Tanya spun on Vukovich, her beautifully sculpted face turning into a dark scowl.

"You. Fucking. Asshole."

Vukovich tried to seem nonplussed as Tanya stormed away, his hands extended to Owen and Brody, "Come. There is nothing to be afraid of, at least not yet."

CHAPTER 32

August 2016 – Dibrovno, Western Ukraine

Brody battled the uneasy feeling of his guts sloshing around as the Polish built Sokół helicopter rose and fell with each undulation in the earth. Twin 900 horsepower turbo shaft engines powered the big rotors whomping away above the vibrating ceiling, Owen the only other passenger in the spacious cabin. Movement out of the corner of his eye caused Brody to turn and see Vukovich working his way back from the co-pilot seat. Vukovich crouched down in the passageway, seemingly oblivious to the floor tilting with each juke of the powerful helicopter.

"This is madness," Brody yelled at Vukovich over the incessant thrumming of the helicopter's blades.

"Don't talk like that," Vukovich barked. "You want to sound like one of *them*, to be one of *them*, but you're not. Face it. You're much more like *me*."

"I'm hardly—"

"Global elites are waging war on humanity for no reason other than sheer greed. I know how much this vast inequality grinds at your sense of justice. Are the one percent not rentiers? Are they not parasites? They need to be cleansed from the human host, do they not?"

"It's murder," Owen interjected, his eyes shining like glass.

"Would you rather see millions die?" Vukovich responded. "That's what I call murder. Especially when the alternative merely involves removing the few hundred individuals responsible for turning progress back centuries."

Dibrovno swept into view.

The helicopter slewed around into a hover. Owen stared out the window at the citadel. Built by the Kievan' Rus and improved upon by their Polish-Lithuanian conquerors the castle was legendary; in its time withstanding over 50 Tatar and Cossack attacks plus one epic Ottoman siege. His stomach pushed up with the helicopter's descent, but his eyes remained glued to the fifty foot high outer walls studded with crenellations, casemates, and multi-level gun emplacements. It was a historian's dream. Rounded towers provided observation platforms along the outer wall's ten foot wide perimeter. As they dropped lower the massive stone inner walls surrounded the helicopter, wrapping around a courtyard featuring an imposing gatehouse and entryway bracketed by two U-shaped stone towers plus bear pits. Timber buildings lined the inner courtyard, including a barracks that looked as if it could comfortably house several hundred combat soldiers. The plunging aircraft settled onto the flagstone courtyard with a thump, the whipping blades slowing as the twin turbines powered down.

Vukovich slid open the shed sized cabin door, waving them out. They cleared the landing pad in a running crouch, passing through an open wooden door that slammed shut behind them. Oil lamps and candles flickered in the poorly lit antechamber.

"Am I missing something?" Brody said. "You guys scrape up the cash to buy Castle Wolfenstein but putting in a few light bulbs was asking too much?"

Owen smiled, but then two muscular figures emerged from the shadows to push Owen and Brody toward a stone spiral staircase that had been built into the tower wall. Owen leaned over to Brody, whose vision had only partially adjusted to the darkness, "The living quarters should be above us, the lower level is traditionally where they put the dungeon."

Vukovich directed them to head down. Brody shivered, noticing his companions hardly seeming phased by the drop in temperature. They hit bottom inside a narrow rock walled tunnel. In the gloom Brody could just make out reinforced planks spanning a door held in place by heavy bolts. In spite of the door's imposing size and strength, it appeared misshapen, bowed outward as if something ferociously strong had slammed into it from the other side. He gulped.

Vukovich nodded to his assistants who affixed blindfolds over their captive's eyes. Brody struggled against the cloth at first, but gave up when he heard Vukovich's men grunting followed by the groaning huge door swinging open. A hand wrapped around Brody's bicep, guiding him forward. Behind him an echoing boom announced the door closing. After what felt like marching forever they again came to a halt. Brody heard renewed grunting, coupled with what sounded like a large toilet tank's lid being slid aside. Rough hands pulled him a few more steps then cool air hit his face as someone jerked his blindfold free.

He stood in a room. Light glimmered from two oil lamps mounted near the ceiling. A stone slab that must have been the door leaned against the wall. Just inside the doorway sat a small wooden table and chair. Two intricately carved wooden boxes dominated the table's uneven surface. Heavy wooden beams above added to the room's claustrophobic feeling. Owen was led across the hard packed dirt floor to a stone wall. There the guards fastened iron manacles to his wrists, a tense feeling palpable in the confined space. Old fashioned skeleton keys locked each manacle into place. Vukovich signaled the grateful guard's to leave.

Owen stepped away from the wall, but the jingling chains allowed hardly any movement. In taking up the slack he could almost, but not quite, work his hands free. After another pull he gave up trying. It was getting harder to coordinate his limbs and he was tired of fighting. He leaned back to savor the dank air washing over his glistening face.

Brody eyed the boxes. The one to his left featured a woodcarving of a wolf pack cavorting under the moonlight. The other box displayed a figure human in its posture and the set of its legs. However, a thin layer of fur covered its body, the werewolf's face unmistakable.

"How about you clue us in on what we're doing here," Owen said, dipping his head and wiping his brow.

"It's a test of trust," Vukovich replied, grabbing a box and inserting the key. The box popped open.

Brody's eyes widened at the sight of his pistol.

"It's loaded," Vukovich announced as he held the weapon up.

Brody eyed Vukovich. The soft yellow light cast by the lanterns flickered across the creature's otherwise shadowed face. *It was obvious why Owen was chained and he was free. Could he do it? Could he shoot Owen? A man he had come to consider his friend? Though he was an accomplished marksman he had never had reason to point a gun at another person. Sure he had drawn it. But that had been a prophylactic measure, not the real thing. There hadn't been anyone looking him in the eye as he decided whether that person would live or die.* As he glanced over at Owen he again considered the gun and the awesome responsibility carried within its compact frame.

Vukovich closed the box and locked it. He leaned over the other box, opening it much more carefully, holding his body back awkwardly from Kateryna's semi-automatic resting inside. "Unlike your weapon this has but one round. I would show you, but I have a bit of a medical issue with the bullet's unique composition."

Vukovich locked it back up and turned toward Brody, "Your friend will become the most lethal foe you've ever faced. In my world he's young, out of control, and easily handled. In yours he will have speed, strength, and senses such as you have never seen," Vukovich said. "Each weapon has utility. It's up to you to figure out how to use them."

"Assuming I believe you, then why are we here?"

"Amidst these tunnels there's an escape path," Vukovich said. "If you cannot find it then you will need to choose between taking your friend's life, and saving your own."

Owen stared wide eyed, his temples pounding a primitive beat. Every inch of his body felt wet and slippery, his breath coming in strained gasps.

"Unlike you, Owen doesn't get a choice," Vuckovich said. "Tanya disobeyed me, and he's paying for her disobedience."

"What about Cindy and Kateryna?" Brody said. "What will happen to them?"

"Cindy faces her own choice. Though, and as it may be, what happens depends upon what transpires down here. The librarian is in Karlovic's hands now; there is nothing that can be done about that. But you intrigue me the most."

Brody seethed, fear for himself superseded by his concern for his friends.

Vukovich watched him and smiled, "People with your connections, compassion, sense of justice, and your drive to make things right..." He trailed off, his expression like that of a college football coach recruiting a star player, "A human like you comes along maybe once in a lifetime," Vukovich said. He smiled at Brody then dropped the keys onto the table and walked from the room.

"That's just great," Brody said, scowling at the open doorway.

"Love," Owen whispered.

"Huh?" Brody spun. His heart tightened at the sight of his friend.

"It's what I would have wanted to accomplish with my life. To have lived a life full of love shared with a wife, a couple of kids, maybe some cats or dogs." He sat on the floor, his back pushed against the wonderfully cool stone wall, legs splayed out on the hard packed dirt.

Brody didn't respond, irritated by an intruding thought of Julie. *Why did she let Donnelly—*

"There's no reason to be scared," Owen said, misreading the look on Brody's face. "You're the one with the guns. You better use them."

"Why?" Brody said as he sat down next to Owen. "Because Vukovich says you're a werewolf? It's not so simple for me. I need to see with my own eyes."

"Sometimes you have to believe."

"*He* would have been proud of you."

"I was so wrapped up in Tanya…" Owen trailed off, eyeing Brody. "Nobody would blame you for killing a monster."

"You're not a monster, you're a man.

"Sometimes there isn't a difference, is there?"

"This isn't one of those times," Brody said. "Now, hard as it is, try and forget about Ernie and what happened on that mountain. Kateryna and Cindy are in danger. They need us, and I think I know a way out. Before we made that second to last turn I swear I could—"

Owen toppled over on his side, groaning and clutching his stomach, one foot kicking out from under him. Brody reached out, then jerked his hand back. *Touching Owen was like touching a hot iron.* Brody searched around, *the boxes.*

Owen's head shot up, vision blurry but clear enough to see Brody going for the guns, "You don't have to put me down yet."

"No worries buddy," Brody said as he checked the weapons. "If you turn into a dog the Humane Society will be the last place I'll take you."

In spite of his agony Owen giggled as he imagined the look on the veterinarian's face at the sight of Brody showing up with a werewolf on a leash. Then another bout of painful cramps hit, and he began flopping around like a fish on the deck of a boat.

Brody tore his eyes away from Owen's contortions to confirm his .45 held a full clip of lead bullets and the Polish semi-automatic *Vis* a single silver bullet. He slipped the *Vis* between his belt and the small of his back, dropping to his knees at Owen's side, his .45 in hand. "Hold still. I'm gonna shoot your manacles off."

"OH MY FUCKING GOD IT HURTS!" Owen's eyes rolled back. A horrible popping noise filled the room. It was as if a bunch of kids had gotten ahold of the wrapping bubbles in a shipping box, squeezing one after another.

The sight and sounds of Owen's vertebrae bursting up along his spine sent Brody's stomach spinning. Owen pushed him and he fell back on his butt, the sudden shock helping him choke off the urge to vomit. He rose, backpedaling and staring wide eyed as Owen's skin darkened, thick fibrous hairs growing into a pelt.

Owen's bloodshot eyes corkscrewed around and fixated on Brody, a last bit of humanity pushing through, "RUN. PLEASE. RUN!"

Brody reflexively stepped back as the last of what had been Owen slid from the gasping man's face. Owen's hands lengthened, blood streaming from his fingertips as his cracking nails grew into wickedly curving claws. However, at that exact moment when everything inside told Brody to bolt, he froze - transfixed as Owen's mouth opened impossibly wide, his skull bulging outward accompanied by an incessant rhythmic growling and shaking as his jaw and nose elongated and merged into a broad muzzle. Covered in a gray pelt, the werewolf eased up onto one knee, breathing deeply.

Brody stared in numb horror. Even kneeling the werewolf loomed as tall as his six feet standing. One clawed hand rested on the beast's knee, the manacle biting into his wrists. His other powerfully muscled arm extended back toward the wall, the chain stretched taught. Owen's broad chest rippled and flexed, flaring into a neck as thick as a running back's thigh. Balanced on top of the Hulk-like form perched the wolfish head of the immense carnivore, muzzle wrinkled in a snarl, eyes downcast as he caught his breath from the wrenching transformation.

Brody braced to fight.

The werewolf looked up, mouth opening into a shark like grin. In one swift motion the werewolf tore the manacles from his wrists and stood, his head slamming into the ceiling, dust sifting down from the jarring impact.

"Do not move a fucking muscle," Brody commanded. He leveled his

.45 on the werewolf's head, his hands so slippery with sweat he was afraid he would drop the gun.

The werewolf's ears perked up, two fuzzy triangles.

A ray of hope flared in Brody's mind.

Then the werewolf took one small step forward.

"Owen, I said no."

The giant beast *moved*.

Brody hadn't even realized he pulled the trigger when the .45 bucked hard in his hand. The bullet blasted a broad hole in the werewolf's face, shattering one of the beast's molars before ripping under his right eye and plowing out the top of his skull, accompanied by a spray of highly oxygenated blood and fatty brain matter painting Brody's face and the low slung rock ceiling above. The werewolf's head jerked backward as if he had been hit by a baseball bat. His body tumbled thereafter.

The salty smell of blood and acrid taste of gunpowder rent the air. The werewolf lay motionless on his back, blood caking his fur and seeping onto the stone below. A sharp ringing echoed in Brody's right ear, which had been turned away from the door and into the small room. Something wet dripped from it. He reached up, and then pulled his fingers away. They were sticky with blood. At least his other ear still worked.

Motion drew his eyes to the room's far side.

The werewolf eased into a sitting position, touching his torn face and open skull. Gleaming white bone, and pink flesh studded with prickling hairs began reforming the beast's lupine head as a wet squishing noise like an old man gumming his pudding filled the air.

Brody's heart thudded in his chest, his mind reeling.

It can't be.

But it was.

I'm so fucked.

He spun and ran.

CHAPTER 33

August 2016 – Dibrovno, Western Ukraine

He ran.

He ran until his muscles screamed and the blood pounded in his temples as his body caromed off a tunnel wall. He ran, every stride opening more distance between him and the monster lurking somewhere in the dark labyrinth. He ran, his labored breathing coming like a freight train, sweat soaking through his chaffing clothing. He ran harder yet.

Rounding yet another turn Brody slid once more into a slick wall. He bounced off. This time however, his rubbery legs gave out. He hit the ground hard but willed himself back to his feet. Wheezing, he dredged up the energy to move. His right leg buckled, dropping him to one knee. Fingertips splayed out on the hard packed dirt he caught his balance and rose up again. He took two more steps that felt like slogging through cement and stopped, bent over, panting like a dog chained to a hot porch. He stood that way for several minutes, gathering himself for another push.

A thick viscous fluid slid down his nose. Brody's hands flew across his face, wiping away the werewolf's clinging blood. Something soft and pulpy fell into his palm. He stared in confusion, then in sickening recognition as the bile rose in his throat. It was a piece of the werewolf's brain.

He flung it aside, rubbing his soiled hands on his pants, feeling his terror subside a bit more as he realized that as recently as the week before he likely would have fainted had he been in a similar situation. Standing a bit taller, he winced at the muffled ache throbbing along the side of his head. Though the ringing had subsided, the pain reminded him he had blown out an eardrum. He turned his good ear back the way he had come.

The wind whipped through the tunnels.

He stiffened and peered into the darkness.

That wasn't the wind.

He began walking, not knowing where he was going but needing to move. The werewolf's presence loomed everywhere. He held the .45 stiffly outstretched before him, stumbling every now and again as he acclimated to his shot equilibrium.

If I can just get out of here, I'll make things right. By the time I'm done they won't have a choice but to prosecute Donnelly. I do that, and maybe Vukovich will call off the dogs before he creates a war the likes of which this world has never seen. I do that, maybe I can help Cindy and Kateryna. But first I need to get out of here. Think.

A row of blinkering oil lanterns marched along the tunnel's stone walls. Spaced out roughly every twenty feet and mounted head high each cast tidy arcs of light. The dim illumination left impenetrable shadows everywhere in-between, the darkness as dense as an Upper Peninsula iron mine. He glanced over his shoulder, hearing another roar, this one louder and clearer.

Brody felt the *Vis* still snug in the waistband of his pants. *There was a chance Vukovich wasn't lying.* If so he couldn't afford to waste the weapon's single round. This left the .45. He had seven bullets. It couldn't stop the werewolf, but it could—

Something furry scuttled between Brody's legs. He looked down. It was a rat, running from the direction of the last roar. Another body raced across the top of his head.

That was no rat.

The skin crawled up the back of Brody's neck as he bent over, his free hand brushing frantically forward. It came away sticky with cob webs, something thumping onto the ground in front of him. The spider was as big as his palm.

Another roar echoed down the tunnel.

The spider skittered away.

At least they had the common sense to flee.

Brody picked up his pace, cursing himself as he went. On the way into the tunnels he had heard the faint sound of rushing water. When Owen changed however, he had bolted like a screaming three-year-old girl running from a clown. The water forgotten, as was the path of rights and lefts he had painstakingly memorized on the way in.

The next roar sounded louder.

He crouched into a jog, cramping stabs of pain lancing his side at even this moderately increased effort. He hadn't gone far when he came to a three way intersection, a lamp marking each corner. He inventoried the dropping levels of oil in each one, hearing and seeing nothing that would help.

The werewolf called out yet again, taunting his prey.

Brody's scent guided the hungry beast's path forward like a runway attendant signaling a passenger jet. If he didn't make a quick decision he faced the unenviable choice of putting a silver bullet in his friend or meeting a gruesome death delivered by fang and claw. He scrunched his shoulders in frustration, eyeing the nearest lamp to his right as it emitted a curl of smoke that drifted up before bending off to the left.

Which tunnel, dummy?

Rumbling growls edged closer.

Brody pivoted to his left. The lamp on that corner was sending wisps of smoke drifting around the corner behind it. He didn't have a clue which way to go, and couldn't come close to making up his mind. In despair, he turned to face back the way he had come, weapon up and ready in a two-handed shooting stance. He decided to put the creature down with the .45, using the werewolf's recovery time to open up more distance between them while taking whichever tunnel his legs carried him into.

At least the light from the lamps provided a clear line of sight.

Brody braced himself to shoot.

Seconds ticked by like hours.

He waited for the beast, but only a slight breeze whispered around the corner, chilling his sweat slicked face. Still shivering he glanced over at the third lamp. Then he glimpsed back to peer along the gun's barrel and down the tunnel again. He still didn't hear or see anything. After another moment he edged closer to the nearest lamp's welcoming heat, only then noticing the greasy tendrils of smoke drifting back—

His eyes widened in stunned realization.

The smoke. It drifted back.

He twirled around, the smoke from the other lamps flowed in the same direction, across the intersection and toward the tunnel leading to the left.

The smoke was being pulled!

The hair stood up on the back of his neck the same time Brody realized that his bad ear had been turned in the direction he had come, leaving him deaf to the approaching—

He whirled as his healthy ear picked up the scraping of claws on rock and dirt. He fired before he even saw his target. A huge clawed hand reaching for Brody's head jerked away, a piercing howl of pain echoing down the narrow tunnel. The snarling werewolf didn't go down however, the red streak flowing from his bulging deltoid drying in an instant. Worse yet, his frenzied face showed no evidence of having been shot at close range less than fifteen minutes before.

In the hazy darkness Brody slammed another round between the creature's furrowed eyebrows. The flash from the jerking barrel lit up the tunnel, the echoing muzzle blast sending dirt cascading down from the ceiling. This time the werewolf jackknifed into the ground with a loud thump.

Brody ran, following the smoke. As desperately as he wanted to bolt all out, every so often he stopped and listened. However, he heard nothing other than the growling from his relentless pursuer. Frustration mounting, he ran for as long as he dared before stopping once more, straining to hear.

There!

He grinned as he heard water gurgling behind the tunnel wall. Then it vanished, drowned out by a roar bursting from dismayingly close behind. Brody pivoted and fired. The bullet slammed into the beast's chest. Brody accelerated away as the tunnel flattened into a long straight away widening in height and breadth. Knowing the additional space worked against him he slowed enough to spin and backpedal while winging off another round.

He missed.

The werewolf bounded close, arms outstretched, eyes glowing with need—

Brody centered his gun on the target and tapped two rounds smack into the beast's mouth. Blood and teeth exploded everywhere. With only one bullet left in the pistol he sprinted off, lungs and legs burning. His thoughts were turning to the *Vis* stuffed in his waistband when he slewed around a corner, senses assaulted by the deliciously deafening sound of rushing water.

His flashing grin of triumph and joy turned to terror however, when his feet slipped out from under him. Brody slid at least a dozen feet on the wet rock before crashing to a stop against an outcropping. Bright lights flashed behind his eyeballs, a loud gasp of pain hissing free from his lips. He staggered upright, his back aching horribly. Stalagmites hung like immense icicles from an arching rock ceiling. The dank grotto like cave sloped down to dark water in front of him. Brody winced again when his foot slid an inch, his tightening back radiating pain. He glanced down at the underground river flowing several feet below his toes and across the cavern's width. It slipped under a solid stone wall stopping roughly one foot above the churning surface. He shook his head in confusion.

There had been a lamp on the tunnel wall outside the cavern, but it shouldn't have been kicking off enough brightness for him to see so well.

Then he understood. Moonlight was reaching inside.

Brody jumped in surprise as a furry shape tumbled behind him, arms and legs reaching everywhere before snagging the wall with a clawed hand. Straining for leverage, the raging werewolf pulled itself up. One side of its mouth had healed. But the other was a tangle of rent flesh and shattered canines stretching into a flapping open tear along his cheek.

Brody drew the *Vis*. He had no idea how well a werewolf could swim and he was not about to find out. The pace of healing seemed to quicken every time he shot it. He leveled the Polish semi-automatic on the werewolf, praying he wouldn't have to use it as he yelled to be heard over the water, "I HAVE SILVER BULLETS. STOP, GODDAMNIT."

The werewolf's ears pointed toward him, ripped cheek stitching itself together.

Brody wanted to believe enough Owen remained to consider what he said.

Fuck Vukovich and his choices. There has to be another way.

Brody risked a quick glance down.

The werewolf growled.

Brody settled his feet on the slick rock, finding his purchase at the same moment an idea clicked inside his head. He turned his attention back to Owen, knowing what he wanted to do, how to do it, but far from certain he could pull it off.

The werewolf's powerful legs twitched, propelling him into the air, mouth agape, fangs and claws shining against the gray and black background of the cavern's ceiling and a pulsing red light affixed high on the wall.

Brody's mind worked in slow motion, his feet pushing off and back flattening above the water. He aimed as carefully as he could even as the creature plummeted toward him. Brody fired, the roar of the gun drowned out by a high pitched keening yelp unlike anything he had heard before from the werewolf.

Brody smacked into the brutally cold water, the impact ripping his breath away. The rushing current yanked his legs into the numbing depths. As his torso was pulled under he strained his neck upward to take one last desperate gulp of air, catching sight of Owen's crumpled form on the water's edge, a deep red furrow running across his chest and the side of his throat.

A ray of hope flashed through Brody before the water splashed over his head.

Chapter 34

October 2016 – Washington D.C.

Jimmy Donnelly shifted in his seat, trying to control his anger.

"I appreciate your visit." Senator Emily Wayne said. "Nonetheless, as evidenced by this summer's Congressional hearings your bank is out of control. Given its importance to the global financial system I have a problem with your failure to understand that's an issue."

"Look here, Senator—"

"No, you look here. Your bank is loaded up with unacceptable levels of risk."

"Risk?" Donnelly sneered. "That's called leverage, and it's what our bank does."

"If you ask me, it's more like a cash advance thrown down in a casino." Wayne said, "Your commercial deposits might be leveraged at ten to one. But the investment side takes that, and the hot money coming in from god knows where and cranks it up to something like two hundred to one. You have the nerve to call what you do banking, but that's not what I see. I see a hedge fund, and a poorly run one at that."

Donnelly couldn't remember the last time someone had the nerve to talk to him in such a manner. "You hold on a goddamn minute."

"I haven't even mentioned the laws that your bank has broken."

Donnelly fumed at the direction the meeting with his biggest public critic had taken. *She was so fucking naïve. It wasn't his job to give a rat's ass about anything but returning value to his shareholders, time to put this uppity bitch in her place.*

"Law breaking?" Donnelly said. His eyes blazed with a creepy energy, lips parting as his anger intensified. "Then why don't you hit us with another fine. The shareholders can afford it."

Senator Wayne's eyes widened at not only the expression in Donnelly's eyes but the sight of his unusually large teeth.

"If we get in trouble I can stick my hands into Uncle Sam's pockets any time I want," Donnelly said with a smirk. "So spare me the bullshit about the law and stay the fuck out of my way."

He abruptly stood and strutted from the room.

The first thing the Senator did after he left was to lock the door behind him.

October 2016 – UC Davis Lab, California

Exasperated beyond belief, she once again refocused the electron microscope. The subject came from a perp suspected in a young woman's grisly rape and murder and it was taking her far too long to finish the forensic analysis. Behind her two lab assistants were chatting away about last night's adventures at the local watering hole. If that wasn't bad enough, the news had been left running on the TV: *"Attorney General trumpets settlement against America's largest bank. Questions linger as to why no top executives were indicted—"*

"Turn that off," Dr. Cynthia Davila snapped over her shoulder as she mixed the subject material with a dilute solution of ammonium molybdate, and focused in again, annoyed with herself for losing her temper. She had seen what happened to other professional, albeit minority, women who expressed their anger. Time and again, she had willed herself to overlook various indignities lest she be labeled as some sort of brown-skinned-bitch, but not this time.

Besides, she couldn't stop thinking about Owen and Brody. Though, that was only part of it. By returning home when she did she had abandoned Kateryna to a fate nobody deserved. Least of all the determined and earnest librarian who had suffered so much but may have been the difference between her coming home at all or ending up in an unmarked grave in the Carpathians. She once again considered the highly unique agreement she had agreed to just before being given a first-class ticket for a flight home from Kiev.

At that thought Cindy refocused the microscope again even though it didn't need it, telling herself she was doing important work.

Nevertheless, she couldn't hide from the truth. It was not nearly as meaningful as the work she had turned down.

October 2016 – London, England

Cusick stared as the ceiling, his wife snoring next to him. Shadows from the ebb and flow of the moonlight danced on the bedroom walls. As usual, he couldn't sleep. He had already checked on his kids, he would check twice more. It had been like this ever since he quit on Vance. At that Cusick thought of the homeless guy, Patrick. He glanced at the nightstand, his service pistol like a lump of coal in the semi-darkness.

It was loaded.

Cusick's heard pounded in response to what he was thinking about doing. He breathed deep, fighting back against the panic attack before it got going. He was getting better at controlling them even as they came with greater frequency. He sat up, grabbed his smart phone and walked into the bathroom.

The house was quiet, but he glanced out the bathroom window anyway. Before he went back to bed he would walk his home's perimeter as had been his habit each and every night since Patrick had been killed. He was about to turn away from the sink when he stopped. He turned back to the mirror, staring at his reflection, his face shadowy but clear enough in the silvery-blue light.

He didn't know how long he stood there, thinking of his wife and kids and what it would mean for them if he made the call. He thought about what it would mean for them if he didn't. He shut the bathroom door.

Vance answered on the first ring.

October 2016 – Kiev, The Ukraine

"A good day to you, sir," Brandner said, the bell jingling as he stepped into the English language book store. Tucked into a narrow side street, it was a gathering spot for the few non-military American ex-pats who remained in the city.

An employee looked up from a leather ledger, his large glasses lending him an owlish appearance in spite of the broad shoulders straining his shirt, "Can I help you?"

"I'm here to pick up my order. Your associate called me earlier this morning," Brandner said.

"Ah yes," the employee said. "That would be the Soviet General Staff Study on the Battle for Lviv?"

"Not exactly," Brandner replied. "I ordered the study of the Second World War Korsun'-Shevchenkovskii Operation."

"Quite right, my mistake," the employee noted. He appeared not a bit chagrined and almost bored as he reached under the counter, past a fully loaded sub-machine gun to snatch up a brown paper wrapped parcel.

Brandner nodded and took the proffered package. He didn't pay, nor was he asked. The bell over the door jingled as he left, travelling opposite the direction he came. He stopped every few store fronts, pretending to shop, using the glass to scan the street behind him. After a half-hour of this he was sure he wasn't being followed. He relaxed, swinging back around to take a more direct route to his office. Inside the parcel was a special report from Roberts and instructions regarding his remuneration, however he didn't hurry. The report was a formality.

Though they never did find out why Brody had shaken his surveillance, it didn't matter. Brody had reappeared in Kiev ready to play nice, checking in regularly with his MVS liaison while working out of the Bureau's offices at the consulate in Kiev. The calls between Brody and Quantico had been tapped and conclusively showed that the professors Brody visited with had not been helpful. Moreover, he had failed in his mission to track down Karlovic.

Roberts bought all of it and ended the operation. Though Brody's conversations with the Bureau seemed legit, Brandner hadn't survived forty years in this line of work being the believing sort of person. Nor had he spent the same amount of time hunting Karlovic only to see an FBI agent twenty years his junior move in at the last minute and steal away what was his Holy Grail. As such, he had made sure word got out to the right people that Brody, and possibly the Bureau, were still on the hunt.

The payoff was more than he could have imagined. Forewarned, Karlovic had eluded Brody. The FBI agent ended up leaving the Ukraine empty handed. For Brandner, who had been tailing Brody, things couldn't have turned out better. He had just about given up hope he would ever get near Karlovic. Now, not only did he have a fresh trail but he would follow it wherever it led.

October 2016 – Detroit's Western Suburbs

Brody stood in the home's book shelf lined front room. The sky unloaded in fat pounding drops as the booming echo of thunder reached through the rattling window. He gazed at an old maple tree, its crimson leaves showering down onto the slightly overgrown lawn. Somebody bumped into him, grunting an apology. The home had been good sized when built, but it wasn't 1977 anymore.

It was the loss of this home that finally broke Mr. Granger. His wife had tried to cheer him up, explaining that it wasn't his fault; that they would win on appeal; that the kid from two doors down had grown up to be an FBI agent and that he would figure out a way to help. None of that mattered. Donnelly's bank stole the house anyway.

Late one night Mr. Granger took the shotgun that once belonged to his father, a proud Marine and combat veteran of Guadalcanal. That night, seventy years after his dad's war ended, Mr. Granger strode down his driveway one last time, having lost a new war he never knew had been declared. He crossed the street and walked into the park carved from the woods. There the proud father of three and grandfather of four kneeled on the baseball diamond, and blew his brains out.

Now, less than one week later, Brody stood in the Granger's dark front room, hands clenched tight behind his back. It had been raining for days, seemingly since Mr. Granger had died. Brody figured he had spent enough time hating himself. Besides, one of the side effects from being hunted and nearly killed by a werewolf is that it tends to focus the mind.

He spun hard on his heels, accusing faces finding something of interest to contemplate on their paper plates. His neck prickled with the thought he was no longer welcome in his hometown. Walking from the kitchen and down into the family room he glimpsed Mrs. Granger sitting on her couch, her proud back drooped in the face of shattering loss. His onetime best friend sat holding her veiny hands. Chris was a veteran of the second Iraq war, but he looked like the same skinny kid from a childhood spent so long ago. Both looked away as Brody approached.

He marched past, anger simmering as he slid open the door wall and strode outside onto the small covered deck. The rain hammered at the wood roof, the staccato sound melding into a roaring rush pounding at his ears. Brody stood there as droplets pressed through gaps in the slats, running into his eyes. He didn't blink, inhaling the cool wet smell and once again thinking about the lie that had been his career.

After several moments he reached into his pocket and fingered his old Swiss army knife. His parents had found it in a box of his childhood mementos. They gave it to him just before the funeral. They meant well, but the only memory it dredged up was that of his failed raid on Frank Castro's fort.

Brody's smart phone began buzzing in the breast pocket of his suit jacket.

The wind picked up, shrieking now.

It was going to be a hard winter.

The phone continued to ring.

Two months before he had memorized the number splayed across the display. Still he let it ring. A small part of him couldn't believe what he was about to do, but he didn't know any other way. At that, he thought of past promises and realized that losing hope in the system was strangely liberating. He swiped the smart phone's screen, a feeling of anticipation and dread sweeping through his body.

"Is everything ready?"

"Are *you* ready?" A woman's voice answered.

"We follow my rules. That means no violence. Got it?"

"Yea, sure."

Brody didn't respond. He once had an entire team backing his every move. Now all he had was *her.*

"Do you trust me?" The woman's voice cut in.

He hesitated, watching a swale of grass filling with water before replying, "Without you I wouldn't be here."

"You don't trust me, do you?"

"It doesn't matter. He's mine, not yours. Understand?"

"I'm so ready to do this."

"You know where to be, and when," Brody said, swiping the phone off and dropping it into his pocket.

He had recently come to an important understanding about this world.

It needed the bad. Though not to balance the good as many thought, there was less of that than most realized. No, sometimes it took doing bad to stop even worse things from happening.

At least he hoped that was true.

CHAPTER 35

October 2016 – Connecticut

Brody crept down the wooded hill side, the full moon gleaming in the crisp night air. He shivered as the silvery clouds slid east with increasing vigor, thinking of a time when being in the forest made him peaceful and wondering when he would get that feeling back. Reaching the edge of the tree line he crouched next to a majestic pine.

To his right a slope led to the shore of Long Island Sound. Before him loomed a French Renaissance style mansion. He checked off the salient points from his briefing. It featured twelve bedrooms and sixteen bathrooms as well as numerous other rooms for play, work, and showing off. A brick paver patio, outdoor kitchen, and sumptuous gardens sprawled behind the home. On the manor's far side were tennis courts, a putting green, separate twenty car garage, and a helipad. If everything went right he knew exactly where to find the homeowner; Jimmy Donnelly.

The wind whipped up, the calm of the moment disappearing along with the branches eerily blowing about. In a few minutes it would be Halloween. In Detroit it was *Devil's Night*, a night of once otherwise harmless pranks that had turned to vandalism and arson when some realized tomorrow would not be a better day.

A cloud drifted in front of the moon, shadows shimmering across the lawn. Brody sprinted from the trees. He slid to a stop on the slick grass at the garden's edge, catching his breath next to a row of boxwoods before stepping onto the brick paver patio. A security guard appeared, a Mossberg twelve-gauge tactical shotgun pointed at Brody.

"He made it," The security guard whispered into a collar mounted microphone.

Brody relaxed ever so slightly, still more than a bit incredulous that *she* was delivering on her promise.

An alarm began to blare. Nodding toward Brody, the guard lowered his weapon and dashed off toward the beach. Flood lamps clicked on from one end of the grounds to the other, armed figures sprinting through the unnatural light's harsh glare.

Cloaked by the security team's mobilization Brody approached the home's darkened lower level, pausing at the open door. Two months ago he wouldn't have imagined doing something like this regardless of whatever childhood stunts he had once pulled. However, his face hardened as he remembered an old photograph he had seen at Mr. Granger's funeral. It was a picture of him and Chris, along with their dads. They were at their father-son bowling league's year-end party. A first place trophy stood before them, their father's arms proudly draped around the shoulders of their sons...

Brody shook off the memory and stepped into the house, reaching into the soft leather holster under his arm and drawing the heavy .45 long-slide semi-automatic pistol. He had lost his old .45 in the river outside Dibrovno's castle two months prior and had wanted something that hit harder. The AMT version of the .45 fit the bill and then some, its brushed stainless steel finish and wide target style trigger providing the pistol with an intimidating look to match its power. He moved off in a crouch, his weapon up in a high ready position. Within minutes he cleared the luxuriously appointed basement and began climbing a winding staircase to the first floor. Focused on the task at hand, he failed to notice the pair of dark clad figures that had slipped inside behind him.

Brody reached the top and padded down the first floor hallway, his footfalls hardly registering on the hand woven rugs. A muffled voice escaped from a set of French doors near the front of the house, a light shining out into the hallway. Brody peeked around the corner. Jimmy Donnelly stood behind a large desk, barking orders into his smart phone. A glass topped wooden box sat on the desk. The box was open, a paper certificate next to it.

"It's a what?" Donnelly said. He wore a powder blue robe and was speaking rapidly, "Somebody spotted by the beach? Do we need to call the cops? No? Okay, I want a report."

Brody holstered his weapon and took a deep breath, walking in as Donnelly set down the phone.

"Come with me," Brody growled, flashing his badge.

"Surprise, surprise," Donnelly smiled. "I've often wondered when you'd grow a pair."

Virtually nothing had changed since he had last been in the CEO's presence. The only other time Brody had ever seen someone so arrogant with power had been when he saw video footage of the drug lord Pablo Escobar at the height of his cartel's reign.

"Follow me," Brody commanded.

"I'll change first."

"We have to go," Brody said. "Now."

"The front door is this way," Donnelly said, knocking into Brody as if he were in a high school hallway and trying to signal his dominance.

Brody's free hand wrapped tight around Donnelly's bicep, steering him in the opposite direction.

"What're you doing? My security will be back in a few—"

"They won't," Brody said. "Walk."

Everything the guards did was logged. So *she* had created a fake situation, and those carefully managed events unfolding outside would be recorded to provide *the company* shelter from liability.

They arrived at floor to ceiling double doors.

Brody gestured.

Donnelly pushed them open. Deep shadows obscured much of the room. Donnelly reached for a light switch. Brody grabbed his wrist, shaking his head no. Donnelly glared at Brody who ignored him and turned to walk into the room. He came to an abrupt stop. A stuffed and mounted timber wolf towered on a pedestal, snarling in a permanent rage. Brody stared past the wolf to see at least a dozen other dead animals similarly displayed.

"What? Don't you have a trophy room in your house?" Donnelly said.

Brody waved Donnelly toward the far end of the high ceilinged room. There, an intricate Afghan rug of at least twenty square feet covered much of the hardwood floor. Donnelly plopped into a weathered leather club chair. Brody eased into the matching chair opposite him, glancing around.

"How's Julie?" Donnelly said.

Brody face flashed red, the blood buzzing hot in his ears.

"It didn't have to be this way," Donnelly said. "All you had to do was look the other way and—"

"You know I couldn't do that."

"She loved you."

"She used me."

"No she didn't," Donnelly said. "I did."

"Same thing."

"If you believe that, then you're dumber than you look."

"Where is she?"

"Fuck if I know, but that's hardly news to you. So why don't we knock off the chit-chat and you tell me why you're really here."

"I'm curious," Brody said. "At what level do you define success? One hundred lives ruined per week? One thousand lives per month?"

"Cut the sanctimonious crap, Brody," Donnelly said. "Virtually every great American has gotten to the top by cheating, or as our esteemed leaders in the political class do it — being paid off by other people. The working class you so desperately hoist onto a pedestal does the same thing. They just aren't as good at it."

"Bullshit."

"Oh Brody, you simple, simple man," Donnelly said, "Years ago this home's builder pulled me aside and told me he hadn't been reporting all his income. The IRS had him dead to rights and he needed my help. Then again, it seems that my entire adult life every other blue-collar contractor that I hire wants cash payments. Give up, Brody. Everybody cheats."

"You're not a plumber for chrissakes," Brody said. "If you screw up, then the entire economy crashes."

"My position in life isn't an accident," Donnelly said. "Get over it."

"If you're so important then why did you need the taxpayer when your precious bank nearly imploded?"

"It's not that simple," Donnelly huffed, for the first time showing that Brody was getting to him.

"Let's make it simple. Why did you foreclose on an old man's house when it was paid for? Why shouldn't you be held responsible for his suicide? Shaking people down wasn't enough, was it?"

"What makes you think *I'm* responsible?"

"What part of 'the government has been reading everybody's email' don't you understand?" Brody said. "Wake up, Donnelly. In spite of everything you've done I'm giving you a choice. Take a deal and roll over on your buddies. Give me what I want and you'll only do a few years in a country club prison. Then you can fade out into retirement."

"People like *me* don't go to jail, you delusional sonafabitch."

"People like you?" Brody said. "It's time to give the taxpayers a better return on their investment. Take my deal or—"

"Go to hell."

Brody played his last card, "I got you dead to rights, emails, phone transcripts, you name it. I've documented your greasy little fingers all over multiple frauds and this time I ain't going up the chain of command. You've got that angle pretty much covered, but that's not everything. Last chance, work with me or I'm going public."

"They'll crucify you," Diamond said, but he had an unsure look on his face.

"That's where you're wrong," Brody said. "This summer's congressional hearings made you famous. There's no hiding now. I go public and you'll be the poster boy for every bad banker out there. You and your buddies have gotten away with so much shit, the people are so fucking angry, and Congress will be so embarrassed you played them for public fools that they'll have to do something. And you know it."

The outside alarm and flood lights clicked off.

A low rumbling growl echoed through the room.

Brody shot upright in his chair. *No, no, no. She was supposed to handle the diversion, that's it. What was she doing?*

"What was *that?*" Donnelly said.

A different growl pierced the air.

Brody spun around, turning his back to Donnelly, eyes searching the opposite end of the huge room, straining to see...

A click came from where Donnelly had been sitting. Brody's heart plummeted into his stomach, hand plunging into his jacket, jerking his .45 free as his peripheral vision caught sight of Donnelly standing, arm raised, a snub-nosed revolver pointed—

The gun's deafening report echoed through the room.

The bullet's impact slammed him back into the chair, his .45 tumbling from his hand. Brody stared in numb fascination at a spreading patch of red seeping from his left shoulder and across his jacket. Then the pain hit, white-hot and radiating up his neck. He clenched his teeth in response, not wanting to give Donnelly the satisfaction.

"Oops, I meant to kill you," Donnelly said. "If it's any consolation I was considering your offer."

"Fuck off," Brody replied through lips pursed tight against his pain.

"You're not much of a cop," Donnelly said. "I thought patting down a suspect was police procedure 101. You must have missed that class."

Brody's angry lunge upward stopped before it really began, the sudden movement sending a sharp stabbing pain lancing into the base of his skull. He fell back into the chair, his mind flashing back to the empty box on Donnelly's desk and the voluminous pockets on the front of Donnelly's designer robe.

A long murmuring snarl rippled through the room. *It* sounded close.

"Nice touch," Donnelly said, glancing over his shoulder. "Did you actually think I would've given up if you threatened me with a police dog? Well, I'm not some chicken-shit-camel-fucker and this isn't Abu Ghraib."

"You pompous ass," Brody said, his voice strengthening as he willed himself to accommodate the pain, "You have no idea what you're talking about."

"I'll take care of Rover in a second," Donnelly said. "It's time to say goodbye."

Brody defiantly glared at Donnelly.

The banker aimed the unfamiliar weapon.

Something rippled in the shadows.

Donnelly never saw *it* coming. A hairy hand clamped down on his wrist and squeezed, the revolver thumped harmlessly onto the floor. Each of the carpal bones in Donnelly's wrist shattered in a series of sickening crunching sounds. A second werewolf appeared and lifted Donnelly into the air then dumped him into a chair.

Brody used his functional right hand to retrieve his pistol, his left arm hanging limp at his side. To stem the bleeding he grabbed one of the decorative pillows next to him and stuffed it under his jacket and against the open wound. A kaleidoscope of stars exploded behind his eyes. After several moments of controlled deep breathing he managed to avoid fainting, focusing his attention on the primeval scene unfolding before him.

There was something horrifyingly captivating about the delicate grace with which the werewolves' moved. A thin sheen of silky hair covered each beast; one werewolf black as night, the other gray. A distinctive white streak of fur creased the gray werewolf's upper chest and side of his throat.

Brody recognized the reminder of his handiwork. His heart beat like it was full of hummingbirds as nightmarish memories of the castle tunnels settled heavily in the pit of his stomach. His good right hand holstered his next-to-useless .45 and trailed down his side.

Inside a jacket pocket his fingers curled around his back-up weapon - a compact Walther PPK loaded with silver bullets. It had cost him a fortune, though he couldn't imagine shooting who he surmised to be Tanya or the gray beast he had recognized right away as Owen. On the other hand, he should do something but the mere act of getting his hand into his pocket had been torturous.

So now what?

The black werewolf leered at Donnelly. Her muzzle wrinkled back, glistening fangs shining luminously in the moonlight. She could taste the delightful smell of the man's terror escaping from the pores of his skin. The man's vanity only made him more savory. Too much time in the tanning booth had turned his leathery skin into a crisp crust protecting the marbled mouthwatering layers of flesh waiting within.

Brody watched, again toying with the idea of drawing the Walther. *He didn't have to kill them. The silver bullet he had winged Owen with had laid him out as if he had been run over by a truck. Then again, his carefully aimed shot in the tunnels had been luck. No matter how good of a marksman he liked to think he was, just getting the short barreled Walther centered on target with the pain he was in and with those two monsters charging him would be a feat, no less trying to wound both of them in the shoulder or leg—*

"You have no idea what you've done," Donnelly abruptly said to Brody as the black werewolf grasped the banker's ankle, spinning him onto his back. Before Brody could even think to respond the black werewolf's hand reached under the robe and through Donnelly's boxer shorts. Razor sharp claws sliced into the pulsating flesh, gripping tight. A high pitched staccato scream burst from Donnelly's mouth as her arm pulled back accompanied by the wet tearing sound of flesh and fibers, the banker's torn organ flopping limply in her grasp.

Donnelly's head thrashed about, hysterical at the sight of his crimson covered penis and testicles grotesquely mashed together between her slippery fingers. The black werewolf casually flung her arm to the side. Donnelly's genitals hit a picture window with a loud splat, one of his testicles grotesquely stuck in place, the remainder of the steaming mess sliding down the glass in one glistening red streak.

Whining like a dog looking for a treat the gray werewolf licked at the gouts of spurting blood slathering Donnelly's stomach, arm braced on the floor to steady his huge frame, virtually intoxicated by the salty taste seasoned with fear. The werewolf's mouth opened, tearing through the pink flesh, snout pushing past the fatty folds of skin, reaching inside. His jaws worked once and he eased back, a ropy section of squishy intestine dangling from each side of his dripping muzzle. He tossed his head. Chewy lumps flew up in the air like so many fat sausages, blood droplets scattering like paint from a roller before plummeting into the werewolf's open maw. He licked his rubbery black lips, delighting in the smoothest tasting elixir he had ever known. Every tangy drop sliding down his throat made his head swoon like the first time he had experienced the everything-is-right-in-the-world-feel brought by heroin.

The black werewolf's body tingled as she watched. It had been years since she shared a meal with a lover, no less one for which she could savor every morsel without any moral compunction. The majority of her kills had been depressingly the same. Her victims dispatched with such humane speed they didn't have time to realize what happened. This man's crimes however, meant she could do whatever she wanted. She hadn't felt *so wolfish* in a long time. She leaned in, mouth clamping down, ripping away a fat chunk of meat from the writhing man's spongy thigh and rolling its sweetness around in her mouth, swallowing the ragged piece in one juicy gulp.

The gray werewolf elbowed her aside. He lunged forward to tear at his prey's softy palpitating internal organs. His huge body splayed flat on the floor as he buried his entire snout inside the banker's stomach in an orgiastic fury of hunger, feverishly snapping his jaws through the tearing popping flesh. Donnelly's screams increased to a mindless volume. He picked up his head, rolling eyes taking in his torso jerking under the werewolf's assault as his chest cavity cracked under the pressure. Moist, meat-covered rib bones thrust skyward.

Brody stomach summersaulted in one dizzying loop after another. He convulsed and spun away, his mouth lurching open as his stomach shot up his burning esophagus in great retching heaves. Wiping his hand across his mouth Brody shuddered again, this time with nothing left to give.

A strange garbled noise compelled him to turn back. When he did he stared in horror.

Donnelly was still alive.

The man's eyes locked on Brody's, the cold reptilian energy inside extinguished, bloody lips mouthing his final request, *"Kill me."*

Brody drew the Walther before he realized he had acted, wincing in pain but managing to level the pistol's barrel on the grey werewolf's chest.

The big beast didn't have to be told what was in the weapon, the exposed scent of silver confirming why he had sensed an aura of danger cloaking Brody since they had entered the room. He stepped back.

Brody switched his aim to the black werewolf.

She glared at Brody, her face a mask of dripping snarling menace.

Brody swallowed, his wound throbbing.

She took one step forward.

Brody raised his aim point from her chest to her head as he acknowledged it had to be Tanya. No one else he knew was even close to matching her aggressiveness.

Tanya growled, but stopped. Her huge clawed hands squeezed into fists.

He stared her down, finger tightening on the trigger.

Tanya's eyes drilled into Brody.

Another second passed.

She nodded and stepped aside.

Brody waved the Walther at Donnelly's revolver.

Owen kicked it over.

Brody bent and flipped the Walther into his left hand, nearly dropping it as a wave of eye watering pain radiated through his crippled arm and shoulder. His right hand picked up the revolver, aimed, and fired. The top of Donnelly's head exploded in a cloud of red mist.

Tanya snarled, jerking Brody's attention away from the meat on the floor that had once been a man.

He stared back, wordlessly conveying his frustration and anger, then throwing the revolver aside.

She cocked her head to one side, mouth opening in a grin of approval.

He turned and walked from the room.

Brody leaned against the kitchen island. He rechecked his impromptu field dressing, having used his belt to bind his left arm to his body, cinch the pillow tight over his wound and staunch the bleeding. Pain still throbbed through his shoulder but it had dulled into a manageable ache.

What part of you missed the reality that somebody might actually die if you let the monsters out to play? Then again, Donnelly was a sociopath. Granger wasn't the only victim, far from it. How much longer before his old neighborhood became like the one where they found Cameron?

At that, he thought back to the awful last night in Dibrovno and the events that had followed...

The river had spit him out under the bridge in downtown Dibrovno. He had made it to his car and was back in the Ukrainian capital later that morning. There, he followed up on Kateryna's cryptic dinnertime comment about seeing the Maidan Nezalezhnosti. The clever librarian had sold it well, making it seem as nothing more than the rambling of a drug addled mind. However, Kateryna had been signaling where she and Karlovic would be and when.

Maidan Nezalezhnosti was Ukrainian for Independence Square. On August 24, 1991 the Ukraine formally gained its independence from the Soviet Union. Each year that event was celebrated in Kiev's main square, with the twenty-fourth falling this year the day after he returned from Dibrovno. He briefed his fellow agents as to Karlovic's impending appearance. In an effort at maintaining airtight security they had told no one outside the office. Early the next morning they staked out the square.

Two hours later they had spotted Karlovic with Kateryna in tow. As they made their move a man had approached Karlovic and the three of them disappeared into the crowd. Regardless of the fact the Bureau had a rat Brody had lost perhaps his best chance at saving Kateryna. Nevertheless, given how close he had come to getting their person of

interest the suddenly magnanimous AG had declined to push for his dis-
missal. Plus, having said nothing about werewolves he had headed off a
trip to the looney farm.

He used the hard won praise as leverage toward one more shot at
working within the system, indicting Donnelly, and hopefully stopping
Vukovich in the process. All of which would have granted him enough
breathing space to make another stab at finding Kateryna and Karlovic.
Vance had a buddy at the NSA with the proper security clearances. He
helped Brody uncover an email chain between Donnelly and the Vice
President in charge of their bank's Mid-West operations. In a damn-
ing exchange they specifically discussed the suspense account program,
the bank's euphemism for its extortion racket aimed at people like the
Grangers. Wilson had forwarded the criminal referral Brody and Vance
put together. The AG's office shut it down with a tersely worded state-
ment based on prosecutorial discretion. It was the legal equivalent of are-
you-fucking-kidding-me. That happened one week before Granger killed
himself—

Something padded into the room behind Brody. His neck tensed at
the same moment a half gnawed human arm thumped onto the quartz
countertop, a large presence hovering over his shoulder. He didn't look,
fingers slipping into his pocket and wrapping around the Walther in
case *they* had decided to turn him into a Happy Meal.

A hand gripped his shoulder.

Brody twisted to see a *human* hand, followed by perhaps the most
incredible sight of the night.

Tanya stood before him resting one hand on a sweeping hip, acting
as if there were nothing more normal than having god-knows-how-
many pints of burgundy colored bodily fluids painted across her nude
body. Behind her loomed Owen, still in werewolf form.

Brody ignored Owen and lit into her, "What the fuck was that all
about?"

"You can't change the nature of the beast," Tanya said with a shrug.

"I don't care what you are," Brody said. "What just happened—"

"Was on me, and deliciously so I might add. I love the way the
wealthy taste. Their grass-fed-organic diets add so much more flavor
to their meat than the corn and preservative addled flesh of the rest of
you Americans."

"Don't you get it, Tanya? That's a fucking crime scene back there."

"Versus what?" Tanya laughed, "Your extra-judicial attempt to threaten a man into pleading his guilt."

"Do you have any idea what's going to happen?"

"Oh my," Tanya said. "You still believe that some establishment figure's life is more valuable than that of others less fortunate."

"You shouldn't have been in that room," Brody replied. "You made things worse."

"You believe in justice, why not retribution?"

"Violence doesn't make things better," Brody said, noticing how Tanya's eyes were glowing as if she had just experienced the fucking of her life.

"Don't worry, killing gets easier."

"It's a sin."

"Only if you don't eat what you kill."

"That's not what I meant." Brody realized her canines were still elongated. However, as much as he wanted to open some distance between them he was not about to back down.

"You don't know what you mean."

"Gimme a break, Tanya. The fucking commandment—"

"Refers to murder not killing," Tanya said. "Do you, of all people, really want to play the religion card? If so, need I direct you to Exodus, chapter twenty-one, verses—"

"That's enough," Brody said.

"I hope so. Because you need to stop pretending you're something that you're not," Tanya said, noticing Owen's hesitant looks directed at Brody. "Relax," She said to him, her jutting breasts jiggling as she pointed at Brody. "He's not going to shoot you again."

Owen whined and touched the streak of white hair running up his chest and across his neck. The silver bullet fired into him under the castle had accomplished Brody's goal of getting them out of Vukovich's game alive, albeit just barely. Though the bullet had missed major organs, it had grievously injured Owen. It took him weeks to recover. Nevertheless, with his first change behind him at least now he could mostly control himself.

Brody peered around Owen's frame to see a group of security guards, wearing what looked like doctor's scrubs, carrying cleaning materials, and heading for the trophy room. Brody turned back to Tanya, impressed by her team's professionalism but not knowing what to think of her appearance. He couldn't help but stare, wondering whether he should be aroused or disgusted by her blood smeared nudity.

Owen snarled as if he could read Brody's mind.

"Will you two grow up?" Tanya said, turning toward Brody. "And stop staring at my goddamn tits."

"This isn't some sort of half-assed rebellion," Brody said. "You can't just kill people. Or did you conveniently forget everything we talked about?"

"You forget that the rich stay wealthy because they and those that protect them are violent," Tanya said, wiping her forehead as a glob of blood slid down from her hair. "You forget that once the middle class dropped violence from their playbook they rolled over and died. You forget that it's called class warfare for a reason."

"Give me a break, Tanya. Violence isn't how—"

"The system's *broken*," Tanya said. "Ernie was right, there's no such thing as justice."

Outside, the wind whooped up.

"Do you know how it is a rapist can break a woman's back?" Tanya said.

"*What?*"

"My best friend Inez and I were fifteen when the Germans came to Dibrovno. One night a drunken group of soldiers broke into Inez's house and raped her in front of her parents and younger sister."

Brody swallowed thickly, thinking of the hell that had been Tanya's human life.

The wind kicked up louder.

"The tough wooden floors in those old houses were built for functionality, not comfort. When the rapists bent poor Inez's legs to her shoulders that coiled up spinal column, on that hard floor with no support... Her mother later told me that Inez's back snapped like a chicken's neck."

"Jesus Christ, Tanya."

"Years later I found out what happened to those men. They survived the war, living long lives filled with more joy than Inez could have dreamed. You talk about justice but I know how rare that is," Tanya said.

"I'll hold up my end of the deal. Just remember that power changes people, even ones like you."

"That's the least of our worries."

"Let the elites ready themselves for war, they have no idea what's coming," Tanya said.

"Listen to me," Brody said. "They've armed the police to the fucking teeth. If anyone even thinks of trying another American revolution they will get crushed."

"What are we going to do about it?"

"I need actionable intelligence. That means I don't just get Kateryna back but I get definitive information on Karlovic's whereabouts, understood?"

The wind screamed savagely, rattling the big windows above the sink and quartz countertops.

"Agreed," Tanya said, extending her hand and looking him in the eye.

He took it, feeling hopeful.

Tanya let go and stepped outside. Owen followed as the children of the night ran free.

Brody waited a moment and then walked out the door into Halloween morning. Dead leaves crunched under his feet, a cold October rain pattering down.

They had changed things.

Forever.

The howling rose on the night air.

Acknowledgments

As is usually true, a book is a collaborative effort. Special thanks to artist Dean Samed for creating the cover and not only going past my initial expectations but doing so in a timely and professional manner. I also thank Claudia B. Logan of Oxbow Creative for her editorial services. Furthermore, I would be remiss if I did not mention the work of Michelle Lovi from Odyssey Books. Michelle ably navigated the process of formatting, printing, and distribution. I couldn't be happier with the final product she created. Finally, I would like to thank my friend, Steven Mercatante. A World War II historian and author, he provided needed insight into the mechanics of researching military history matters. In addition, he edited the content set during the Second World War.

About the Author

S.M. Douglas is married with children and lives in Southeast Michigan.

Follow the author on Facebook, Pinterest, Twitter, Goodreads, Google Plus, or at www.smdouglas.com